Delicious Prey

A Dark Mafia Romance

Sonja Grey

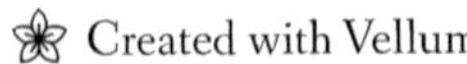
Created with Vellum

Contents

Also by Sonja Grey

If you'd like to be a part of my mailing list and get a free novella and bonus epilogues for every book, then please go to: **subscribepage.io/lKtqfy**

All series are interconnected and can be read as stand-alones, but they're more enjoyable if you read them in order.

Russian Boxing Club Series

My Russian Obsession

My Russian Temptation

My Russian Salvation

Stand-Alones

Grumpy Bratva Hitman

Delicious Prey

Fedorov Bratva Series

Caught by the Bratva Boss

Savage Savior

Arrogant Bratva Bastard

Medvedev Bratva

Devil from Moscow

Bratva Devil

Filthy Devil

Blurb

It was my testimony that put him away for life, but now he's escaped and standing in my bedroom.

Lydia:
Kirill Chernikov is a deadly hitman for a powerful Bratva,
and it's my eyewitness testimony that puts him away for life.
He's the monster who killed my dad...at least I think he is.
The truth is I didn't see his whole face that night.
I saw a tall man with a powerful, deadly build, and one hell of a chiseled jaw.
The police convinced me it was Kirill, and he's the one I pointed out in the courtroom.
After he was sent away, I thought it was over, but it's only just begun.
Turns out he's a little, I mean a lot, obsessed with me.
He sends me letters from prison, has someone watching me at all times,
and tells me I'm not allowed to date anyone.
I'm his and only his.
I should be disgusted.
I'm not.

He makes me want things I shouldn't, and when he escapes, I'm the first thing he comes for.
He makes it clear that he won't be spending another night away from me ever again.
He's a man who doesn't like to be disobeyed.
And he's decided I'm his.

Kirill:
I've spent my life building a reputation that ensures everyone fears me.
I have no attachments. No one gets close.
But all that changes when I see Lydia.
I can't get her out of my head.
I'm an obsessed man with nothing but time.
I may be in prison now, but I'll be escaping soon,
and when I do, I'm coming for her.
Once she's in my arms, I'm never letting go of my delicious prey.
I'm going to devour her piece by piece.

Before You Read

This book contains all the elements you would expect from a dark mafia romance. If that's not your thing, then you might want to skip this one. :)

For the animal lovers:

There are five dogs in this book, and all five make it to the end. No animals will ever come to harm in my books. :)

Chapter 1

Kirill

I take the drink Ivan offers me, but when he waves at the leather chair in front of his massive desk, I remain standing.

"Always so fucking stubborn," he mutters in Russian.

The head of the Teterev Bratva pours himself a vodka and lights a cigarette. His cold, brown eyes meet mine. We've been working together for a decade, ever since I turned fifteen and proved my worth to him by taking out a competitor who was trying to creep into Ivan's territory. No one else could get the hit on Mikhail, but I'd managed it. When I'd brought Ivan the man's head, he'd hired me on the spot. I've been his best hitman ever since. The pay is good, the work is relatively light, and I get to do what I love. It's a win-win.

"So tell me about last night," he says, filling his lungs and blowing the smoke out through his nose.

I take a drink and rest my arm on the mantle of the fireplace that takes up a ridiculous amount of space in his office. Ivan's never been a subtle guy, though, and that's why he likes me. We both like to make statements. I may live in the shadows, but everyone is aware of my work. Together, we've kept the Teterev Bratva at the top of the food chain by ensuring that everyone else is too scared to fuck with us.

"You're too damn tall to hover," Ivan says, taking another drag of his cigarette.

I smile and toss back the rest of my drink before sitting in the chair opposite his desk. Stretching my long legs out, I unbutton my suit jacket and meet his eyes.

"Last night went well, very well, actually."

Ivan smiles. "Details, Kirill. You know I like the details."

I lift my hands and give a small shrug. "Not much to tell. He's dead. Two shots to the head. No witnesses."

"You never leave witnesses."

He's right. I never do. I'm also not stupid enough to have witnesses in the first place, but sometimes it just can't be avoided. The few times it has happened, it's been a quick fix. Unfortunate, yes, but the alternative is to let them go and possibly identify me later, which is not something I can allow, no matter how much they may beg and promise that they'll never tell a living soul about what they've seen. You can't trust someone who's begging for their life. They'll always tell you whatever they think you want to hear.

Ivan stubs out his cigarette and pours us both another drink. The gold of his wedding band clinks against the glass decanter. His office is devoid of family photos, but I've met his wife and three kids on more than one occasion. I've even met all three of his mistresses. Ivan's a man who keeps busy. I've told him before that every single one of them is a liability, that men like me will always see them as targets, a way to send a warning or to hurt and weaken him enough so another man can come in and take over, but he refuses to heed my advice. He maintains he loves them all and could never part with a single one. I told him he's full of shit and just likes to get his dick wet. If I was anyone else, that comment would've gotten me killed, but Ivan had just laughed and nodded his head in agreement.

"That I do, Kirill," he'd said with a laugh. "It keeps a man young."

He's been head of the Bratva ever since his dad died, and now that he's nearing fifty, he's been even more paranoid than usual. He's convinced everyone is just waiting for him to show the slightest sign of weakness, and once they see it, they're going to pounce. He's not wrong. That's part of what last night's hit was about. The Faretti family killed one of his men a few days ago, and the man I killed was retaliation. Ivan had lost a low-level drug runner, but I'd taken out a man who was much higher up in the ranks.

"So how'd you manage to get Lorenzo?"

I smile and shake my head. "I don't reveal my secrets, Ivan. You know that. I'm the best for a reason. I don't trust anyone. I have my ways, and I always get the job done. That's all you or anyone else needs to know."

Ivan laughs and lights another cigarette. "Fair enough." Grabbing his iPad, he pulls up a file and then scoots it across the desk to me. "I need this one taken care of tonight."

I arch a brow at him. He knows I require more of a heads-up so I can fully prepare for the job.

"I know, I know," he says before I can speak. "I just found out he's in town less than an hour ago, and he's leaving tomorrow morning. This is the only window we have. It has to be tonight, and I'll pay double, of course, for the inconvenience."

When I see who the file is on, I meet Ivan's eyes again. "You sure you want to do this? There's no going back after you give me the okay."

"I'm sure," Ivan says. "The fucker needs to go. His dad needs to know how serious I am."

I look back at the photo of Matteo Faretti, knowing his death is going to start a war. It's going to trigger something that will be impossible to stop once it's in motion. I remind Ivan of this.

"Enzo will never let this go if you have his son killed. You'll have to destroy the entire Faretti family."

Ivan waves away my concern with the cigarette still clutched between his fingers. "If he wants a war, then he'll get one. He can either get the fuck out of my city, or I'll take down his entire family."

When it's obvious Ivan isn't going to change his mind, I put my focus back on Matteo's file, memorizing every detail of it until I know the man better than he probably knows himself. He's staying at one of the bigger hotel chains, and I'm sure the security around him is going to be an absolute bitch, but it's nothing I can't handle.

"Consider it done." I set the iPad on his desk and stand up. "He'll be dead before the sun rises."

Ivan smiles, but it's not friendly. He's already envisioning the war that's about to start and the victory that he assumes will be an easy one. I'm not convinced Ivan's going to win it, but that's the beauty of being a hired hitman. If the Teterev Bratva gets taken down, I can just find another one. My services are in no short supply. Everyone wants to hire the ghost that never gets caught. My loyalties are to no one but myself. That's why I'm still alive, and I intend to keep it that way.

"I'll transfer the money into your account," he says as I turn to leave. I don't bother looking back at him. With the short notice he's given me, I don't have any time to waste.

When it's close to midnight, I walk onto the roof of the hotel and make my way to the side that faces the ocean. The penthouse suite is right below me. Vadim, the man I regularly use to scope out locations for me, already informed me that Matteo is inside with one of his many mistresses. He has two guards positioned outside his door and one inside with him. It's almost like he's inviting me to come inside. Sometimes it's just too damn easy.

Stepping to the edge, I look down and smile at the adrenaline rush it gives me. Hundreds of feet below is the unforgiving brick veranda. It's too far away and too dark for me to see it, but I know it's there. Taking a few steps to the right, I watch the small balcony that extends from Matteo's suite, waiting for any sign of movement. I'd studied the hotel's layout, so I know this particular balcony leads directly into the bedroom, a place his guard is unlikely to be. It's a warm enough night for the French doors to remain open, and that's exactly what careless Matteo has done. He knows it's an unscheduled visit into the city and that his visit has remained hidden, and it's made him lazy with his security—a mistake he won't live to regret.

As soon as I hear the over-the-top moans from his mistress, I smile and grip the edge of the building, slowly lowering myself down. Most people look at my height and muscular body and assume I'm not very agile, but they're wrong. I'm actually a pretty nimble motherfucker, and once I'm hanging over the side of the hotel, I close the short distance to the balcony, landing without any noticeable sound.

Staying crouched low, I keep myself hidden and take in the scene before me. His redheaded mistress is riding him hard. Her large, fake tits are bouncing like they'll never stop, and I'm happy the man will at least get to go out with a view. Unfortunately for her, she decided to accompany him on this little impromptu visit. If I was a nice man, I'd let them both climax before I kill them, but I've never been accused of being nice.

With my gun in hand, I creep into the room, grabbing a throw pillow from one of the chairs on my way. They're so into what they're doing that they don't even realize what's happening until it's far too late. One sharp push sends the redhead on top of Matteo, and a second later the pillow is against her back and I'm firing the shot that will kill them both. The pillow and the silencer on my gun suppresses the sound enough to keep it in this room. The bullet went through her heart, killing her instantly, but I can hear Matteo's wheezy breaths as he fights it. I lean closer so he can see me.

"No hard feelings, Matteo. It's just a job."

He's trying to glare at me, but he's too weak to pull it off.

"You died fucking, man. No better way to go," I tell him, trying to make him feel a little better about the situation. The hate in his eyes lets me know it's not working. I laugh and put the pillow over his face, knowing I don't have time to fuck around with this. I'm guessing his mistress is known for being a loud lover. A few minutes of silence and the guard right outside the bedroom door is going to get curious.

Pulling the pillow away, I make sure he's dead and then tuck my gun away and run for the balcony. I lower myself down to the suite below and then do it one more time, landing on the balcony of the room that I reserved for the night under the name Mr. and Mrs. Hyde. I slip through the French doors that I left unlocked and close them behind me before pulling back the thick curtains. Turning on a light, I strip out of my black clothes and peel off the leather gloves. I take a quick shower and change into a pair of grey joggers and a white T-shirt. Lounging on the big, comfy bed, I put in an order for room service. I've worked up an appetite and a medium-rare steak will really hit the spot.

I send Ivan and Vadim a thumbs up and pick up the remote, surfing through the channels while I wait. I've just found a good comedy when my food arrives. A delicious meal, a funny movie, and an easy two million in my account—not a bad night at all.

I sleep like a baby and wake up a little after sunrise. After another shower and more room service, I send a text to Vadim, asking him how things are looking.

Not good, man. The Faretti family is going crazy. Enzo has men all over the city. There's a few outside your hotel. Use the employee side entrance. I'll be waiting.

I grab my bag and leave my keycard on the nightstand along with several hundred dollars. The room is paid for and completely untraceable to me, and I'm sure as hell not going to waste my time checking out when the Faretti family has eyes on the place. Taking the stairs, I quickly head for the back of the hotel, and then walk my ass into the kitchen like I have every damn right to be there. It's amazing what a nice suit and a pissed-off look will allow you to get away with. Men scurry out of my way while the women sweep their eyes over me in appreciation. I ignore all of them and walk out the door and over to Vadim's black Audi. As soon as I'm in, he takes off, shaking his head at me while maneuvering us into the flow of heavy traffic.

"What the fuck is Ivan thinking?"

I shrug and put my sunglasses on. "I'm not paid to worry about that. I did my job. That's all I care about."

"Enzo is fucking pissed. Matteo was his only son, his goddamn pride and joy. He's just started a war."

"Not my problem, and not yours either," I remind him. "You work for me, not the Teterev Bratva. You and me, we're on the outside. We go where the money's good, and right now, Ivan's the top payer. I'll take out who he wants me to take out, and all the other jackasses can worry about the war on the ground."

Vadim laughs and drives me to my house. I'm a paranoid bastard, so I've gone through a lot of trouble to make sure no one knows this is where I live. Vadim is the only person who knows my address. To everyone else, the large house on the hill with the private beach is owned by sixty-year-old Thomas Skylar. He's a retired investment banker, never married, no kids. I have enough land to ensure my privacy and more security cameras than all of London. If anyone steps foot on this property, I'll immediately be alerted to it. I also have four very well-trained Belgian Malinois who are very aware that they're allowed to bite anyone I haven't told them is okay. So far the no-bite list includes one name: Vadim.

"You coming in?" I ask when he pulls down the long driveway and stops in front of the four-car garage.

His eyes scan the yard, and I know he's looking for my dogs. He's scared to death of them. I laugh and smack his shoulder.

"They're not going to bite you. They've been told not to."

He scrubs a hand over his light beard. "Yeah, you say that, but, I mean, they're dogs. They could easily change their minds."

"That's not how it works. I command. They obey. It's as simple as that."

He laughs. "I bet your ego loves the fuck out of that."

My smile says it all. I do like being obeyed.

Vadim's quiet for a second, and I know what's coming before he even says it. He's the closest thing to a friend I have, and the only person I even halfway trust.

"You took out the mistress?" he finally asks.

"I did. It was unavoidable. They were fucking when I shot them."

He's cautious when he says, "Maybe you could've waited until she fell asleep."

My harsh laugh makes him turn his head to me. "I think you might be in the wrong line of work. There's no place for a conscience in this business. I couldn't have waited because she was a smoker. As soon as they'd finished, she would've walked out onto the balcony and had a cigarette, which is exactly where I was. Even if she hadn't been a smoker, they could've left the room, they could've ended up fucking all night, or Matteo could've just decided to leave early. I couldn't risk it. I had the opportunity, and I took it. End of story. She was fucking the mob boss's son. She knew the risks associated with that. It's not like he just picked her up for the night and she had no idea who he was."

"True enough," he admits.

"Get your head back in the game, Vadim. We still have work to do. There's another hit scheduled for tomorrow night."

"Yeah, I'm good," he assures me.

"Go get laid. It'll help calm your nerves."

"It's eight in the fucking morning. How the hell am I supposed to pick up a piece of ass this early?"

I laugh and smack his arm before opening the door. "I could do it."

"Jackass," he mutters, making me laugh even harder.

He drives off while I give a sharp whistle. Within seconds, four large dogs come running towards me from various directions. Each dog is assigned a section of the property. They never cease to amaze me. I swear they're smarter than a lot of people I know. When they're close enough, I drop down and pet them, rubbing heads and bellies and scratching behind ears. I lead them to the large automatic feeders I have set up and the four bowls of water, making sure they've eaten enough and have fresh water. After they've had a drink and eaten some breakfast, I send them back to work.

The house is large and devoid of everyone but me since I don't trust maids and cooks. I don't mind cleaning up after myself, and I know my way around a kitchen. Walking to my office, I check the security feed across the three large monitors on my desk. I didn't get any alerts on my phone, but I need to check it anyway. Paranoia keeps you safe in this business. Satisfied, I pull open the folder on my next target. There really is no rest for the wicked.

Chapter 2

Lydia

I look down at my high school diploma and wait to feel something —a sense of accomplishment, a flicker of pride, hell, even just a bit of relief, but there's nothing. All I feel is the need to move onto the next item on my life's to-do list. Graduate high school, check. Graduate as valedictorian, not a check, but still pretty damn close. Graduating fifth in my class had been enough to get me a full scholarship to my state university, and that's all I really care about. Go to college and get the fuck out of this town were soon to be checked off, and I couldn't be happier.

Weaving my way through the crowd of families who are all still posing for photos, I walk my solitary ass back to my car. I hadn't expected my dad to show, and I pretend it doesn't sting that he didn't prove me wrong. My dad and I have a strained relationship. My mom died when I was little, leaving my dad alone with a small daughter that he had no idea what to do with, so he kind of just didn't do anything. I raised myself, microwaving my own meals, making sure I always got my bath in before bed, and that my homework was always done, while he racked up gambling debt. I knew my only way out of this place was a scholarship, so that's what I'd put my focus on as soon as I hit high school. I was obsessed with it, giving up any chance of making friends or having a social life. I tell myself it was worth it as I drive away and ignore the sting of jealousy at seeing the laughing groups of friends, the boyfriends who are hugging their girlfriends, and the proud parents who can't stop smiling. Yeah, totally worth it.

I drive across town to the ranch-style house that's been my home since I was born. Carrying my diploma and cap, I stop to check on the irises I helped my mom plant when I was little. The purple flowers follow a line all along the front of the house, stopping at the border of yellow dahlias that flank the entire length of the sidewalk. I have few memories of my mom, but I remember she loved to work in the garden. She was always planting something new or watering the array of flowers she already had. Every time I put my hands in the soil or see a new bud open and bloom, I feel close to her.

When I step inside the house, I'm not at all surprised to find it empty. My dad is no doubt at the casino on the outskirts of town or at a private poker game. Either way, he won't be back for a while, and depending on how much he loses, he'll either slip in quietly or make a racket just to let the world know he's pissed. He's not a violent man; he's just not an affectionate one either. I get slight nods when he notices me and the occasional grunt of approval on very good days. Mostly we live a very quiet life, one where I bury my head in my textbooks and he works and then goes off to lose almost everything he just made. Occasionally we meet up for a TV dinner.

Peanut comes running in before I've even got the door shut. I drop to my knees and scoop my little Yorkie up, giving him a gentle squeeze and more kisses than he probably wanted. This little guy is my whole life, and I'm not ashamed to admit it.

"How's my little Peanut?" I scratch behind his ears and laugh when he gives an excited wiggle. Setting him down, he bolts into the kitchen, waiting for the dog biscuit that he knows is coming. Laughing, I follow him. He's already sitting patiently, giving me the cutest puppy-dog look, and when I hand him the treat, he takes it and runs off so he can eat part of it and then bury the rest, as per usual. There are half-eaten dog treats buried all over this house. I found one the other day in an old purse under my bed, and he'd been none too pleased at having his treasure unearthed.

While he's busy, I put my stuff away and then try and find some supper. Thirty minutes later, I'm sitting in front of the TV with a plate of pizza on my lap while Peanut sprawls across the cushion next to me, chewing on one of his many toys.

"Let's try this movie tonight," I tell him, clicking on a comedy that I've been wanting to watch. He lifts his head as if appraising my choice and then gets back to chewing. Instead of a wild graduation party, I get pizza and a movie with my best friend, who also happens to be my dog. Pathetic? Maybe, but it could be a hell of a lot worse. At least I won't end up with my head in the toilet or making a horrible life choice like losing my virginity to some horny guy who won't even remember the most likely very short encounter it would've been.

"Cheers, Peanut." I raise my slice of pizza to him and then sit back to watch the movie. Once the credits start, I'm stuffed and pushing away the bag of Twizzlers I decided to eat for dessert. I don't know why I can't ever just eat a couple of those damn things. Anytime I open a bag, it's kind of a done deal that I'm going to eat them all.

I groan and pat my stomach. "Why'd you let me do that?"

Peanut gives a soft yip and licks my hand before crawling into my lap. I pet him for a while before deciding it's time for bed. Keeping him in my arms, I put my dishes in the sink and carry him up to my bedroom. After getting ready and crawling into bed, I lay on my side and curl my body around Peanut, keeping a hand on him so I can pet him as I fall asleep. It's how I've slept with him since I found him wandering around two years ago. He was scared and way too thin, and I hadn't thought twice about bringing him home. Without a collar, I'd taken him to the vet to see if he was microchipped, but there wasn't one. He'd become mine right then and there. I think he's the best present the universe has ever given me. I kiss his nose before falling asleep with the warmth of his little body against mine.

A loud noise rips me from my deep sleep. My hands immediately look for Peanut. As soon as I feel his fur, I relax a little. He gives a soft whimper when there's another loud thud and then the sound of a chair being scraped across the floor. This wouldn't be the first time my dad's come home drunk after a night of gambling, but something about this feels wrong, and my half-asleep brain can't figure out why.

I get out of bed and grab Peanut when he runs over to the edge, whining for me to pick him up. Cradling him in my arms, I give his head a kiss and quietly make my way out of my room and down the hall. I don't know what's happening, but something tells me to not shout into the darkness for my dad to ask what the hell is going on. Tiptoeing down the hallway, I clutch Peanut to my chest. Right as I turn the corner, I hear what sounds exactly like two muffled gunshots, and it freezes me in place. When I lift my eyes, I see my dad sitting in our dining room chair. It seems like it takes my brain an impossibly long time to process the blood that's spreading across his shirt. His head hangs down, chin resting on chest, and I don't realize I'm crying until the tears fall on Peanut, making him give a soft whimper.

A sound pulls my attention to the right, and my whole body starts to shake when I see a man standing near the backdoor. He's huge, his head only a few inches lower than the top of the door, and he's dressed all in black. The hood of his sweatshirt is pulled low, keeping his face hidden. When my eyes fall to the gun at his side, everything inside me grows cold.

"Please," I whisper, and it's all I can manage. When he doesn't do anything, I beg in a shaky voice, "Please don't kill me."

Without a word, the man turns and leaves, giving me a brief glimpse of his lower cheek and jaw, both covered in a light, dark stubble. He's gone in seconds, and when I rush to my dad, I know he's dead before I even check for a pulse. My cell phone is still sitting on the counter, and the call to 911 is barely coherent. I eventually get the words out, and several minutes later, I hear sirens in the distance.

The police find me huddled in the corner, my face buried in Peanut's soft fur. When I refuse to part with my dog, they give up and let me bring him to the police station. I spend the next several hours going over my story and feeling completely disoriented.

"He was tall, you said?" Officer Jenson asks me yet again. He looks like he's not that much older than me, and when he scrubs a hand over his reddish blond mustache, I can tell he's getting frustrated with me.

"Yes, he was tall."

"But you didn't see anything else?"

"No. He just left. I barely got a glimpse of his face."

"You saw his face?" he perks up at this as Officer Roberts walks in. He's older, more like mid-forties instead of mid-twenties like Jenson, and he clearly doesn't share his younger partner's view on staying physically fit for this position. His large gut strains hard against the buttons of his shirt.

"No, not really," I say with an exhausted sigh. "He turned and I got just a brief glimpse. He had dark stubble. That's really all I can tell you."

The cops look at one another before Roberts lays a photo down on the table in front of me, right next to the stale coffee I've resisted drinking. The man in the photo is gorgeous in a scary-as-hell kind of way. His dark hair is thick and cut in a short style, his jaw chiseled and covered in a light stubble, and there's a scar running down the left side of his face and slicing through his cheek. That's not the scary part, though. It's his eyes. They're staring right at the camera, and they're the coldest damn things I've ever seen. They're completely devoid of all emotion, the stormy grey color just enhancing the overall terrifying feel of the man.

"Who is he?" I ask, my voice barely more than a whisper. I keep my eyes on the photo, unable to pull my gaze away.

"His name is Kirill Chernikov," Roberts says, "and we believe he's the man who killed your father."

I'm so surprised, I meet his eyes. "What? Why?"

Officer Roberts sits in the chair opposite me and rests his hands on his belly. "We picked him up near your house tonight, and he fits the description you gave."

"I didn't really give a description," I remind him, but he chooses to ignore me and instead reaches a paunchy hand across the table and points at Kirill.

"This man is a hitman for the Teterev Bratva. The guy's a fucking ghost. We think he's responsible for hundreds of murders all over the city, but so far we've never had enough evidence to put him away."

Roberts breaks out into a smile, and then reins it in when he remembers that we're here because I just watched my father get murdered.

"With your eyewitness testimony, we can finally get the bastard."

Jenson chimes in with, "We need to make sure he doesn't get away with it this time. You have the power to put the man in prison who just murdered your father. Don't you want that?"

Roberts waves his hand at Jenson, clearly telling the guy to back off a bit, and then he leans in closer, putting his beefy arms on the table between us and softening his expression. "Lydia, we know he did this. He was in the area, he's a known killer, and he fits the physical description you gave us. This is as cut and dry as it gets."

"But why would a hitman want to kill my dad?" I shake my head. "It just doesn't make sense."

In the same calm voice he's been using, Roberts says, "Lydia, you're a smart girl. I know you're aware of your father's gambling problem." He lets out a sigh as if it pains him to say any more, but he continues nonetheless. "The truth is he owed a lot of money, and some of that debt he'd racked up was to some very dangerous men."

I feel a pang of anger towards my dad's stupidity for getting involved with the fucking mafia, but then guilt replaces it when I remember it cost him is life. Looking down at the photo of Kirill, I run my fingers through Peanut's fur, letting his small presence comfort me. I try to imagine the man in the photo standing in our doorway. When I cover part of the photo with my hand, eyeing just the jaw and cheek, I can see how it could be him. They're both chiseled with dark stubble, and the guy is huge, way taller than the average man with broad shoulders that could easily be the same as the person I saw. What are the odds that a known hitman would be in the same area on the night that my dad is murdered? It's the only thing that makes sense, and when I start to nod my head, I hear the relieved breath that both officers give.

And just like that, it was a done deal. The next few weeks are an absolute nightmare. I went from being a high school graduate to a clueless adult who has to figure out how to arrange a funeral and find a job. Once the bills start arriving, I nearly have a panic attack. My dad's savings is enough to keep everything running for a little bit, but it's not going to last long. I've never felt so scared and alone, and I have no idea what the fuck to do. There's no way in hell I can keep everything going and go to college. I'd briefly spoken to a realtor who made it clear that nothing was selling lately, and if I did manage to sell this place, I'd barely bring in enough to cover what's owed on it. My only option is to stay here, get a job, and try to keep everything running as usual.

Every night I wake up from nightmares, images of my dad slumped over, except in my dreams, the tall man shrouded in darkness doesn't let me go. His face becomes Kirill's, and all I can do is stand frozen and helpless as he raises his gun and fires it at me, hitting me right in the chest, just like he did to my dad. I wake up screaming while Peanut whines and licks my hand, trying to coax me back to reality.

Daily I have to remind myself that my dad is actually dead. I'm so used to not seeing him. In a way, it's like nothing has changed. I can't honestly say that I miss him, because I don't feel like I ever really had him. I mourn him in my own way, though. I mourn the fact that I'll never get to know him, and I mourn the loss of the only family I had left.

By the time the trial starts, I'm still an emotional wreck, but at least I have a job, and I'm managing to get the bills paid. Thanks to my dad's life insurance I have enough to cover the lawyer fees, but there's hardly anything left over. The police assure me that the men my dad owed money to won't come after me, but I have a hard time believing them. They say that there's way too much publicity surrounding me right now and that they'd never risk it, but what happens when all the attention dies down? I try not to worry about it, but it's impossible not to.

I'm more of a mess than usual today. My hands won't stop shaking, and I feel like I'm going to pass out and throw up, each urge fighting with the other, but my body refuses to pick one, so I just sit here shaking while a war wages inside me. Maybe I'll get lucky and throw up before passing out on the witness stand. That would be the cherry on top of this fucking nightmare.

"We're ready for you now, Miss Moore."

I look over at the woman who's been assisting my lawyer. Stephanie's in her late twenties, and today her honey-blonde hair is pulled back into a stylish bun. Her blue eyes are the perfect mix of professionalism and sympathy, but underneath that is a hunger that will serve her well in the profession she's chosen. She's just as cutthroat as the others. It's just hidden behind a deceivingly sweet female face. I'm so glad she's on my side and that I won't have to face her on the stand.

"I don't know if I can do this," I admit, hating how shaky my voice sounds.

She squats down, managing to make the move look smooth and practiced, until she's eye level with me. Her black skirt is tucked demurely under her, so if anyone's looking, all they'll see is a few inches of toned thigh and calf.

Squeezing my hand, she says, "Lydia, you can do this. You're stronger than you think, and we're going to go in there together, and we're going to get that bastard. We're going to get justice for your father, and once all this is over, you're going to feel so much better. Seeing him behind bars will give you peace. It'll help you move on."

I nod my head and take a deep breath. I know she's right, and I also know I have no choice. I have to do this. Everything hinges on me going in there and identifying the man who shot my dad. A soft but insistent voice in my head reminds me that I didn't actually see who shot my dad, but I shush it, because it has to be Kirill. It fucking has to be. There's no other explanation.

Stephanie gives my hand another squeeze before standing and waiting for me to do the same. She gives me one last encouraging smile and then leads the way into the packed courtroom. I keep my head down, avoiding everyone and wishing like hell I could've brought Peanut with me. When I'm called up, I go on shaky legs and then swear that I'll tell the truth. It *is* the truth, I tell myself. Kirill Chernikov killed my dad, and he's going to pay for it. He's a known killer, and he was fucking there, one goddamn street over from our house. With my resolve firmly in place, I finally raise my eyes to face the monster who ruined my life.

I'm not sure what I'm expecting, but his smug face isn't it. He's staring right at me, those cold, grey eyes piercing right through me while a smirk tugs at his full lips. The man is huge. His body seeming way too big for the chair he's in. I found out from the police that he's six-five, and he looks every inch of it today. His suit has to be bespoke. There's no way in fuck that came off a rack. It's molded to him perfectly and obviously made to his exact measurements.

The more I look, the more he confuses me. If someone pointed him out to me and told me he was a successful owner of some company, I wouldn't bat an eye. He exudes power and authority, like he's a man who's just used to being obeyed and getting what he wants. But he's not some arrogant CEO, he's a fucking hitman for a powerful, dangerous Bratva. The cruelty that lives within him feels like it's right below the surface, making me wonder if I ran over to him and raked my nails across his chiseled jaw, would I let it out? Would that tear in the skin expose him for the monster he is?

I break eye contact first, and I don't have to see him to know that his smirk has grown. I can feel it from where I'm sitting. After answering a million questions about the night my dad was shot, I'm finally asked the one that I've been dreading.

"Can you identify the man who shot your father?" my lawyer asks.

Using every ounce of courage I possess, I meet Kirill's eyes yet again and point my finger at him. "It was him," I say, my voice no longer shaky. It's strong as it echoes through the courtroom. "He shot my dad." Before I look away, Kirill winks at me.

Turns out Stephanie was wrong. After Kirill was sentenced to life in prison, I didn't feel better. I still have nightmares. I still wake up screaming, and my life is still a stressful mess of working at a job I never wanted and worrying about bills that I never should've had to pay. I went from being an excited, somewhat carefree eighteen-year-old to being an adult who's stuck in a life I never wanted. I didn't think it could get any worse, but then the first letter arrived six months later. I found it tucked under a rock right outside my front door.

My dear, sweet Lydia,

Prison isn't all that bad. It's given me a lot of time to think, and you're what occupies my thoughts. I'm not going to lie. I was very angry at you for a long time. My first six months here were spent thinking about how badly I wanted to make you pay for what you've done, but the more I tried to hate you, the less I did.

I'm not sure what you've done to me, zaika. I confess that I've become a bit obsessed. I keep seeing your beautiful face, exactly how you looked when you pointed me out to the courtroom. So scared, yet so strong and determined to do what you thought was right. God, I'm hard just thinking about it. I wish I could've crossed the distance between us and traced a line along your neck with my lips, breathing in the scent of you before running my tongue along your skin. I'd give anything to feel the rapid beat of your pulse against my lips. One day, zaika.

First, I need to explain to you what's going to happen. I'm stuck in prison for now, but I won't be staying here forever. I'll get out, and when I do, I'm coming for you, sweetheart. You put the wrong man in prison, and I want to know why. I have someone watching you, so don't go getting any ideas about alerting the police to my letters. I will continue to write them, and you will write me back. Put the letters under the rock, just like how you found this one, and one of my men will make sure I get it. If you tell the police, it won't change anything. It will just really piss me the fuck off, and trust me when I say you don't want to do that.

One more thing before I stop. You are not allowed to date anyone.

You are not allowed to fuck anyone. You are not allowed to touch anyone. You are mine, Lydia, and I don't fucking share. Break my rules, and it will end in blood. That is the only warning you will get about this. I expect complete obedience in this and in all things. No one touches you but me.

Write me back, zaika. I want to know everything about you, so I better not just get two sentences from you. I'm bored, and all my time is spent thinking about you. I need something more substantial than the little information I have. I want to know you, the real you.

Talk to you soon, sweetheart.

Kirill

P.S. Pet Peanut for me.

Chapter 3

Kirill

The first letter I receive from Lydia leaves a lot to be desired. My little bunny, my *zaika*, has already decided to disobey me. My hand aches with the need to spank her perky ass, but her punishment will have to wait. A lot of things will have to wait. I pace the small, solitary cell they have me in and read her letter yet again.

> *Kirill,*
>
> *Stop writing me. You're a fucking psycho, and you killed my dad. I have nothing to say to you.*
>
> *Lydia*
>
> *P.S. Fuck off.*

I'm pissed, but it doesn't stop me from bringing the letter to my face and trying like hell to breathe in some hint of her scent. I swear I catch a soft whiff of jasmine, but that might just be my imagination. I like her spunk, not that I'll ever admit that to her, but she needs to learn that I'm not a man to disobey. She sent me to prison. She should be damn grateful I haven't put a hit out on her ass. The first six months of being here were a blur of nothing but pure rage. I'd tried so hard to hate Lydia and spent most of my time devising just how I was going to make her pay for putting me in here, but all the scenarios ended with me tying her to the bed while I spanked her bare ass and she begged me to fuck her. It was infuriating to say the least. The more I learned about her, the more intrigued I became. It's safe to say I'm a bit obsessed.

Sitting down, I grab a pen and some paper and remind myself that this isn't going to happen overnight. I'm a patient man, and I have nothing but time. My *zaika* will learn to love me. She doesn't have a choice. First I write a brief note to Vadim, the man now in charge of keeping a close eye on Lydia, instructing him to gently convince her that writing me is the wise choice. I also ask him how my dogs are doing. As a man who prides himself on having zero attachments, I have to admit that I miss them like crazy. The next letter is all for my girl.

Zaika,

I forgive your angry, insulting letter, sweetheart, because I know you're grieving. I'm sorry I can't be there to help you feel better. It must be terrible to go through this all on your own. My dad died when I was around your age. I'm not going to lie to you. I will never lie to you, Lydia. You'll carry around his death for the rest of your life, but it will get easier.

I stop and smile at the thought of my father. He'd been a mean son of a bitch who liked to beat my mom. Killing him had felt damn good, and the memory always makes me grin. I don't bother mentioning those details to Lydia. Every relationship needs a bit of mystery.

I expect a letter from you very soon. I will not fuck off, as you so rudely suggested. I'm here to stay, zaika. There is no getting rid of me.

Write me a letter and tell me about yourself.

Kirill

Satisfied, I fold the two pieces of paper and put them in an envelope. When Tony walks past my door, I hand him the letters. He takes them with a grunt, barely even bothering to glance through the small window. I catch sight of his ruddy, chubby cheeks, and then he's gone. I won't see him again until tomorrow. I don't know what he's so pissy about. I'm spending a goddamn fortune to keep him on my payroll. His kids will go to college because of me. All he has to do is keep me in my nice solitary cell and be my little messenger boy, delivering things between me and Vadim. Easy way to make a million.

Ensuring I would get a solitary cell wasn't hard to do. Even after paying off Tony, I had to make it seem a necessity, so the first day I was here, I killed someone, crushed his goddamn throat when the stupid fucker tried to pick a fight with me. Tony had stepped in and taken control while also earning him a little bit of respect from his fellow correctional officers. I tower over most men, and I've always worked hard to keep myself in top physical condition. Most people give me a very wide berth. I'd let the little guy have his fun, though, and humbly followed him to my new cell. I'm not worried about my safety in the general population. I can take care of myself, but I don't like company, and a roommate would no doubt annoy the hell out of me. I'd rather not deal with it. Plus, no one gets to see what belongs to me.

Sitting on my cot, I rest my forearms on my legs and stare at the wall in front of me. I've taped up several photos of Lydia that Vadim has sent me. I've already memorized every detail of her face—the big, blue eyes, the long, dark hair that shows hints of red when she's in the sun, and the slight build. She's perfect, and she's going to be what gets me through this hell. She will be my salvation, the reason I wake up in the morning, and she will be what helps me keep my sanity in this cell that feels like it's constantly growing smaller.

This isn't the first time I've been locked up, but it's damn well going to be the last. I spent a few months in a real shithole in Russia when I was eighteen, and that place makes this place look like the fucking Hilton. I can survive this. I can fucking survive anything.

Keeping my eyes locked on the photo of Lydia in a white sundress with little pink flowers on it, my mind oscillates between wanting to fuck her so hard she'll barely be able to walk when I'm done, each hard thrust a reminder of why she shouldn't have pointed me out in that courtroom, and wanting to fuck her slowly and treating her like the delicate little thing she is. I don't want to break her, at least I don't think I do, not fully anyway. Maybe just a little bit. Maybe just enough to show her who's really in control, and it sure as hell isn't her.

I stare at the wall until my supper tray arrives. It's as unappetizing as every meal that's come before, but I eat it all anyway, barely tasting the watery mashed potatoes and hunk of meatloaf. Spearing a green bean on my plastic spork, I keep my eyes on Lydia and finish the rest of my food.

It takes two weeks for me to get a return letter. My little bunny held out longer than I thought she would. Her strength both amazes and infuriates me. Tony's leading me back to my cell after my two-hour daily break. I spend most of it lifting weights, only taking a quick shower right before it's time for me to go back to my small dungeon. When he locks me in, he hands me a small package.

"You're a good man, Tony," I tell him, but he just scowls harder than usual.

"Yeah, they'll probably give me a medal for this."

"It's hard to make a living nowadays. You're ensuring your family will be taken care of. Can't fault a man for that."

He ignores my little pep talk, and I try not to laugh. He's a greedy dick, who's willingly put himself on my payroll, a hitman for a notorious Bratva. Not Tony's finest hour. Of course, if he hadn't taken the money, my man would've had to kill him, and then someone else would be standing here delivering my messages. It makes no difference to me who it is, just as long as the job gets done.

Opening the package, I groan when I see a sealed baggie with pink, lacy panties in it. Resisting the urge to tear into it right away, I set it aside and grab the letter that's written in Russian.

Boss,

It took a little convincing, but after breaking in and rearranging her living room furniture, she finally decided it was in her best interest to write. She's following her usual routine, going to work and walking her dog, but she's constantly looking over her shoulder and looks like she's lost a bit of weight. She also spends a lot of time in her flower garden. Everything seems normal, but she still wakes up screaming every night.

I found this pair of underwear in a pile of dirty clothes. Thought you might want them. Don't worry, I didn't touch them with my bare hands or sniff them. I don't have a death wish.

Your dogs are doing good. They haven't eaten me yet, so I'm taking that as a good sign. The Teterevs and Farettis are still slowly killing one another. Rumor has it Ivan is very, very pissed. Without you, he's not nearly as strong as he was.

Vadim

He's smart enough to not include a picture of my dogs. No photos of anything to do with my house. Ever. The mention of Ivan worries me a bit, but there's nothing I can do about the shitstorm he paid me to create. He can get his own ass out of trouble for once.

I pick up Lydia's letter, pleased to see that it's longer than the last one. It's not as long as I want, but still, progress is progress. I run my fingers over her pretty cursive, and this time when I smell the paper, I'm positive I get a whiff of jasmine. Just that one smell is enough to have my cock straining against my pants. Savoring every second of this moment, I lay back on my thin mattress and read my girl's letter.

Kirill,

Congratulations, you've scared me enough to write your goddamn letter. Who the hell broke into my house? Why would you have someone do that? Do you have any idea how terrifying it is to know that a hitman has people breaking into my home? Are you going to kill me?

I don't know what you want from me. I saw you that night. I saw you kill my dad. I couldn't just not say anything in that courtroom.

You have ruined my life, Kirill. I worked my ass off in high school so that I could get a full scholarship, and I had to give all that up. I work forty hours a week as a cashier in a grocery store, although I'm sure you already know that, you fucking psycho, and I don't see my life getting any better. I may not have been close to my dad, but he was still my dad, and you murdered him. Why did you let me live? What kind of hitman leaves witnesses? Maybe you're just not a very good one...

I have to stop because I'm laughing too hard to continue. God, my little bunny has balls of steel. Slipping a hand into the orange pants they issued me, I lazily stroke myself while I keep reading.

Will you leave me alone if I ask nicely? Please, please, please leave me alone, Kirill. What's done is done, and you're in prison for life now. I think you should just accept that and try to move on. I know I'm trying to. I've done what you asked, and I didn't go to the police, but I want you to stop now. No more letters, no more breaking into my house, just no more anything. Let me live my pathetic life in peace.

Lydia

P.S. Don't ever mention Peanut again. It feels like a threat, and I swear to God, if you hurt my dog, I will find a way to fucking kill you.

P.P.S. Please fuck off.

As soon as I finish her letter, I reach for the sealed plastic bag and rip it open, pawing at her lacy panties like a fucking animal. I work myself harder and bring them to my face, taking in a lungful of her pussy's sweet scent. God, she makes me fucking feral. I tighten my grip on my shaft and pick up the pace. Unable to resist, I bite the crotch of her panties between my teeth and run my tongue over the used strip of fabric, the same strip that was nestled against her sweet cunt. Her name echoes through my mind as I explode in my goddamn hand. The force of the orgasm leaves me breathless and my heart pounding in my ears.

"Fucking hell," I groan when I pull her panties out of my mouth. I give them one more sniff before cleaning myself up and grabbing a pen and some paper.

Dear Zaika,

So many questions. You are a curious little bunny, aren't you? I'll try to answer them all because the last thing I want is to disappoint you.

First, I would never hurt Peanut. I've never hurt an animal in my life, and I never would. I have four dogs of my own. They're beautiful Belgian Malinois, and I can't wait for you to meet them. I've never brought a woman to my home before, but I'm going to bring you.

I'm sorry you're stuck working a job you hate, but it won't be for long. I'd give you money now, but we don't want to look too suspicious, now do we? Just know that once I'm out of here, you'll never have to work another day in your life, sweetheart. I will take care of you and give you anything you want. My little bunny deserves nothing less.

There's something you should know about me, Lydia. I'm a man who likes to be obeyed, and you refused to write me like I asked, so I had a friend give you a gentle nudge in the right direction. You are a stubborn little thing. I'm guessing you'll be walking around with my handprint on your ass more times than not. I think my girl needs some discipline. Don't worry, baby, I'll always make it enjoyable. Pain mixed with pleasure always. Despite what you may think, I'm not a cruel man. Never to you, anyway.

Spanking aside, I am not going to hurt you, Lydia, so please stop worrying about that, but you're very right about one thing: I don't leave witnesses. You're still alive. Do the math, sweetheart. I know you can. You were almost valedictorian.

Are you getting enough sleep? I'm told you're still waking up screaming. I'm more sorry than I can say that you have to wake up alone. I've never wanted to take care of anyone before, but I want to take care of you, Lydia. I look forward to the day when you welcome that instead of fear it.

Tell me what your favorite movies and books are. What kind of music do you like? You like to plant flowers? When did that start? What's your favorite kind? I want to know everything about you.

You have no idea how much I love the part in your last letter where you beg me. I can't wait to hear it in person, except you won't be begging me to leave; you'll be begging me to stay.

Thanks for the pink, lacy panties, zaika. You smell fucking divine. Before I wrote this letter I had them in my mouth, running my tongue over the used fabric while I jerked myself off. God, the things I'm going to do to you, sweetheart. I can't fucking wait.

I'm always thinking about you,

Kirill

P.S. Don't forget what I said about other men. I know you're a virgin, and you'd better damn well stay that way. I will kill any man who dares to touch you. That pussy is mine, sweetheart.

P.P.S. Write back soon!

Chapter 4

Lydia

I stare at the letter in my hand and read it yet again. This man is crazy. Worse, he's *obsessed* and crazy. That's like crazy on top of crazy, and all of that is focused on me. I have no idea what to do. The obvious choice is to go to the police and hand all this over, but I don't trust them to be able to keep me safe. Kirill has a man watching me, obviously, and the fucker broke into my home *while I was sleeping* without me even knowing. That thought alone is enough to get me to keep my damn mouth shut.

Peanut nuzzles my hand and gives it a quick lick. "It's okay, buddy," I tell him. "I won't let the crazy bastard get you."

He looks up at me with absolute trust and love, and I know I'd do anything to keep him safe. He's the only family I have. I briefly wonder if Kirill was telling the truth about his dogs. I'd looked them up online, and I'm not at all surprised that they're the kind of dog that could easily rip a man's throat out. Like owner like pet. I look down at Peanut's sweet face and kiss his nose. He may not be fierce enough to protect me in quite the same way, but this little guy has saved me over and over again in more ways than I can count. I'll take that over brute force any day.

I read over the end of his letter again. Kirill may be completely off his rocker, but I don't understand why he keeps trying to convince me that he's not a threat or why he even wants to write me. Everything about this confuses me. He's never denied what he is to me in his letters, and he's already sentenced and knows that there's no way in hell confessing to the crime is going to make things worse at this point, so why keep hinting at his innocence?

The little voice in the back of my head reminds me that I didn't see the man who shot my dad. I caught a glimpse of a cheek and chin. That's hardly identifying someone. They don't do cheek and chin line-ups for fuck's sake.

My mind keeps going back to the mention of my pink panties. I'd been looking for them a few days ago and just assumed they were around here somewhere, but now I know that he had his creepy underling steal them. I remember exactly what Kirill looks like. His face haunts my every waking thought and also my dreams. He scares me, but there's no denying he's the most attractive man I've ever seen. The thought of him jerking off to my panties, well, goddamn, that does something to me when I know that it absolutely should not. I stuff the thought down deep, way, way deep, because I'm not willing to admit how fucked up I might be.

"We're gonna bottle that shit down deep, Peanut."

He gives a soft yip, encouraging me in my not-so-healthy coping choice. Pushing the letter aside, I decide it's time to take some serious action. Kirill has set his sights on me, and I think it's because he sees me as his. He's fixated on me and thinks that I belong to him, but what if I take away the one thing he thinks he has a right to? If I find some random dude and lose my virginity, then I'll no longer have what he wants. He said there's a man watching me, but he can't watch me all the damn time. He can't be everywhere at once. A plan starts to form as I nibble on a piece of red licorice. It's not brilliant by any stretch of the imagination, but it just might work.

Two hours later, I'm petting Peanut goodbye and slipping out my front door like I'm not up to no good. I'm carrying my reusable grocery bags, swinging them as I walk in a causal, *hey, just going grocery shopping* kind of way for anyone who might be spying on me. While I head downtown, I notice my car is still making the wonky noise that I've been pretending I don't hear for the last couple of weeks because I don't want to deal with it. I park in front of the grocery store I work at and walk in. As soon as I'm through the entrance, I bolt for the employee breakroom, giving a quick nod to one of my coworkers before slipping out the private door in the back. I race across the dark alley, hoping that all the perverts in the area took the night off. I make it down the narrow alley unscathed and practically run to the nightclub at the end of the street.

I pay the ridiculous cover charge, get my hand stamped so no one will sell me alcohol, and then disappear into the dark club. It's Friday night, so the place is packed. Loud, thumping music vibrates up from the floor, and when I start to weave through the crowd, I get a few smiles from the guys around me. When I see a guy who looks close to my age with a friendly face, I smile back, figuring he's as good as anyone. This isn't about love. This is about making myself undesirable to the guy who's stalking me. Clearly, this has all the elements of a good life choice.

"Hey," he says, walking over and leaning down so I can hear him over the music. "What's your name?"

Now that I've reeled a man in, I have no idea what to do. I've got a few chaste kisses under my belt. That's what I'm working with here, and a huge flaw in my plan becomes painfully obvious.

"Lydia," I finally stammer out when he's still waiting for an answer.

"Pretty name." He wraps an arm around my shoulder and pulls me closer to the bar. "Want a drink?"

"Um, I'm only eighteen." I hold up my hand like he's asked for proof. Deciding this may not be the best idea, I try to wriggle out of his grasp, but he squeezes my shoulder tighter and smiles even bigger.

"Don't worry about it," he says with a wink. "It'll help loosen you up."

He waves the bartender over and orders a drink for me while I study his profile. His light brown hair is long enough to curl in the back and every once in a while a piece will fall across his forehead, making him brush it away in a practiced move. Light brown eyes meet mine, and I quickly look away. He gives a soft laugh before handing me the freshly made drink. He's wearing a ring on his left hand, and I recognize it as being from the university I'd been given a scholarship to.

"Drink it. It'll make you feel better."

I take the glass, but I don't drink it. Something flashes across his face, but it's gone before I can decipher it. He nudges my hand.

"Don't be scared, Lydia. I won't let anything happen to you."

"What's your name?"

He gives me a big, charming smile, revealing a perfect set of teeth. "I'm Kyle."

I nod and look around the crowded club. The dance floor is packed, every table is filled, and by the looks of it, most people are well on their way to getting shit-faced. I suddenly feel very stupid. This is not how I want my first time to go down. I have no idea who this guy is, and the way he keeps trying to get me drunk has alarm bells ringing all through my brain. I'm here. I managed to sneak past whoever the hell is watching me, which means I can just lie about fucking some random dude. I don't need to actually make the horrible mistake of doing so. God, I'm an idiot.

Shoving the drink back at Kyle, I give him an embarrassed smile. "I'm sorry. I need to go."

"Hey, wait." He grabs my arm, refusing to let me go. "Why are you leaving? You just got here."

I jerk my arm away. "I changed my mind. I'm leaving."

He tightens his fingers, and for one horrible moment I'm afraid he's not going to let go, but then he gets control of himself and lets out a harsh laugh.

"Whatever. Get the fuck out of here."

Surprised by the hard tone of his voice and the cruel look he's giving me, I quickly turn and push my way through the crowd, knowing how damn close I just came to making a huge mistake. Once outside, I run down the sidewalk, checking over my shoulder every few seconds to make sure Kyle isn't following me. It's no longer Kirill's man I'm afraid of. I let out a huge sigh of relief when I make it back to my car. On the drive home, I promise myself I won't ever attempt anything that fucking stupid again. I'll figure out another way to get rid of Kirill.

I'm convinced I've gotten away with my stupid stunt, that is until I open my front door the next morning and find a small box with a note underneath it. The box is wrapped in red paper with a silver string tied around it, ending in a big, loopy bow. Grabbing the box and note, I bring them inside and lean against the kitchen counter. Pulling the string, I slowly untie it and then lift the lid.

"Oh my god!" I yell when I see the finger inside. When I see the part that's been snipped and notice the white bone surrounded by red flesh, I drop the box and dry heave. The finger rolls across the kitchen floor, and as soon as I see Peanut lunge for it, I let out another yell and dive for him, scooping him into my arms before he can wrap his little teeth around it and take off running, no doubt wanting to bury it with his half-eaten treats.

"Sorry, Peanut," I whisper and pet his head to calm him down.

My eyes stay locked to the ring that's now lying on the tiled floor. I recognize the university ring that's still wrapped around the meaty part of the finger, right below the knuckle. Kyle's finger is on my goddamn kitchen floor. I'm so frazzled I can barely think. I grab a pair of tongs from the drawer and grip the finger before carefully putting it back in the box and closing the lid. I scoot it to the edge of the counter and reach for the note. My hands are shaking so badly that I have to set the note down so I can read it.

Zaika,

I am disappointed. Is someone testing their boundaries? I'm guessing after seeing the present I left for you, you now know just how serious I am about this. I warned you of this, Lydia, and if you want someone to blame, sweetheart, you can pick that finger up and point it right at your beautiful face. No one is allowed to touch you but me.

Before you get yourself in a huff about my caveman ways, let me first say that you got damn lucky last night. That jackass slipped something in the drink he was so desperate for you to take. Ever heard of date-rape drugs, sweetheart? Do you have any idea how crazy it makes me to know that you were in danger and that I'm stuck in here and can't do a goddamn thing about it? I'm not there to protect you myself, zaika, so I need you to be extra careful until I can be there with you.

I lift my head and sigh. I knew something felt off about the way he was constantly pushing that drink at me. I glance over at the sealed box, trying to muster up some sympathy because that really must've hurt like a bitch, but right now I'm tapped out, so I turn back to the letter instead.

I'm guessing your plan was to just sleep with some random guy. Maybe then I'd leave you alone because clearly I only want you since you're a virgin? Am I close?

Jesus Christ, is this guy a mind reader?

Let me set your mind at ease, Lydia. I'm not going to lie and say it doesn't thrill me to no end that you've never been with a man, that I'm going to get to be your first and only, but I would feel the same way about you even if you'd slept with your whole goddamn high school. I'd kill them all, naturally, but it wouldn't make me feel any differently about you. Feel better?

I snort out a laugh to my empty kitchen. No, Kirill, that does not make me feel better.

I suggest we put this little slipup behind us. You tested things, and a douchebag lost his finger. Lessons learned all around. Don't make me teach you another one, sweetheart.

This is my second letter to you, and I'm still waiting for a response. Be a good girl and write me back. I want to know how you're doing.

Kirill

P.S. I have several photos of you hanging on my wall, and in my favorite one you're wearing a white sundress with pink flowers. I dream about you in that dress, zaika. One day I'm going to slide my hand between those pretty thighs of yours and cup what's mine. Will I find your pussy wet, sweetheart? I bet it will be.

I step back and take in a much-needed breath. I didn't know about the photos. I didn't know his cell was covered in pictures of me and that he stared at them all day, every day. He's never going to just forget about me. I'm guessing a man like Kirill never stops until he has what he wants, and for whatever reason, he wants me.

Eyeing the box that holds Kyle's severed finger, I debate what to do. I can't just throw it out with the garbage, can I? What if it somehow gets traced back to me? In the end, I decide to bury it beside one of the rose bushes in my backyard. Peanut sits and watches, looking like he thinks I'm losing my mind. Maybe I am. I dig a shallow hole and then envision a curious, hungry squirrel getting ahold of it and running off. I can just imagine drinking my coffee in front of the window, watching the cute little thing run off with Kyle's college ring glinting in the sun. I dig deeper and then set the box in before filling it back up.

I would be feeling some serious guilt right now if Kyle had been a sweet guy. I'm hoping the next time he wants to drug a woman, he'll look down at his nub and reconsider. I snort out a laugh and then shake my head.

"I'm losing my mind, Peanut."

He jumps in my lap and lets me carry him back inside. I get ready for work in a daze, and by the time I'm giving Peanut his goodbye hug, I'm more confused than ever about my situation. Things could be worse. Kirill could want to kill me. His letters could be filled with death threats and vivid descriptions of all the ways he's planning on torturing me. Instead, the man wants to fuck and take care of me.

He's a psycho a little singsong voice says in the back of my head. Pushing everything from my mind, I get in my car and head to work. I'm halfway there when I realize my car is no longer making the wonky, clicking noise. When I park, I notice the little sticker in the upper corner of my windshield is brand new. Someone fucking fixed my car and got my oil changed. God, Kirill's man was busy last night. Instead of being freaked out, I'm actually kind of relieved. I don't have the money for car maintenance, and now I don't have to worry about it. Maybe if I mention that I don't like to take out the garbage, Kirill will add that to his man's to-do list. I bark out a laugh into my empty car and then shake my head.

"This is not normal," I mutter. "This is so not fucking normal."

I scan the nearly empty parking lot, not at all surprised when I don't see anything out of the ordinary. Whoever's watching me is damn good at his job. The rest of the morning passes by with the same monotonous boredom that I'm accustomed to. There was an exciting moment when I got yelled at because I couldn't honor an expired coupon, but other than that, it was a typical morning.

I'm so used to keeping to myself that it takes me a second to realize someone's joined me at the small corner table I always eat my lunch at. I look up and meet Chris's eyes, unable to hide my surprise at seeing him.

"Sorry, I didn't mean to startle you," he quickly says.

Chris is a few years older than me, and he's been nothing but nice to me since I started working here. I get the distinct impression he feels sorry for me.

"No, you didn't startle me." I laugh at his expression. "Okay, maybe a little bit, but it's okay."

He opens his container of lunch and says, "Sorry you got yelled at earlier. People can be such assholes."

"It's all right. I briefly thought about just slipping fifty cents to the woman to make up for the coupon loss, but I thought that might just make her yell even louder."

"Probably," he agrees before taking a bite of his pasta.

We finish our break talking about the manager who just up and quit and the schedule for next week. Chris seems on edge, and it isn't until I'm gathering up my stuff that he finally says, "Do you think maybe we could hang out sometime?"

I'm so surprised that I don't say anything, just stand there looking at him while he grows more uncomfortable with each passing second. I finally find my voice.

"Oh, um, I'm not so sure that's such a great idea." I'm not thinking about Kirill when I tell him no. I just have no desire to date Chris. There's nothing wrong with him. He's a really sweet guy, but there's just nothing there for me.

That's because he's not a tall, gorgeous hitman with a sexy Russian accent.

I shove the annoying thought away and try to look at Chris without comparing him to the grey-eyed devil who haunts my every thought. It's impossible not to, though, and poor Chris falls short on all counts. He just doesn't stir anything inside me. He'll be a great boyfriend for someone, that someone is just not going to be me.

I can see the disappointment on his face, but he covers it as best he can with a friendly smile. "Sure, yeah, you're right." He lets out a soft laugh. "Rumor has it I might be promoted to manager, so I guess it would be frowned upon anyway."

"Yeah, definitely," I say, trying to make it seem like that was the reason all along. "Don't want to piss off the bosses."

He runs a hand through his blond hair but is careful to avoid my eyes. "Guess I'll see you around, Lydia."

"I'll be here." I give a dorky laugh that I wish I could take back as soon as it leaves my mouth. I swear I catch a glimpse of relief on his face, like he's just now realizing the bullet he dodged with my messed-up ass. Yeah, Chris, I've got issues. Better run fast and far before my insane hitman stalker comes after you.

Later that night, I debate what to do. I think about writing Kirill a letter, but then decide that the best thing is for me to just ignore him. If I keep to myself, then he won't have any fingers to chop off, or worse, and this will give him the opportunity to prove that what he says is true and that he won't hurt me. The idea of not writing him agitates me, which is all the more reason to not write him. He's getting under my skin, and that won't lead to anything good, at least not for me.

The next morning, my doorstep is empty, and I pretend that I'm thrilled about it and ignore the slight annoyance I feel at not having a new letter to read. It's my day off, so I throw on some old clothes and spend the morning planting some new flowers. I'm brushing dirt off my jeans and not paying attention to where I'm going when I trip over the hose and fall on my ass. I stick my arm out to break my fall and end up landing on my wrist in a way that sends a white-hot flash of pain up my arm as my breath leaves my lungs in a painful hiss.

Peanut runs over to me when I groan and clutch my arm to my chest. I look down, breathing out a sigh of relief when I don't see a bone sticking out anywhere, but stretching out my arm and trying to wiggle my fingers sends another jolt of pain straight through me.

"That's probably not a good sign," I tell Peanut. He sniffs my hand and gives a soft whine. I think about my measly bank account and the huge deductible on my insurance and decide that it's probably not broken. "Nothing a little aspirin can't fix," I mutter and slowly get my ass back up to standing. At least I had enough sense to fall on my left arm.

An hour later I'm petting Peanut goodbye and walking to my car. Fuck this. My wrist is twice the size it was and the aspirin isn't doing shit to dull the pain. I keep my arm glued to my chest and drive one-handed to the emergency room. Once I've signed in, I sit down and wish like hell I had someone here with me. My bastard of a mind immediately imagines what it would be like to have Kirill by my side. God, he probably would've done some over-the-top man move like carrying me in bridal style while yelling for a doctor. I smile at my own stupid fantasy. There's no one here to take care of me, so I sit in the uncomfortable, plastic chair for three goddamn hours until they finally decide to call me back.

After x-rays and an examine that brings tears to my eyes as the doctor prods my tender arm, it's finally decided that I have a nasty sprain, and I need to immobilize it for a couple of weeks. He wraps it in an elastic bandage and tells me to buy a sling. I do get a nice prescription from some painkillers, though, so not a wasted trip at all.

I dread checking out. I'm scared to death the bill is going to empty my measly savings, but when I tell the receptionist my name, she smiles and says, "Okay, Ms. Moore, you're good to go."

"Huh?"

"I said you're good to go. Everything's taken care of."

"What do you mean? Don't I have a copay?" I briefly wonder why the hell I'm arguing with her. If it's a clerical error, then I should just be grateful for the good luck and get my ass out of here before they realize the mistake.

"Your bill has been paid," she says, speaking slowly in the hopes that I'll get it this time.

"Who paid it?"

"A nice gentleman paid it while you were in the exam room."

I shoot my head around, running my eyes over everyone in the waiting room, but aside from a man holding a bleeding hand and a woman with a screaming toddler, the place is empty.

"Is he here? Do you see him?"

She arches a manicured brow at me. "No," she says even slower, making me feel like a real dumbass. "He left before you came out."

"What did he look like?"

"Tall, light brown hair with a slight beard, hazel eyes." A soft smile plays at her lips. "He was very handsome."

I thank her and then race to the pharmacy. With my pills in hand, I drive home, the pain in my arm fading to the background while I think about what just happened. Kirill paid my hospital bills, and I have a description of the man who's been following me, of the man who broke into my home. Shutting my car door, I walk to my house and stop by the front door. I turn around, scanning the street I live on. I don't expect to see anyone, but at least now I know who I'm looking for.

Peanut goes nuts when I walk in, scampering around my feet while whimpering and sniffing all the hospital smells. Too worn out to do much of anything, I let Peanut out to use the bathroom and then send a message to Chris, letting him know I've sprained my wrist and asking if someone can cover my shift tomorrow. He immediately responds and tells me it's not a problem and hopes I feel better soon. With that taken care of, I pop a pain pill and lay down on the couch. Peanut cuddles up beside me, and the next thing I know it's morning.

Even with my drug-fuzzy brain, my first thought is still of Kirill. I stumble to the door, and when I open it, I can't help but smile when I see the giant care package that's waiting for me. I grab the basket with my good hand and lug it inside. Peanut runs over and sits down beside me while I look through everything. There's a bouquet of red roses, a sling, a heating pad, some ice packs, several bags of Twizzlers, my favorite hot chocolate, some really comfy-looking pajamas, and there's even a box of Peanut's favorite milk bones. When I give him one, he wags his little tail like crazy before bolting down the hall. I open the letter last.

My sweet zaika,

I heard you had a little fall yesterday. I'm not a man who cares about much, Lydia, but when I found out you were in the emergency room all alone, it made this damn cell feel even smaller than it already is. I can be patient, at least I thought I could be, but my need to take care of you is overwhelming at times. I'm sorry I wasn't there with you, that I couldn't drive you to the hospital and wait with you. I'm sorry I couldn't be there to take care of you. You would not have had to wait three hours if I'd been there with you.

I hope this stuff helps in some small way. Be sure to wear the sling, zaika. Baby the arm, don't use it, and be sure to ice it regularly and then later you can move on to the heating pad. Be careful with the painkillers. Don't take them if you're going to be driving. You'll find enough money in this envelope so that you can take the week off. I'm sure Chris will understand. I know what you're thinking, zaika, but don't worry. I won't be taking any of Chris's fingers. He's a smart man and decided to take the hint. I'm not cruel, Lydia, but I guess you'll learn that in time.

I've been told you can eat your bodyweight in licorice, so I hope this is enough.

I'm always thinking about you,

Kirill

P.S. I know it's the left wrist you sprained. Write me a damn letter.

P.P.S. I hope Peanut likes his treats.

I smile at the note, rereading it again, and I don't care that I should hate him. The basket and note are sweet. Horrible people don't do this. They don't buy you comfy pajamas and your favorite snacks and write sweet letters. I open the first bag of licorice and start eating while I count out the money, which is way more than I make in a week. I send Chris a text, telling him I'm super sorry but that I'm going to be on painkillers and really need a week to rest. I also tell him I'll work extra shifts next week if he needs me to. He responds for me to not worry and to rest up, so that's exactly what I decide I'm going to do. I'm taking the week off, and I'm going to relax with Peanut and focus on resting my arm.

I also make the decision to quit fighting this whole pen pal thing. If Kirill wants a letter, he's damn well going to get one. It's not like I have a crowd of family and friends to spill all my thoughts to. I write him a ten-page letter, telling him all about me. I tell him about my mom and how she taught me to love gardening, about the strained relationship I had with my dad, and about Peanut and how I found him. I even tell him about my nightmares and how his face is always in them. I expose myself to him in a way that I've never done before, and it feels oddly therapeutic. Exhausted, I put the letter in an envelope and set it under the rock by my front door.

And that's really how it begins. For the next year, we send each other letters. Sometimes I wake up and find my house filled with hyacinths, the flower I told him was my favorite. Other times I'll come home from work and see that a repair's been done to the house. What was once unsettling has slowly morphed into comforting. As fucked up as it is, it's nice to know someone is looking out for me.

I'm still not entirely sure what I think about Kirill, but after hundreds of letters, I feel like I know him better than I've ever known another living soul. He still sends an ache straight between my legs when he tells me all the things he wants to do to me, but I know he's never getting out of prison, and a part of me is sad about that. I try not to beat myself up too much about my thoughts towards him. He still hints at his innocence, and I feel myself starting to believe him.

Chapter 5

Kirill

It's been almost two years since I was brought here, and it's time for me to get my ass out. The letters from Lydia surround my cell. Some are stacked up on my shelf, some are taped to the walls, and others, my favorites, are on my mattress, nearly split in places because of how many times I've read them. She's opened herself up to me over the last year, and the woman I thought she was pales in comparison to the woman she actually is. I worry about what she'll do when she sees me in person. I'm fully aware that she's spilling her most inner thoughts to a man she believes will never be set free, a man she's convinced she'll never see again. I expect her to grow distant, to fight me, and to fight her feelings for me, but like I told her before, I'm a patient man, and I'll wait as long as it takes.

The letters I've gotten from Vadim are more disturbing. After holding out as long as he could, Ivan has made peace with Enzo. Vadim thinks Ivan made me the bargaining chip, that he put all the blame on me and convinced Enzo he had no idea I was going to kill Matteo. I wouldn't put it past Ivan to do something like this. I'm the perfect scapegoat since I'm already in prison. He can claim ignorance, strike a deal with Enzo and end the war. I can't say I'm shocked by it. I'm going to kill him for it, of course, but I can't say I'm surprised. I've always known what a coward Ivan is. He likes to put on a good show, but he's always depended on others to do his dirty work. You can't ever fully trust a man who orders the deaths of others but refuses to get his own hands bloody.

A lot of enemies are going to be waiting for me on the outside, but I can't keep my little bunny waiting any longer. I need to be with her. Enough time has passed for things to settle down about her dad, and I've been a model prisoner since coming into solitary confinement. All eyes are not on me, and I intend to take advantage of that.

Tony is less than thrilled. He leans against the wall while I finish up my weightlifting circuit.

"It's not a big deal, Tony."

I almost laugh at how big his eyes get. "Not a big deal? You want me to help you walk right the fuck out of here?"

"I do, and you will." I meet his eyes, making it very clear that he has no say in this. "You will be paid an additional million dollars for your help. Obviously, you won't be able to come back here, so you'll have to run with your family, but you'll all be alive, and you'll have money."

"And if I don't help you?"

The side of my mouth lifts up in a smirk. "Then you won't all be alive, and you won't have money. Your choice, Tony."

"Not much of a choice," he mutters.

"Cry me a fucking river," I tell him, working on my bicep curls. "I've been living in a goddamn sardine can for almost two years for a crime that I should never have been convicted of."

"You've killed more people than we even know about, hitman."

I give him another smirk. "Yes, but you didn't catch me for any of those. That's not what I'm serving time for."

He lets it go, but I can tell he doesn't agree with my reasoning. After my workout, I take a quick shower before Tony leads me back to my cell. Later that night, he comes back to slip me a package from Vadim and to let me know he'll do it.

"I never doubted you for a second." I grab the note and give him a wink that makes him scowl even more than usual. "See you bright and early, Tony."

After he walks away, I open the package and smile at the maintenance uniform and baseball cap and visitor's badge. I laugh when I see the ID at the bottom, complete with my face and the name John Smith, because apparently Vadim wanted to make it as boring and inconspicuous as possible. He's also included a messenger bag because he knows I won't leave here without my letters and photos.

> *Everything's set for tomorrow. Security feed will be set on a loop, and I've convinced a couple of the other guards that it's in their best interest to look the other way. Try not to sound so Russian, John. I'll be waiting for you outside.*

I can't stop smiling. I'm more than ready to leave this place behind. I'm tired of this tiny cell, I'm tired of having the goddamn toilet less than two feet from my bed, and I'm really tired of fucking my damn hand. Running my finger over my favorite photo of Lydia, I smile and feel my cock start to strain against my pants.

Soon, baby, very soon.

Too excited to sleep, I carefully pack up all my letters and remove all the photos from my cell. I have quite the collection now. Vadim sends me new ones regularly, and there are so many that the white cinderblock walls are almost fully covered. The last thing I add are the pink panties that are, I admit, not looking so great. They've been used so much that they're starting to fall apart. I'm not worried, though, because soon I'm going to have the real thing. By the time I'm done, the bag is filled and my cell looks as empty as it did the first day I arrived.

After managing only a couple hours of sleep, I stand up and peel off the orange pants and shirt that I hope to never fucking see again and step into the maintenance uniform from a company called Smith's Plumbing. John is stitched onto my shirt pocket. The finishing touch is the baseball cap, and when I look in the small, unbreakable mirror above my sink, I can't help but smile.

I'm ready when Tony unlocks my door. He takes one look at me and mutters a "Jesus fucking Christ," while shaking his head and locking my cell back up.

"You don't like it?" I ask, looking down at my uniform and picking off some imaginary lint while I try not to laugh.

"Try not to look so tall. It'll be a fucking miracle if we can pull this off."

"I don't need a miracle, Tony. I have money." I don't mention that I also have threats, because I'm pretty sure Tony is already aware of that. Attachments, like I told Ivan so long ago, will always be weaknesses, and men like me will always find them. I realize Lydia is now my weakness, but I'm not some dumbass who's going to allow her to be used against me. I'm going to make her untouchable. No one but me will ever be able to get their hands on her.

Tony and I leave the solitary confinement wing and slowly make our way to the front of the prison. I hunch as best I can and try to keep the left side of my face hidden to hide my noticeable scar. My badge gets examined, I try to sound as American as possible, we get buzzed through, and on and on it goes until there's only a few feet between me and my freedom. The guards in here have all been paid off. I can tell by the look in their eyes. It's the perfect mix of fear and disgust—fear at being so close to a man who they know is capable of killing them in more ways than they can count, and disgust that they so willingly took my money to look the other way. Ah, the moral dilemma. I smile at them to try and ease their conscience, but that only seems to make it worse, so I just give a small laugh instead. Tony glares at me. I shrug and relinquish my visitor's badge.

Once I'm outside, I look up at the overcast sky and breathe in a lungful of fresh air. God, I've missed this. The prison still hangs on me, making me feel in desperate need of a hot shower. I look over and see Vadim's black Audi.

"See ya, Tony," I say, smacking him on the back before I walk to Vadim's car.

As soon as I sit my ass in that plush passenger seat, I let out a sigh of relief. Vadim grins at me.

"Good to see you, boss." His eyes run over me. "Goddamn, did you get even bigger in there?"

I laugh and say, "Lifting weights helps keep you sane. Let's get the fuck out of here. How long will the security feed loop through of the solitary confinement wing?"

"Twenty-four hours if they don't catch on. It's just repeating yesterday."

He drives us away from the prison, but when he starts to turn towards my house, I stop him. "No, I want to see her."

"Kirill," he starts, but I cut him off.

"I just want to see her for a minute, and then we can go to my place." I look down at my uniform. "I don't want her to see me like this, but I have to see her."

He takes a right, knowing I've made up my mind. "It's her day off. She's been spending them in her backyard. Usually she'll spread out a blanket and read a book while Peanut plays."

"I hope you're not developing a crush on my girl," I say. I'm joking, kind of. He's been watching her for me for almost two years. It's only natural that he might develop feelings for her. I study him carefully, because what he says next will decide very quickly what needs to happen.

Vadim briefly meets my eyes and shakes his head. "Don't even think about it, Kirill. The second I took this job, Lydia became like a sister to me. That's how I think of her." When we hit a red light, he meets my eyes again. "Always. I've never thought of her in any other way. No way in fuck am I trying to come between you and your girl." He smiles and adds, "I don't have a fucking death wish."

Over the years, I've picked up the ability to tell if someone is lying, and I'm relieved to see that Vadim isn't. Lydia is the only person on earth who I would never kill, no matter what, and Vadim is the only one that I would feel deep regret about.

"Glad to hear it," I tell him, noticing the way his shoulders relax when he realizes that I believe him. He parks a few houses down from Lydia's and then eyes my outfit.

"This is like the start to a bad '70s porno."

I laugh and open the car door, but before I can step out, he points at the glove box. When I open it and see the box of dog treats, I smile and grab a couple. "Thanks, man."

My heart races a little faster with each step I take. I've waited so long to see her, and now that she's almost in front of me, I'm like a fucking kid at Christmas. All I want is to open my present and play with it. Standing in front of her house, I run my eyes over the flowers in the front. I have so many pictures of her in this yard, and it's hard to believe that I'm here standing in it right now.

Walking around to the back, I keep myself low so she won't see my head above her privacy fence. Peeking through the slats, I have to bite back a groan when I see her sprawled out on her back in nothing but a bikini top and a pair of shorts. My mouth waters at the sight of her. It's been over two years since I've been with a woman, but even if I'd had access to women, I wouldn't have fucked any of them. She's the only one I want. I watch her for several minutes, and when it's obvious she's sleeping, I can't resist the urge to get closer.

I open the gate, and as soon as Peanut spots me, I can tell he's about to start barking. I toss the dog treat his way, and the little guy bolts to get it before happily trotting off. Jesus Christ that dog is cute as hell, but he's one lousy guard dog. She needs my dogs around her, protecting and guarding her at all times.

When I'm standing above her, everything else disappears. She's even more gorgeous in person. I still remember exactly how she looked the day she testified against me, but after only seeing her in photos for two years, I'd almost forgotten just how beautiful she is in real life. Her face is tilted to the side, her lips slightly parted in sleep, and the rise and fall of her chest is damn near hypnotizing. I run my eyes over her, taking in every single detail—the delicate slope of her neck, the slight flush to her skin from the sun, the curve of her perfect breasts, the hips that I'm dying to sink my fingers into, and the legs that I swear I can almost feel wrapped around me. My cock is rock-fucking-hard, and it takes every ounce of willpower I possess to keep me from taking it out and jerking myself off right above her. I wonder if she'd wake when my cum hit her skin.

Now isn't the time, I remind myself, and instead squat down next to her. I spot the bottle of sunscreen and smile. Squeezing some out, I very slowly leave her a little message on her lower belly. She lets out a soft moan, making me freeze in place, but then she quickly falls back into a deep sleep. I finish up and am about to leave when I see the corner of one of my letters sticking out from underneath her. She must've been reading it when she fell asleep. Smiling like an idiot, I risk leaning down to bring my face close to hers. Closing my eyes, I breathe in her jasmine-scented shampoo and nearly bust a nut in my goddamn pants.

"Soon, *zaika*," I whisper.

Standing back up, I hold another bone out for Peanut, letting him sniff my hands and get used to my smell. I pet him for a few minutes and then quickly leave. Vadim looks relieved when I open the door and get in.

"Thank god, I thought she'd caught you."

"All in good time," I tell him. "I need to go home first and get cleaned up. I don't want to smell like prison when she sees me. I need to make a good impression."

"She's going to freak the hell out when she sees you."

I look out the window at the passing houses and nod. "She will, yes, but it's nothing I can't handle."

He doesn't say anything else, just drives me home. The sight of my house cheers me up instantly. I'm still reeling from being outside the confines of my shitty cell, and even though the house has always been beautiful, it looks like a fucking palace right now. As soon as the car stops, I get out and whistle for my dogs. They come barreling towards me seconds later, and I drop to my knees to greet them. Laughing, I hug and pet them while they go crazy, licking and wagging their tails as their paws tap dance around, too excited to sit still.

I speak to them in Russian, noticing the way they also run up to Vadim. It's obvious they've grown to love him, and he seems much more at ease with them.

"Thanks for taking care of everything while I've been gone," I tell him while still petting my dogs.

He lifts a brow at me. "Did prison make you soft?"

I laugh and stand up, giving Grisha one last pat since he's the only one still whimpering with joy. "Not a chance in hell," I tell him. "If anything, I'm meaner than ever."

He laughs and follows me inside. The place looks just like how I left it. It's obvious that Vadim's been cleaning and keeping everything aired out and ready for my return.

"The fridge is stocked," he says, opening it to show me the packed shelves. My eyes run over the food that I've been dreaming about while locked up. It's crazy how much a person can crave fresh fruits and vegetables, anything that isn't processed, lukewarm, and tasteless. I grab a handful of grapes and pop one in my mouth.

"Holy shit that's good," I say, closing my eyes and savoring the tart juice.

"So what's the plan?" he asks, leaning against the counter across from me.

"I'm going to get cleaned up, and then I'm going to get Lydia."

"What about Ivan and Enzo?"

I shrug. "They don't know I'm out yet. I'll handle them both, but it'll be on my timeline. Let them sweat it out. Ivan's going to shit himself when he realizes I've escaped," I say with a laugh.

"He is," Vadim agrees. "He's gotten a lot weaker since he lost you. Everyone can sense it, and the stress is eating him alive."

"Good." I finish my grapes and grab a bottle of water. "I'm going to get cleaned up."

"All right. I'll let myself out. Call me when you need me." He runs a hand through his hair and gives a soft laugh. "I have no fucking clue what to do with myself. My entire life has revolved around you and Lydia."

"Take a few days off. You've earned it."

He raises a hand in a goodbye and walks out while I head up the stairs. I ditch my clothes and walk naked into my bathroom. I turn the water on as hot as I can tolerate and stand under the spray for what feels like hours. It's pure heaven. I wash the prison grime and stink from my body and hair before finally turning off the water. Drying off, I wrap a towel around my waist and then shave. Prison haircuts aren't the best, and it's shorter than I like to keep it, but it'll have to do for now.

When I step into one of my handmade suits, I start to feel human again, and when I add in my favorite cologne, I start to feel like *me* again. As soon as the sun starts to set, I grab my car keys. It's time to go get my girl. I leave the house with a smile on my face, and the purr of my Porsche's engine just makes my smile grow. By the time I park outside Lydia's house, I'm the happiest I can ever remember being.

Under the cover of darkness, I slip into her backyard again and watch her through the open windows. She's pacing the kitchen, worrying her bottom lip while petting Peanut. Looks like someone found the message I left for her. I give a soft laugh imagining the look she must've given when she'd seen the word *mine* written across her skin from the sun. I'd hoped she would remain outside long enough for her skin to tan around the sun-screened word, and it looks like my wish came true. My poor sweet girl is all in a tizzy. I can't wait to make her feel better.

I lean against her house and watch her until she finally cooks a pizza, disappearing into the living room with it when it's done. I'm going to need to improve her diet. She can't live off frozen pizza and licorice. It's not healthy. I wait until I see the lights go off downstairs before picking the lock and stepping inside. I take my time, looking around her house and learning more about her. She's not a slob, but she's clearly not a neat freak either. I smile at the stacks of paperbacks in the living room, the shoes that were obviously kicked off as soon as she walked in the front door and the used mug she left on the coffee table. Looks like she had hot chocolate after her frozen pizza.

When I'm sure she must be asleep, I grab another dog bone and head for her bedroom. Stepping in, I see Peanut lift his head, but he doesn't bark. He recognizes my scent now, and when I hold up a bone, he wags his tail and jumps off the bed, walking over to me and sitting for his treat. I hand it to him, and then watch him run off, shaking my head at how trusting the little guy is. Oh well, she doesn't need Peanut to protect her. She has me.

I stand at the edge of the bed and watch her sleep. She's curled up on her right side, the blankets kicked off, revealing the pink tank top she's wearing, and when I see her pants, I smile. They're the ones Vadim put in her care package after she sprained her wrist. She knows I've escaped, she saw the message I left for her on her skin, and I know she's scared, but even after all that, she still chose to sleep in the pants I gave her.

Not wanting to wake her, I sit in the chair by the window and watch her. I can't take my eyes off her sweet face. She's twenty now, not the naïve eighteen-year-old I first saw, but the added two years have only made her even more beautiful to me. I straighten when I see her brow furrow and her fingers tighten around the edge of her pillow. When she starts to whimper softly, my body instantly reacts. My hands clench into fists as my cock strains against my pants. I would kill for this woman, I would do anything to keep her safe, but that doesn't mean her scared whimpers don't turn me the fuck on.

Before the first scream is even out, I've closed the distance between us.

Chapter 6

Lydia

The nightmare surrounds me, clinging to me in a claustrophobic embrace that makes it hard to breathe. Even after all the letters Kirill has sent me, it's still his face I see in my dreams. He's the one pointing a gun at me, and he's the one who pulls the trigger. I gasp for air and reach for Peanut, but he's not beside me. Before I can sit up to call for him, a strong arm wraps around me. My whole body freezes as a panic unlike anything I've ever experienced washes over me. I know who it is before I even hear his deep voice and accent.

"I've missed you, *zaika*," he whispers. His nose grazes the shell of my ear. The heat of his breath hits my skin, and my heart races.

"Peanut," I quickly whisper, needing to know my dog is okay.

"He's fine, baby. Happily eating his treat. He and I made friends earlier." His large hand slides around my waist, splaying out over my lower stomach. I'd nearly had a heart attack when I'd gotten out of the shower and seen *mine* written on my skin. It's faint, but it's definitely there.

"Are you going to kill me?" There's enough moonlight coming in from the window for me to easily see him, but I'm too scared to turn around and face him.

He lets out a long sigh. "I thought we were past all this, sweetheart. I would never hurt you." He nuzzles into my hair, breathing me in like he'll never be able to get enough. "I'm sorry you're still having nightmares. Want to talk about it?"

I snort out a laugh. "Yeah. I have nightmares because you shot my dad, and every night I dream that you shoot me too."

"I would never hurt you," he repeats, and even though he sounds sincere, I remind myself that he's a killer, and he's never once denied that part of himself. I opened up to him in my letters, and I formed an attachment to him that I shouldn't have, but I never once thought he would get out. I thought I was opening up to a man that I would never see again. He was safe when he was just words on a page, a man hidden away who could never escape, but I was wrong. He did get out, and he's in my fucking bedroom.

It suddenly hits me how much trouble my ass is in, and when I try to lurch forward to escape, he tightens his arm around me and lays down beside me, spooning me with his much larger body. When I start to scream, he calmly clamps a hand over my mouth and kisses my temple. His cologne surrounds me, and I refuse to let myself think about how damn good it smells. I shouldn't want him, and I *won't* want him, goddammit.

"I knew this wouldn't be easy for you, little bunny, and I'm sorry about that, but I can be patient for you," he assures me in a calm tone.

When he adjusts his large body, trying to get more comfortable on my bed that's clearly too small for him, I feel the hard length of him against my ass and let out a whimper. He gives a soft laugh that sounds way sexier than it should.

"You can't fault me for getting hard, sweetheart. I've thought of nothing but you for two long years, and feeling your body pressed against mine, well, it's enough to drive even the sanest man crazy, and no one's ever accused me of being sane."

The wet heat of his tongue flicks my earlobe, and the shiver that runs down my spine isn't all from fear. As much as I fight my body's reaction, there's no denying what this man does to me. He murmurs something in Russian against my skin before running his tongue down my neck. I squirm against his grip when I hear the unmistakable sound of his zipper being pulled down.

"Easy, *zaika*," he whispers against my skin. "I would never take something from you that you weren't willing to give. I'm going to move my hand, and I want you to look at me."

He slowly pulls his hand back, and I suck in a quick breath, but I don't turn to look at him.

"Lydia," he whispers. "Look at me."

I turn my head and meet the face that's haunted me for two years. He's just as beautiful as I remember him in that courtroom, even more so if I'm being honest. There isn't enough light to see the stormy grey color of his eyes, but I see the almond shape of them, the dark brows, the slope of his nose, his full lips, and a hint of the scar that runs down the left side of his face. The man is breathtaking, murderer or not.

"I need to ask you for something."

"What?" I whisper, unable to look away.

He runs a finger over my forehead, gently brushing my hair back and trailing a line along my skin. Goosebumps cover my body as my nipples tighten and strain against my thin tank top and a throb starts between my legs.

"I need to hold you while I touch myself."

"What?"

He ghosts his fingers along my neck. "You have no idea how badly I want to fuck you, how desperate I am to touch you, to take you and make you mine."

My body tenses at his words.

"And that's exactly why I need to do this. I won't take what you don't want to give. I'm asking, sweetheart, not taking."

It's hard to think with his fingertips grazing the crook of my neck and the intense way he's looking at me, like he can't quite believe I'm here in front of him.

"What exactly would you do?" I ask, my voice a shaky whisper between us.

The corner of his mouth lifts up the tiniest bit. "I just want to feel you against me while I jerk off."

I look away, unable to meet his eyes after the bluntness of what he's just said. His letters were sometimes explicit about what he wanted to do to me, but reading it is a lot different than hearing it in person.

"And right before I come, I want to lift your shirt and come on your skin."

My thighs squeeze together at his words, causing him to let out a low moan because of course he notices my reaction. He brings his hand down, dragging his fingers along my shoulder and arm before resting it on my hip.

"Will you let me, *zaika*? Will you give me this?"

Against all my better judgement, I nod and whisper, "Yes." I'm not sure why I agree to it, except that my pussy is throbbing, my panties are soaking wet, and despite what I know is right, I crave this man. I want to feel him against me. I want him to make himself come, and god help me, I want to feel the wet heat of his seed on my skin.

He rests his forehead against my head and squeezes my hip. "Did you ever touch yourself while you read my letters?"

I think about lying, but decide there's no point in denying it. "Yes."

His lips graze my ear, and when he gives my earlobe a soft suck, my whole body arches at that one small touch.

"My sweet little bunny," he murmurs against my skin. "Slip a hand in your panties and come with me."

"This is wrong," I whisper even as my pussy clenches and throbs with a need that's damn near impossible to ignore.

"Is it?" He moves his hand from my hip and a second later, he groans, and I know he's touching himself. "Feels pretty fucking right to me."

Knowing he's stroking himself has me clutching at my blankets, desperate to touch myself and join him. The soft bite he gives my earlobe stirs me into action, and before I can talk myself out of it, I slide a hand down my pants.

"Good girl," he whispers. "Fuck yourself, baby. Let me hear how wet your pussy is."

My conscience takes a backseat when I feel how wet I am. Kirill gives my neck a soft nip, kissing and licking my skin while he works himself harder. I stop worrying about the right and wrong of this. All I can think about is how badly I need the release and how damn good it feels to have his strong body behind mine and his mouth on my skin. I've never done anything with anyone, and sharing this with him, well, it feels more intimate than I want to admit right now.

"So fucking wet," he murmurs, hearing the erotic sounds that fill my bedroom. His accent is thicker, his voice strained. He roughly pulls my shirt up, exposing my lower stomach and back. His fingers graze my skin, dipping lower until his hand is close to mine before he lets out a growl and pulls his hand away. His breathing picks up when he starts to work himself again. I want to look. I want to see what he looks like, but I'm too preoccupied with making myself come.

When I bring my wet fingers to my clit and press down, rubbing myself in tight, firm circles, I let out a moan and close my eyes.

"Fuck," he groans. "That's right, baby. Let me hear you come."

I bite my lip, my stubbornness taking over as I try to keep quiet, but the orgasm refuses to bow down to my pride. The force of it pulls a scream from me, and all I can do is let go as it consumes me. My head falls back, exposing my neck even more. He kisses and licks my skin, and when he finds his own release, he growls my name right before I feel the wet heat of him hit my back.

I'm still gasping for air when he lets out a shuddering breath and I feel his body relax against mine. He kisses my neck once more before letting out a sigh.

"I can't wait until you beg me to fuck you, *zaika*."

"What if I never do?"

He gives a soft laugh. "You will."

My hand is still in my pants, lazily stroking my clit because I'm greedy for the aftershocks, when I feel him rub his seed into my skin. He smears it along my back and then runs his wet fingers along my side, dragging his semen across my lower belly.

"Mine," he murmurs close to my ear. "Every part of you will be mine."

I slide my hand out of my pants, and as soon as it's free of my waistband, he's grabbing my wrist and wrapping his mouth around my fingers, sucking hard. A moan escapes when his tongue runs between my fingers, licking up my arousal like a fucking starving man. He opens his eyes and watches me as he slowly pulls back. When my fingers slip free, he licks his lips and gives me a wink.

"You're fucking delicious, *zaika*."

He lets go of my hand and zips his pants back up. Turning back to me, he kisses my forehead and runs the back of his knuckles along my cheek.

"Time to go home, sweetheart."

"I am home."

He laughs. "Hurry up and pack what you can't part with. I'll buy you anything else you need."

Still a bit dazed from everything that's happened, I watch as he stands up and straightens his suit. God, he looks so fucking powerful, and I can't believe I just came next to him. Shame descends on me in full force, and when I roll onto my side and curl into a tight ball, he walks around the bed so I'm facing him when he kneels down.

"Don't, sweetheart." He runs a finger down my cheek in a sweet gesture that seems so at odds with who he is.

"Don't what?"

"Don't regret what we just shared. It's the first of many things we're going to do together, and I don't want you regretting a single one of them."

"You're a hitman," I whisper.

"I am," and the calm, matter-of-fact tone doesn't make me feel any better. "We can discuss this more later. We need to go soon, so hurry up and pack."

"I'm not leaving Peanut," I quickly say.

He smiles. "I would never ask you to." He slides his hand along my thigh and gives me a soft pat. "I'm glad you like the pajamas. I told Vadim to get the most comfortable ones he could find."

"Vadim?"

"The man who's been watching you. You'll meet him soon, *zaika*, now get up."

I take the hand he offers and let him help me out of bed. Grabbing a tub from my closet that I store out-of-season clothes in, I empty it and start to fill it with mementos that I refuse to part with. I toss in a photo album filled with pictures of me as a baby, the framed photo of me and my mom and dad that was taken right before she died, and a few of my favorite clothes and books.

Kirill walks past me, stepping into the closet and coming back out with the white dress with pink flowers in his hand. Without a word, he drops it into the tub. I grab the box where I have all his letters stored and toss them in because they do mean something to me and I don't want to lose them. I refuse to acknowledge the smug grin he's wearing and grab a duffel bag to throw all of Peanut's things into.

Kirill's next to me when I stand back up, and I have to lift my head back to see all of him. I hadn't realized how big our height difference is. There's a small smirk playing at his lips, like he thinks it's amusing as hell how short I am.

"What happens if I don't want to go with you?" I probably should've asked the question before I packed my stuff, but still.

He trails a finger along my neck before hooking it under my chin and meeting my eyes. They aren't as empty as I've seen them in photographs or like they were when I saw him in the courtroom, but they're not sweet and soft right now either.

"Then I will tie you up and carry you out of here. Either way, you're coming back with me, *zaika*. I've been without you long enough. I won't do it again, not even for one night."

"I'll get my own room at your house, right?"

He laughs and picks up the duffel bag and tub. "Get Peanut. We need to go."

I pull my sneakers on and follow him down the hall, hollering for Peanut as I go. When he runs over to me, I put his little halter on and attach the leash. He wiggles his butt, excited for what he thinks is walk time.

"You said you have four Belgian Malinois. Are they going to try and hurt him?"

"I would never allow that to happen. You'll both be safe around my dogs. No harm will come to you when you're with me, Lydia, or to your dog. I don't make a lot of promises, but I can promise you that."

I nod and hurry up and grab Peanut's treats, and even though I can feel Kirill watching me, I reach in the cabinet and grab the two bags of licorice I have, because after this night, I'm going to need them. I ignore the soft laugh he gives and take one last look around my house. The only thing I really can't live without is standing right next to me and wagging his tail. Everything else is just a bonus. Deciding I've packed what I want, I turn to Kirill and say, "I'm ready."

I'm not surprised when he leads me to a sleek black Porsche. Everything about this man screams power and beauty and danger. I study his profile while he loads my stuff in the back and a wave of embarrassment hits me when I think about what we just did in my bed. There's clearly something wrong with me. In my defense, he's beautiful. It's hard to remember what a monster he is when he looks so goddamn sexy.

As if sensing my moral conundrum, he turns just enough to give me a wink before shutting the trunk and opening the passenger door for me, waiting for me to get in. I sit in his gorgeous car with Peanut on my lap and watch him walk around.

"He's a beautiful monster, Peanut," I whisper against his fur. "But I'm not going to fall for him."

He licks my hand, but it feels more like a pity lick. He doesn't believe me. I'm not so sure I believe myself. Kirill starts the car, and I force myself to look away from his hands while he shifts. I enjoy watching them way too much.

"I can still taste you on my tongue, little bunny." He says it in a lazy way, like he's just making some random comment instead of talking about the taste of my pussy still lingering in his mouth. "Fucking delicious."

I have no idea what to say, so I keep quiet. He gives a soft laugh and reaches over to run a finger down my thigh. That simple touch is enough to make me squirm, even though I try like hell to fight it. He gives another soft laugh, moving his hand so he can shift again. He drives us further out of the city, and once we leave the lights behind, it's too dark for me to see anything. Sunrise is still a couple of hours away, and all I can see out my window is a line of trees and then nothing.

"Where do you live?" I finally ask after several minutes of silence.

"I have a few places, but the house I'm taking you to is one that I've kept very hidden. We'll be safe there while I sort some things out."

"Sort what out?"

"Nothing for you to worry about, sweetheart."

It's clear that vague answer is the only one I'm getting. For the rest of the drive, I pet Peanut and stare out the window. The quiet interior and the darkness around us lulls me into a light sleep, but my eyes pop open when I feel the car come to a stop. Looking around, I see a large gate in front of us with security cameras mounted along the top of the ironwork. Kirill rolls down his window and types in a code. Seconds later, the large gate opens before us. He starts down the long, paved driveway while the gate swings closed. It's the longest damn driveway I've ever seen. It's uphill and curvy, and when he comes around the bend, the area in front of us opens up, revealing a large house with dark grey siding and white trim. There's a matching four-car garage, and when Kirill pulls into the last stall and turns the car off, I sit in stunned silence. I have no idea what to do, I have no idea what to expect, and I'm more confused than I've ever been.

"Wait here. I need to introduce you to my dogs."

"Okay."

My voice is nothing more than a shaky whisper, and when he hears it, he turns his broad shoulders and leans closer to me, cupping my face in one of his large hands.

"Trust me, *zaika*."

"Why should I? You're a hitman, and I sent you to prison. How do I know this isn't some elaborate plan to get revenge?"

I'm expecting a lot of things, but his carefree laugh isn't one of them. His thumb strokes my cheek as he leans closer, keeping only a small distance between our faces.

"Sweetheart, if I wanted you dead, you would be dead. It's as simple as that. I could've killed you so many times and in so many different ways."

"Are you trying to make me feel better?"

His lips quirk up in a smile. "Yes."

"It's not working."

His smile grows. "I don't want any harm to come to you, and like I told you in my letters, aside from a spanking when I feel you need one, you don't need to worry about me causing you any pain."

"That sounds a bit barbaric, don't you think? I'm a grown woman, and I don't need my ass spanked."

He gives a soft chuckle. "I'll be the judge of that. Now be a good girl and wait in the car until I get you."

Stepping out before I can argue, he shuts the door and walks to the back of the car. I see four large shapes in the early morning darkness and let out a soft gasp.

"Try not to shit yourself, Peanut." I kiss his head and hold him closer. "I swear I won't let them hurt you."

He nuzzles up against my neck and wags his tail, clearly not sensing any danger. I turn around in my seat and watch out the back window as Kirill squats down and pets his dogs. They seem beyond thrilled to see him, and the huge smile on his face makes it obvious the affection isn't one-sided. He loves his dogs, just like he told me in his letters.

After he's given them all a good pet, he stands back up and walks to my door. Opening it, he holds his hand out to me and says, "Come on, baby. You're safe with me."

I put my hand in his and let him help me out because it's not like I can just sit in the car for the rest of my life, no matter how soft the seats may be. Clutching Peanut even tighter, I stand up and then scoot even closer to him when I look over and see four sets of eyes glued to me, watching their owner to see if he'll give the command to eat me and my little dog. He smiles down at me, thrilled that I'm seeing him as my safe haven. Wrapping an arm around me, he pulls me so my body is pressed against his with his hand splayed across my lower back.

"They need to see me with you," he murmurs, ghosting his lips along my forehead. "They need to smell me on you."

His lips trail a line down my temple, and when he threads his other hand through my hair and cups the back of my head, I let out the breath I've been holding and close my eyes. My body shouldn't respond to him the way it does, but there's no stopping it. My pussy obeys him, not me, and there's no changing it. He kisses my cheek before pulling back with a smirk, fully aware of what he does to me.

"Is this how you introduced Vadim to your dogs?"

His deep laugh surprises me. It's so at odds with his usual serious face. It makes him look younger and makes me forget that he's a heartless killer.

"It's not quite the same way I introduced him," he admits. Threading his fingers through mine, he kisses the back of my hand and scoops Peanut into his own arms before I can stop him. "Relax, baby," he says when he sees how worried I am. "It's important that I'm the one holding him."

I nod, but it's impossible to fully relax, although Peanut looks completely at ease tucked against Kirill's broad chest. Can't say I blame the little guy. Kirill guides me to his dogs. They're sitting and waiting patiently, never taking their eyes off their master. Keeping our hands entwined, he brings them to the first dog's nose, letting him smell us.

"This is Grisha," Kirill says, and then starts talking to them in Russian. We go down the line as he introduces me to the other three: Pyotr,

Igor, and Boris. My heart nearly stops when he holds Peanut out and all four of them crowd around to sniff him. Peanut gives me a *what the hell?* look, but he does me proud and keeps his head held high and manages to keep control of his bladder and bowels. The introduction doesn't seem to faze him in the slightest.

"He's a brave little guy," Kirill says, and I can hear the respect in his voice. He smiles over at me and gives a soft laugh. "He's a terrible guard dog, but he's brave in the face of danger."

"He's not a terrible guard dog," I say, feeling the need to defend my dog.

"I walked into your backyard yesterday, and all I had to do was throw him a bone and he ran off happily. He didn't even bark."

"I guess he sensed that you weren't going to hurt me."

"Well, no offense to Peanut's impressive instincts, but I need you to be protected a little better than that." He looks at his dogs. "These four will kill anyone who tries to come near you."

"What if it's just someone who happens onto your property? Like a delivery guy or something?"

"No one just happens onto my property. I have security cameras everywhere, and all twenty acres are fenced in. If I have a delivery, I meet them at the gate. No one steps foot on my property, and if they do, they aren't here for a friendly visit."

"That sounds really lonely."

He doesn't say anything, just pets Peanut before setting him down. Even though he told me his dogs would obey him, I still have to fight the urge to not immediately scoop him back up, but Kirill's dogs don't pay him any mind, not even when Peanut runs around their long legs, yipping excitedly at them. Igor finally gives him a playful nudge with his nose and then sits back to watch Peanut chase his own tail.

Satisfied that they're not going to eat my dog, I help Kirill unload his car and then follow him into what is apparently my new home.

Chapter 7

Kirill

Lydia follows me inside, wide-eyed and looking cuter than ever. I set her tub down so I can give her a quick tour. Peanut races off to investigate while she follows me into the kitchen. I open one of the drawers and toss her licorice inside, making sure she sees where I've put it.

"Actually," she says, stepping up next to me and grabbing one of the bags, "I'm going to just have a couple of those right now."

"It's five in the morning," I tell her.

She lifts a brow, evidently waiting for me to get to my point.

"That's not a good breakfast."

She ignores me and opens the package, grabbing one of the red sticks and taking one hell of a bite out of it, daring me to stop her. I run a hand over my jaw and debate whether or not it's a good time for her first spanking. My cock is severely disappointed when I decide that would be too much, too soon. I ignore the little look of triumph in her blue eyes when I turn and lead her further into the house, showing her the rooms on the lower level before heading up the stairs.

She's already eaten half the damn bag by the time we walk into the large bedroom upstairs, the one that is now ours. Her eyes run over the large windows that face the ocean and private beach. There's a set of French doors that lead out to a spacious balcony. After taking another bite, she opens them and walks out, leaning against the railing and taking in the view. We're elevated, so the long stretch of beach is below us. The sun is rising, giving us one hell of a view, and I watch her face, wondering if she likes it, if she'll be able to be happy here, or more importantly, if she'll be able to be happy with me. We'll have to move somewhere else since I've escaped from prison, but there are lots of places we can go, and for now, we're safe.

She holds the bag of licorice out to me. I eye it but make no move to grab one.

"I was forced to eat shit food for the last two years, *zaika*. No way in fuck am I going to willingly do it now that I'm out. I'm going to make us a healthy breakfast, and you're going to eat every damn bite of it."

The laugh she gives says it all. It's a *whatever you say, buddy* kind of laugh, and it's annoying as fuck. I'm used to giving orders and having them immediately obeyed.

"Still testing your boundaries, little bunny? Remember what happened last time you did that?"

"You going to cut off my finger?" she taunts, taking another bite of her goddamn licorice.

I grab the bag from her, smiling at the angry look she gives me. Stepping in closer, I corner her against the railing. She's so much shorter than me that I have to bend down more than a foot to get us face to face.

"No, smartass, I'm not going to cut your finger off, but if you don't eat every bite of your food, then I'm going to tie you to the goddamn bed and feed you my cock instead." Her eyes widen, but it's not from fear. I hear the hitch in her breath, and I see the way her pupils dilate at the image I've just put in her head. Her nipples have been hard since I crawled into her bed, and the sight of them straining against the thin fabric has my damn mouth watering.

"Don't worry, sweetheart, I'll make you beg for it first. By the time I let you have it, your voice will be hoarse from all the begging, nothing but throaty, raspy cries for my dick."

Her brow furrows as she fights her need to say something sarcastic, to deny the obvious desire I see written all over her face. With a slight huff of air, she relents and lowers her eyes.

"That's my good girl," I say, laughing at the blush my praise brings to her cheeks. Before I stand, I cup her face and run my thumb over the lips I'm dying to kiss. I've thought about tasting her for so long, but I'm waiting. I'm not going to be the one to close the distance between us. She is.

Her eyes dart to my lips, and I know she wants a taste, but she fights it. Turning her head to the side, she looks at the steep drop below us. The balcony overlooks the side of the hill, and it might not be a cliff, but it would still be one hell of a fall, and definitely not one that her delicate body would survive.

I bring my lips close to her ear. "Worried I'm going to let you fall?"

"No," she whispers. "I don't think you're the kind of man to just toss me off the balcony."

Gripping the railing on either side of her, I brush my nose above her ear, breathing in the scent I'll never be able to get enough of. "And what kind of man am I, little bunny?"

She turns back to face me, meeting my eyes and raising her chin in a move that's partly because she's so damn short, and partly out of defiance. "You're the kind of killer who would want to see it happen. You'd want to see the life leave my eyes."

She's right, but she's also very wrong. "Never with you, sweetheart."

"I think you might be insane."

I laugh before I can stop it. "Maybe I am, *zaika*, maybe I am."

Before she can make any more wise pronouncements about me, I grab her hand and lead her back downstairs. Lifting her up, I sit her down on the kitchen island and start working on breakfast. She needs more vitamins and minerals than what a package of Twizzlers can give her.

"Did you drink milk as a kid? That might explain your height."

She shrugs her shoulders and watches me look through the fridge. "Not really. I mean I had it in cereal, and I really love chocolate milk."

"Why am I not surprised?"

"If you wanted someone tall, then you kidnapped the wrong damn girl, hitman."

I bite my lip to keep from laughing as I search the fridge. "I didn't kidnap you."

"You didn't? What the hell do you call this?"

"No," I say again. "It's called taking what's mine."

She's quiet for a few seconds while I grab what I need, and then she switches back to defending herself. "I didn't just grow up on candy."

"Frozen pizza too?" I ask when I turn around.

She rolls her pretty blue eyes at me. "My dad wasn't much of a cook."

Her dad is a touchy topic, so I sidestep it and say, "Well, you have me to cook for you now, and things are going to change." To prove my point, I pour her a glass of organic orange juice and hand it to her.

She scowls at me, but she takes it. She looks less enthusiastic about the bowl of muesli and yogurt I fix for her. "What the fuck is this?"

I add in some dried cranberries and scoot the bowl towards her. "Every damn bite, sweetheart."

Stirring her spoon around, her lip curls up in a grimace. "I'm not so sure I'm going to like living here."

Laughing, I lean against the counter. "Tough shit. Stop being a baby and try it."

I take a big bite, proving that it is edible. It's actually pretty fucking tasty if she'd just give it a chance. She fills her spoon and takes a small, hesitant bite. When it doesn't immediately kill her, she finishes the rest of the spoonful and digs in for some more.

"Told you," I can't help but say.

She ignores me and finishes her bowl. When I scoot her glass of orange juice closer to her, she rolls her eyes at me again but picks it up and downs the rest of it.

"Happy now?"

"Immensely." I give her a wink and set our dishes in the dishwasher, spotting the yawn she tries to hide. "Time for bed."

She waves towards the windows around us and the sunny light filtering in. "It's morning."

"Yeah, but you didn't get much sleep last night. You never get enough because the nightmares always wake you. Maybe they'll go away now that I'm here."

"That's an interesting theory. The monster in my bed will keep out the monster in my head."

"You're cranky because you're tired, *zaika*."

I cut off whatever she's about to say by picking her up. At first she just lets her legs hang while I cup her ass, but after a few awkward seconds, she sighs and wraps her arms and legs around me. Her body molds to mine, fitting perfectly as I carry her back upstairs. She rests her chin on my shoulder while I savor the feel of her ass in my hand and her tits pressed against my chest.

"What happens now?" she whispers. The warmth of her breath against my neck sends a shiver of pleasure straight down my spine before settling in my balls.

"Now I wait for you to realize you're in love with me."

"Do you think you're in love with me?" Her voice is barely more than a whisper this time, and I have to strain to hear it.

I kiss her shoulder. "I know I'm in love with you."

"You don't even know me, Kirill."

I press her against the wall outside the bedroom and run my tongue over the crook of her neck, pinning her tight enough so I can feel the rapid beat of her heart against my chest.

"I know you, *zaika*. I've memorized all your letters, and I've memorized every line of your body, every detail of your expressions. Sometimes I feel like I know you better than I know myself. I knew the first second I saw you that we would always be tangled up together, a part of us always connected to the other. That look in your eyes," I sigh and rest my forehead against hers. "I will never be free of it."

"Are you sure you don't hate me instead of love me?"

Her breathy whisper hits my lips, and it takes all my willpower to not close the distance, to kiss her so fucking sweetly, leaving her with no doubt about how I feel.

"I don't hate you, baby. I could never hate you." I let out a soft laugh. "I was very angry when I first got to prison, but I knew it wasn't really hate. I was more angry that I couldn't hate you."

I know she's struggling with how she feels about me, and when I see a flash of guilt in her eyes, I give her ass a hard squeeze. "No, Lydia, don't you dare feel guilty about me. I'm not a good man, and my ass deserves to be in prison. I've killed hundreds of people. I don't deserve freedom." I give her a small grin. "I'm just too big of a jackass to accept my punishment."

"I'm not about to argue with the jackass part."

I've never been much of a laugher, but she pulls it out of me so damn easily. She says things to me that no other person on earth would ever dare say, at least not to my face, and all it does is make me laugh. Anyone else would be bleeding out on the floor. I've always known there was something dark inside me, something that was a little off, something that other people didn't have, but she makes that part of me smaller. It's still there, but it's not the main element of who I am when she's around. If I have an inner beast, she tames it into a scruffy little pussycat. I'm not going to tell her that, though. She's smug enough as it is.

Carrying her into our room, I set her down and then bring up the things she packed so she'll have everything she needs. She's still standing by the bed, looking uncomfortable and wary, like I'm going to lunge at her and fuck her at any second.

If only, baby.

"Relax, *zaika*. You're going to be the one to close the distance, not me."

She watches me, her blue eyes widening a bit when I slip off my suit jacket and start to unbutton the white dress shirt beneath.

"What do you mean?"

I undo the cuffs and take off the shirt, smiling when I see her swallow hard at the sight of me. I was in good shape to begin with, but two years of burning off frustration in prison resulted in several more pounds of pure muscle. She eyes the scars and tattoos before her eyes lock on my abs.

Unzipping my pants, I say, "It means that you're going to be the one begging me for sex, sweetheart." My pants fall to the ground, leaving me in a pair of black boxer briefs that aren't doing shit to hide the hard length of me. I palm my dick, giving it a good squeeze that leaves her biting her bottom lip. "I'm not giving you this," I say, squeezing myself again, "until you beg me for it."

"Like that's going to happen," she says, but even I can hear the forced sarcasm in her words.

"That would be a bit more believable if you could take your eyes off my cock while you said it."

That pulls her blue eyes up in a hurry. She glares at me, and it's so fucking cute I can't help but laugh. I kick my pants off the rest of the way and step towards the bed, pulling back the covers and getting in. Stretching out, I clasp my hands behind my head and watch her.

"Get in, little bunny."

She walks to the other side of the king-size bed and slips in, putting her body as far from mine as she can possibly get. Well, that's not going to cut it.

I turn my head to face her. "Closer."

"You said I was going to be the one to close the distance."

"That was about me sliding my cock into you. That's up to you. Everything else is up to me. Now get closer. I want to feel your body against mine."

When she still hesitates, I move one hand out from behind my head and stretch it out to her, beckoning her closer with my fingers. She takes in the *come hither* motion and finally relents. My eyes rake over her tits as she crawls closer, and I make an instant decision that house rule number one is no bras in the fucking house.

She stops a foot away from me, and when I arch a brow, she scoots forward another inch. Hooking an arm under her, I scoop her up and haul her ass closer, not satisfied until her body is nestled snuggly against mine. I'd be offended by her efforts to stay away if it wasn't so damn obvious she wants to be near me. Her body melts into mine, and I smile when she rests her head on my shoulder and cautiously puts her hand on my chest. I pull the blankets over us and run my fingers through her hair. I'm not sure I'll ever be able to stop touching her.

After a few minutes, she whispers, "How did you escape?"

"I paid a lot of money for people to look the other way."

"That's it? Just money?"

I give a soft laugh. "Most people will do just about anything for money. I did also make a few threats. Not everyone will do things for money, but they will do it to protect someone they love."

She lifts up, resting her chin on my chest so she can see me. "Would you really have hurt their families?"

I want so badly to lie to her, to be the man that she wants and wishes I was, but I'm not that man. I never have been, so I meet her eyes and say, "I would do anything to get to you."

"Even killing innocent people?"

"Yes."

I play with a strand of her hair while she thinks about what I've said. "It didn't come to that, if it makes you feel any better. The guards got a lot of money, way more than they make at that shit job, and the one guard who everyone will know helped me, is probably on his way to a tropical island with his family, never having to worry about money again."

"They're going to come for you."

"They will."

She seems worried, and I don't know if it's because she's worried about me getting caught, or if she's worried about her sweet ass being in the middle of it. I'm guessing it's the latter, but a guy can hope.

"Don't worry, *zaika*, they won't catch me."

"How did you become a hitman? You never told me in your letters."

"You're supposed to be resting," I remind her.

"Please," she whispers, and I groan at the sound of it.

"Your begging is my weakness, little bunny."

"Is one please really begging?"

"That's a good point." I raise a brow at her, waiting.

"Why the hell did I just say that?" she asks herself.

I smile and give her hair a soft tug. "Because deep down you really like begging me."

"I'm not so sure about that."

When I still don't answer her question, she sighs and says, "Please, oh please tell me how you became a scary hitman, Kirill."

It's entirely insincere and because of that, it does nothing for me, so I wait for her to do it the right way.

I know I'm in trouble when I see the mischievous glint in her eyes. She lifts her head enough to ghost her lips over my chest, letting me feel the heat of her breath and the soft skim of her lips along my skin.

"Please tell me, Kirill," she purrs, positioning her body so I can feel her tits pressing against me.

I smile and thread my hand through her hair, fisting it tight enough to make her gasp. "Keep teasing me, sweetheart, and I'm going to roll you over and bury my head between your legs and fuck you with my tongue until you're screaming my name."

The look of pure raw lust on her face makes me smile even bigger. "All you have to do is ask, *zaika*. I'll let you fuck my face any damn time you want."

Her cheeks are bright red, and when she tries to get up, I wrap my arms around her and hold her tightly against me. Before I start speaking, I kiss her forehead, and while I dance my fingers along her arm, I start to tell her my story.

"I killed my dad."

Her body stiffens in my arms, but I knew it was coming, so I just keep stroking her arm, running my fingers along the delicate lines of her body.

"I told you that my dad died when I was around eighteen in one of my first letters to you. I just left out the details of how. He was a nasty bastard who liked to drink and hit my mom, and one day I'd had enough. By that time I was already working for the Teterev Bratva with a growing reputation for being able to make kills that no one else could, and one day I went to visit my mom. She opened the door to their apartment with a face so swollen I barely recognized her. I didn't need to think about what to do. I just grabbed my knife and ended his pathetic life."

Lydia lifts her head to look at me, studying my eyes like she's hoping to find some spark of humanity. I don't bother asking if she's succeeded. She's my humanity, Before her, I didn't have any, and now that I have her, she's all I need.

"What happened to your mom?" she whispers.

"She's in Greece with more money than she'll be able to spend in this lifetime. Happy and married to a nice Greek man who knows I will kill him very slowly if he ever dares to raise a hand to her."

"How did you get involved with the Teterev Bratva?"

I run my knuckle along her cheek. "Always such a curious little bunny."

She reaches a shaky finger out, tracing the scar that runs down my face. "How did you get that?"

"Ivan Teterev asked me to work for him after I brought him the head of his enemy. I was fifteen when I dropped the man's head at his feet. This," I say, tilting my face so she can see the vicious scar that mars my skin, "is from a man I was hired to kill. He was a damn good fighter."

"You killed him?"

"Of course. I'm breathing, aren't I?"

"Do you ever let anyone go?"

"No."

Her fingers are still on my skin, tracing the line of scar tissue as she thinks. "You're a scary man, Kirill."

"Not to you, *zaika*."

She meets my eyes. "Now that you're out of prison are you going to work for Ivan again?"

"No, sweetheart, I'm going to kill him. The fucker betrayed me. Before I went to prison, I killed the son of a powerful Italian mob boss, well, and his mistress. They were fucking at the time, and her death was unavoidable. Ivan ordered the hit, and it started a war, a war that Ivan couldn't win with me in prison because the man is a giant pussy and can't fight his own fights. He gave Enzo my name, told him I'd done it all on my own and that it wasn't an ordered hit."

I sigh and grab her hand, kissing the palm of it. "I have a lot of enemies, but they will never touch you."

"Are you sure you should be confessing all this to me?"

"I love you. You're going to be my wife and the mother of my children. I don't want secrets between us."

I've never seen anyone look as uncomfortable as Lydia looks right now. I bring my fingers to her furrowed brow and massage the tension away.

"Relax, little bunny. I'm not going to impregnate you in the next five minutes." I don't tell her that the very thought of it has me painfully hard. I cup the back of her head, pulling her back down to rest against me. "Get some sleep, baby."

Pressing her hands against my chest, she looks around the room and yells for her dog. I hear little claws on my nice hardwood floors seconds before he comes barreling into the room. He does one hell of an impressive jump, managing to get his little body on the bed before running towards her. When she rests her head back on my chest, he makes himself comfy on my stomach, sprawling out and resting his head by hers.

"I'm guessing this is nonnegotiable," I say, hoping she proves me wrong.

"It is," she says, but then she kisses my shoulder, making it impossible for me to even get irritated by the dog who I know is going to be one hell of a little cock blocker. "Night, Kirill," she murmurs against my skin.

"Night, baby." I kiss her forehead and hold her as she falls asleep.

I'm exhausted, but I don't want to close my eyes. I keep watching her long after her breathing slows down and I know she's in a deep sleep. I can't take my eyes off her. Eventually, she burrows in even closer and hikes a leg over mine while her arm curls around Peanut. I'm such a fucking goner. A lifetime of keeping people at arm's length, of never forming attachments, and she instantly has me wrapped around her damn finger.

I have a lot of enemies, and she just became a very big weakness because if she's ever taken from me, I won't survive it. I will lose the last part of myself that's human, and I'll tear this whole fucking world down, leaving it drenched in blood.

Chapter 8

Lydia

When I wake, I reach for Peanut, but all I feel is a hard, male body. Still half asleep, my fingers run over the peaks and grooves of his warm flesh. A deep moan vibrates against the side of my face that's still pressed to his chest. I hear the steady beat of his heart, and it's the most comforting thing I've ever experienced. My whole body relaxes, and I feel safe. If anyone should make me feel ill at ease, it's him, but as much as I've tried to fight it, to refuse to believe what my body is telling me, the truth is that he makes me feel safe. The worries in my head quiet when he's around, the fears disappear, and the world no longer feels like it's closing in around me. I can breathe when he's near, and it's fucking exhilarating.

Unable to resist, I press my mouth to the skin that's so close to my lips and trace the lines of one of his many tattoos with my tongue. He lets out another groan as his cock grows beneath my thigh. I should back off, but I can't seem to stop. The taste of him is on my tongue, and I want more. The warning bells ringing in my ears are a distant hum. I can't hear anything except the sound of his heart and our raspy breaths.

"*Zaika*," he growls, flipping me over so I'm on my back, pinned beneath his much larger body. His mouth is on my neck, kissing a heated trail down to my shoulder while his hard cock presses between my legs.

Grabbing both my wrists in one hand, he pins them above my head and rocks his hips, grinding against my aching pussy. I wrap my legs around him, trying to get him closer. He nips at my skin, biting the crook of my neck hard enough to make me let out a throaty gasp.

"Please," I beg, not even completely sure what the hell I'm begging for. All I know is I need more.

He groans and starts to rock his hips, hitting me exactly where I need him. I gasp and struggle against his tight grip, wanting to touch him, needing to feel him under my hands.

"Please let me touch you," I beg, moaning when he drags his tongue along my collarbone.

"You beg so sweetly," he whispers against my skin, dipping his tongue into the hollow at the base of my throat. "Don't stop, little bunny. Let me hear how badly you want it."

He gives a soft laugh when I give a frustrated groan, but it quickly turns to a moan of pure pleasure when he circles his hips, hitting my clit in a way that ignites a fire within me.

"Fuck," I whimper, rocking my hips up in a desperate attempt to grind against him. I struggle harder against his hand, but all it does is turn me on even more when he refuses to let me go. Being underneath him, powerless to move while my lungs fill with his scent and his mouth travels lower is fucking intoxicating.

Desperate for the orgasm that's just out of reach, I buck up against him again, but all he does is settle more of his weight onto me, so I can't move. His thick cock is a firm pressure against my pussy, and when he slowly thrusts his hips, the friction makes my eyes roll back in my head. The thin fabric of my tank top is the only thing between us, and when he hovers his mouth above my hard nipple, I let out another breathy plea for more.

His name is like a prayer on my lips when he wraps his mouth around my breast, soaking through the thin fabric, giving a hard enough suck for my toes to curl and pleasure to shoot through every part of me. Pinching my nipple between his teeth, he gives me a soft bite.

"Kirill," I moan, feeling almost lightheaded.

"I think you can do better than that." He takes me in his mouth again, running his tongue over my soaked nipple while he grinds against my pussy even harder.

"Oh god!" I scream as the orgasm hits me.

"That's better," I hear him growl before giving me another bite, working me through my release with each thrust of his hips.

I feel drunk on pure ecstasy. My pussy clenches with the force of the pleasure, desperate to be filled by his thick length as I soak my panties and shake beneath him. He gives my breast one last suck before lifting up. His stormy grey eyes run over me, and the raw hunger in them sends another rush of pleasure ripping through me. God, that look alone could probably get me off. It's the look of a man who would tear the whole world down just to get inside me.

His hands run down my body before he slides them under my shirt so he can grip my waist, digging his fingers into my flesh. He brings a thumb to my clit, rubbing me through my pajama bottoms until I'm panting and squirming beneath his touch.

With one hand, he pulls his cock free of his boxer briefs, and when I see him, my mouth drops open. He's huge. I can't take my eyes off the thick, long shaft, the line of veins, or the way pre-cum is already coating him. The man is fucking magnificent.

I'm so hypnotized by his dick that it takes me a second to realize he's snaking a hand down my pants. When his fingers meet my bare pussy, the sound that comes out of me is nothing short of feral. He runs his thumb over my soaking wet clit, and I hiss out a breath.

"Look at me," he growls, his accent thick and his voice strained.

I meet his eyes, seeing the need and want in them. His whole body is tense, coiled tight and shaking softly with the effort of keeping himself in check. He starts to stroke himself, watching me as he does it.

"Please," I beg as he swipes his thumb over my swollen clit again. "Please, I need you."

He gives me a sexy smirk and speeds up his hand, jerking himself off in an almost brutal rhythm while he slides his thumb lower, dipping into my slit. Even though his thumb is way smaller than his dick, it's still the biggest thing I've ever had inside me, and the feel of it pulls a throaty moan from deep within me.

"Goddamn," he groans, sliding his thumb back out to hit my clit again. He keeps up the slow, steady motion until I'm shaking and whimpering and completely lost to the moment. He could ask me to do anything right now, and I'd do it in a heartbeat. I'd give him anything he wanted, and I know he sees the truth of it in my eyes.

"Lift your shirt."

I pull my tank top up without a second thought, exposing my bare breasts to him, loving the sound of his deep groan when he sees me for the first time. I'm small chested, but he doesn't seem to mind in the slightest. There are a lot of emotions running through his eyes right now, but disappointment isn't one of them.

"Keep your eyes on mine, *zaika*," he growls, and I know he's close. I watch him, unable to look away as he brings us both to the edge. We topple over together, each of us moaning the other's name. The wet heat of him hits my skin, covering my stomach and breasts as I clench around his thumb, pulling him in deeper as he growls something in Russian.

Slowly the world comes back to me. My heart rate slows down, my ears stop ringing, and my whole body goes limp. With a sigh, he slides his thumb out of me, giving my clit one last soft stroke before bringing his hand to his mouth. He watches me as he licks my release off his skin. When he's satisfied, he runs his eyes over my body. Dragging his fingers through his seed, he brings them to my lips and raises a brow at me.

I open my mouth for him. He slides in, groaning when I run my tongue between his fingers, lapping up the taste of him. I suck harder as he runs his other hand over my chest, rubbing his seed into my tits and stomach until I'm covered in him.

"Mine," he growls, tracing his fingers along the faint letters written on my skin.

When he slides out of my mouth, I grab his hand and kiss the palm before bringing it to my cheek. He lowers his body over mine, bracing his forearm next to my head. I can't resist reaching up to touch him. My fingers graze the dark stubble that now covers his cheeks and jaw.

"You're so beautiful," I whisper.

He smiles and runs his thumb over my lips. "I think that might just be the orgasms talking."

"I bet you've been with a lot of women," I blurt out, surprised by how much the idea bothers me. When he doesn't confirm or deny, I ask, "Were any of them serious? Have you ever been married?"

He laughs and shakes his head. "Nothing even remotely serious, and the only woman I've ever wanted to marry is you."

"Why didn't you fuck me?"

He raises a dark brow at me.

"I begged," I add, feeling like an idiot.

His lips quirk up a tiny bit before he says, "You call that begging? You have so much to learn, *zaika*."

He laughs again at the confused look I give him, because I really feel like I most definitely begged. Bringing his face closer, his lips barely brush mine as he whispers, "I'll fuck you when you're so desperate for my cock that you'll do anything to get it. I'll know when you reach that point, little bunny."

"I kinda feel like I was there a few minutes ago," I whisper back.

He smiles and shakes his head, letting his nose brush over mine. "Not even close, sweetheart. You're holding back. I want in here," he says, brushing his fingers along my forehead, "and I want in here." He lowers a hand to graze over the heart that's beating a wild, frantic rhythm. "When you give me those, I'll give you the cock you can't stop drooling over."

"I wasn't drooling," I say in my own defense, but we both know it's only because I managed to get my mouth shut in time.

I watch him for a few more seconds, neither one of us in a hurry to get up. The color of his eyes is constantly changing. Sometimes they look more blue than grey, and other times, like now, they look exactly like the sky right before a storm is unleashed. I remember what he said about it being up to me to close the distance, so I do.

Sliding a hand behind his neck, I pull him closer and press his lips to mine. When I run my tongue lightly along his lips, he groans and cups my face, deepening the kiss. His tongue coaxes my mouth open even more, delving inside and laying claim to every damn inch. The kiss is slow, like he's savoring every second of it, and it's so damn sweet I can feel my eyes start to burn as I fight tears.

When he finally pulls back, I keep my eyes closed because I don't want him to see how much this one kiss has affected me. His thumb brushes my cheek, waiting for me to look at him.

"*Zaika*," he whispers. "Look at me, baby."

I shake my head and bite my bottom lip, feeling like a giant dumbass. I haven't even been here twenty-four hours, and I've already lost myself to him. God, this has to be the quickest fucking case of Stockholm Syndrome ever, like in the history of mankind. What the fuck is wrong with me?

"Please look at me."

The worry in his voice is what has me opening my eyes, and the love I see in his when I do makes it impossible to stop the next round of tears. They fall, and there's nothing I can do to stop him from seeing it. He cups the back of my head and leans closer, running his tongue up my cheek, licking the tears from my skin.

"I want every part of you, little bunny, even the tears you cry." He licks my other cheek clean and then rests his forehead against mine. "Why are you crying, baby?"

"It's stupid," I whisper.

"Nothing is stupid if it concerns you. Please tell me."

"That kiss was really sweet," I say, hating that my voice cracks while I say it.

"And that made you cry?"

"I didn't expect you to actually care about me. I knew that you believed you did, but I guess I just didn't think it would feel so real."

"It is real. I love you, Lydia. You're the only woman I've ever loved. I don't let people get close to me, but there was no way I could keep you out. I knew it the second I saw you."

"I shouldn't feel anything but hate towards you. What the fuck is wrong with me?"

"I don't deserve your love. I'll be the first to admit it, but that means I'll appreciate it all the more for the gift it is." He gives me a gentle kiss and brushes a strand of hair from my forehead. "I will never take it for granted, and I will never love anyone but you." He runs his eyes over me, studying me to make sure I'm okay. "Anything else?"

"It's the first time anyone's ever held me like this and taken care of me. I hadn't realized how lonely I've been."

"That's my fault, and I'm sorry you've been so lonely. I'm a selfish jackass when it comes to you. I couldn't stand the thought of another man touching you while I was in prison. Just the idea of it," he stops and shakes his head, clearing it of the image of me with someone else. "I'll spend the rest of my life making it up to you."

"I understand why you did it." I imagine him with another woman, and the spike of jealous anger it brings is quick and brutal. "I wouldn't want you to be with someone else if I couldn't be there with you, so I guess I'm just as big of a selfish jackass as you."

He smiles and gives a soft laugh. "I would never be with someone else, even if you were separated from me for years. I would spend every second thinking of you and trying to figure out a way to get you back."

"You're pretty sweet for a hitman."

He laughs, and the carefree sound of it has me smiling. "You're the only person to ever call me sweet. Even my own mother wouldn't ever use that word to describe me."

He gives me one more kiss and then lifts up, scooping me in his arms and carrying me into the bathroom. The sun is still bright in the sky, so I'm guessing we didn't sleep too long, and when my stomach growls, I look up to see him smirking at me.

"Don't worry, baby. I'm going to fix you lunch after we get cleaned up. I think maybe you like eating healthy."

"I was just thinking about my Twizzlers," I tell him, but he knows I'm lying. The truth is I'd really fucking loved that granola shit he'd fed me for breakfast.

He sets me on the counter and starts the shower. "I can take one after you," he says, but when he starts to leave, I grab his arm, stopping him.

"It seems silly for you to have to wait. I've already seen you naked, kind of."

"I haven't seen you naked, *zaika*, and I'm waiting. I know what I can handle and what I can't, and you naked and wet is not something I can handle."

He leaves before I can argue. His bathroom is huge. There's a large, walk-in shower that could easily fit the two of us with room to spare, and in the corner is a garden tub that I'd very much like to take a swim in. All my things are already stacked up on the counter and in the shower, but I didn't unpack this morning. I look closer and open up one of the drawers, seeing the makeup I use mixed in with lotion and face wash. Some of this stuff I didn't even pack. All of this was already here before he came and got me.

I should be freaking out, but instead I'm just happy to have what I need. I grab my toothbrush and brush my teeth before taking a shower. I try to hurry, but I'm also determined to make sure I'm all nice and shaved. If sexy Kirill is going to have his hands on me, then I want to make damn sure he doesn't feel a bunch of stubble when he does it. With the hot water cascading down on me, I look down at the trimmed hair between my legs. Based on my experience with movies and books, men like a shaved pussy. I debate what to do for several seconds before grabbing the razor and shave gel and getting to work. It's a terrifying few minutes, but when I set the razor aside, I look down and admire my work. I managed to not nick myself, and when I run my fingers over my skin, I can't help but smile. It's silky smooth, and I'm beginning to see the appeal.

Turning off the water, I wrap myself in a towel and step back into the bedroom. He's waiting for me when I come out. He takes one look at my bare shoulders and the water that's still dripping lightly down my skin and lowers his mouth to me. I feel the sharp nip of his teeth at the crook of my neck as he lets out a groan. Without a word, he walks into the bathroom and shuts the door behind him, leaving me with a racing heart and an ache between my legs. I'm starting to think this is just how I'm always going to feel from now on.

Walking to the closet, I step into the large room, not at all surprised to find that it's already filled with clothes for me. I run my hands over the shirts and pants. They're not my clothes, but they might as well be. The long-sleeve tees and jeans are the exact kind of thing I would've picked out on my own. I'm pulling open drawers, trying to find a bra and panties when I hear Kirill's deep voice behind me.

"I told Vadim he wasn't allowed to buy you any lingerie. I'll be ordering that myself."

I turn around, but whatever I was going to say dies on my tongue when I see him standing there in nothing but a towel wrapped around his trim waist. His dark hair is slick from the shower, still dripping a few beads of water onto his bare chest. My brain stops working at the sight of him. Not even his sexy, deep laugh can get me to pull my eyes away from the sculpted chest that I'm dying to lick.

Finally, I muster up the last of my pride and meet his eyes. The amused glint in them isn't helping. "So I don't have any underwear is what you're saying?"

"If you didn't pack any, then no."

Fuck. I'd still been reeling from the fact that Kirill Chernikov was in my damn bedroom and that I'd just enjoyed a joint masturbation session with him. I had most definitely not been thinking about practical matters like fresh undies. Refusing to let him see how much he's riling me up, I give him a soft smile and let my towel drop. His eyes flare when he takes in my freshly shaved body. The tension in his jaw and the way his towel tents out with his obvious erection would make me laugh if I wasn't being pinned into silence by the fierce look in his eyes. He looks like a man who's seconds away from losing all control. That look reminds me that he's a very dangerous man, and I'm in way over my head.

Taking a step closer, he stalks me, slowly closing the distance and making it impossible for me to look away from his powerful body. He's not a man to be fucked with, and I most definitely just fucked with him. Completely naked with my courage dwindling by the second, I take a step back and keep going until my bare ass hits the row of shelves behind me. Without clothes, the size difference is even more obvious. I truly am the little bunny who chose to tease the big, scary wolf, and now he looks like he's about to slowly devour me piece by piece.

When he closes the distance, his cock presses into my stomach, reminding me that there's only a scrap of towel between our naked bodies. He hooks a finger under my chin and jerks my face up to meet his eyes. Definitely an angry, stormy grey right now.

"You shaved." Two words spoken in a thick accent, but they hold so much frustration and desire, so much *want* that I start to shift my weight from foot to foot, squirming from the intense emotions filling the air around us.

"Do you like it like this?" My words are nothing but a soft, breathy rush. It's all I can manage right now.

His cock digs harder into my stomach. "What the fuck do you think, *zaika*?"

I swallow the whimper that wants to come out when he slowly drags a finger down my chest. He follows the curve of my breast before trailing his finger over my taut nipple. When he gives it a soft pinch, the whimper breaks free, and he smirks. He keeps his eyes locked on mine and slowly trails his finger lower.

"Always testing boundaries, little bunny," he murmurs, ghosting his fingers over my freshly shaved skin. Dipping lower, he drags the tip of one finger along my wet slit. "Jesus Christ," he groans.

My body is tense, waiting for him to dip inside as my heart races and my breathing picks up. Before he can do anything, an alarm goes off in the other room. His eyes darken at the sound of it. He gives my pussy a possessive squeeze, pulling a moan from me before he lets go and races out of the closet. Grabbing his phone, he swipes across the screen and studies it for a second and then tosses it on the bed.

"It's Vadim."

Feeling better that there isn't an imminent threat barreling towards his sanctuary, he drops his towel and saunters back into the closet. My eyes run over him, drinking in the sight of all that toned perfection. He isn't the least bit self-conscious, not that he has any reason to be, and I continue to eye fuck the hell out of him while he steps into a pair of jeans and grabs a black Henley. When he pulls the sleeves up, revealing his tatted forearms, I have myself a little mini orgasm.

Fully dressed, he walks back over to me and cups my face, tilting me up so he can kiss me. I grab his wrists, using him as my anchor as I stand on my tiptoes and open my mouth to him. The kiss is hard and hungry and way too short. When he pulls back, he smiles at the heavy-lidded look I'm giving him.

"This isn't over, *zaika*." He lets me go and takes a step back, running his eyes over my naked body one last time. "Get dressed and come downstairs. It's time you met the man who's been watching over you for two years."

After he's gone, I quickly grab a pair of jeans. It feels weird as hell to put them on without underwear, but I do it anyway, and then grab a pink long-sleeve tee. I pull it on and then take a quick look at myself in the mirror, groaning when all I can see are too very obvious nipples poking out against my shirt. There's no way in fuck I'm going down there like this, so I switch the shirt out for a black one and hope that's enough to not make it quite so painfully obvious.

I run a quick brush through my hair and head downstairs. If he didn't want me to flash nipple, then he should've reminded me to pack some damn bras. As soon as I hit the kitchen, Peanut comes scrambling over to me, yipping and running around like he hasn't seen me in days. I scoop him up, grateful that his furry little body will help conceal my bare chest.

"Where have you been?" I ask him.

"He's been taking full advantage of the doggy door I asked Vadim to put in," Kirill says, already getting ingredients out of the fridge.

"Is it safe for him to just run around like that?"

Kirill laughs. "He's got four bodyguards now. Nothing is going to happen to that little guy."

I smile at the image and then turn when I hear a knock. Kirill pulls his phone from his back pocket and uses it to unlock the front door, proving he has one hell of a kick-ass security system going on here. Suddenly nervous, I squeeze Peanut tighter and take a step closer to Kirill. As soon as he sees it, he stops what he's doing and wraps an arm around me, pulling me closer. He kisses the top of my head.

"Don't worry, baby. He's a friend."

"It's just weird finally meeting him. I mean, he's been watching me for so long."

Vadim walks in before he can answer. The man is tall but still several inches shorter than Kirill with light brown hair and a short beard. Like the receptionist at the hospital said, he's handsome, but the sight of him doesn't light my body on fire like the man who's currently stroking the nape of my neck with his thumb.

"Nice to finally meet you, Lydia," Vadim says, giving me a big smile.

"This is so weird," I say, repeating my earlier thought.

He gives a soft laugh. "Agreed. I feel like I know you already."

"Thanks for fixing my car and the drainpipes that one time and all the other stuff."

"I was under strict orders to do anything and everything you needed," he says, pointing at Kirill. "Even in prison, he's bossy as hell."

I laugh, not doubting him for a second. If there's one thing I've learned, it's that Kirill likes to be obeyed. Vadim watches the way Kirill kisses my head and leads me to one of the stools. He lifts me up and sits me in one and brings his mouth to my ear.

"Keep those pretty nipples covered, little bunny. No one gets to see that but me." He gives my ear a kiss and sets Peanut on the ground when he struggles to get free. His grey eyes watch me, and when I hurry up and cross my arms over my chest, he gives me a pleased smile and a wink. His approval shouldn't mean that much to me, but it does.

Peanut runs over to Vadim like they're old pals, because of course they fucking are. Vadim smiles and reaches down to pet him. When he stands back up, they switch to Russian, discussing who the hell knows what while Kirill prepares a couple of chicken breasts. I watch him, amazed at the ease with which he moves around the kitchen. It's obvious the man is used to cooking, and he looks sexy as hell while he does it, especially with his deep voice speaking Russian.

Whatever they're talking about, it must not be good. Kirill's eyes narrow and his jaw tightens, but it's not because of sexual tension this time. He just looks pissed. Putting the chicken in the oven, he scrubs a hand over his stubbled jaw and growls something out in Russian before grabbing a knife and cutting board. I'm not at all surprised to see how at ease he is with a sharp blade. He cuts through the cucumber and tomatoes in seconds instead of the many minutes it would've taken me. I lean my arms on the counter and rest my chin in one hand, watching him prepare our lunch. He gives me another wink when I meet his eyes, and my heart does that same damn flutter it always does when he looks at me like that.

When there's a lull in their conversation, I look over at Vadim. "How did you get into my house?" I've been curious about it for so long, and I don't want to miss the opportunity to get some answers.

He gives me a guilty smile. "I took your key while you were sleeping and had a copy made. It's a lot easier than picking the lock every time."

Well, that's unsettling. "How did you always know where I was? That day I snuck out and went to the club, there's no way you could've seen me."

"I put a tracking app on your phone."

"Holy shit," I whisper.

"Don't worry, I didn't like watch you sleep or anything." He darts his eyes to Kirill. "I was under very strict orders about what I could and could not do."

"You stole my underwear," I remind him.

He laughs and holds up his hands. "Again, I was under strict orders. I used a pen to lift them up and then stuck them in a bag, and that was that. It wasn't quite the perverted affair you might be imagining. Now, what the hell happened after they were delivered, I don't ever want to know."

"No, you don't," Kirill agrees, giving me another wink.

My face heats up, because I know exactly what happened after they were delivered. I vividly remember reading that detailed letter.

"I woke up this morning and had no idea what the hell I was going to do with my day," Vadim admits. "I almost drove to your house out of habit."

"I told you to take a vacation," Kirill says, checking on the chicken.

"I will once everything is taken care of." He checks his watch and looks back up at us. "I need to get going." He says something in Russian and then turns back to me. "Sorry again for all the spying. I hope it didn't freak you out too much."

"It's okay. It did at first, but then it was sort of oddly comforting to know someone was looking out for me."

Vadim meets my eyes. "He was always looking out for you."

I nod and return his wave goodbye before he turns and walks away. Kirill fills two bowls with salad and then cuts up the chicken breasts, adding them in with some homemade salad dressing.

"He seems nice," I say. When he doesn't say anything, I add, "So what did you two talk about?"

He grabs the bowls and starts to walk away. I hop down and follow him through the French doors and out onto the veranda. My hair whips around from the breeze coming off the water, and when he sits down at a table under an awning, I take the seat opposite him.

"Not going to tell me?"

He smiles and walks back inside. I wait because I know he's got to come back at some point. Returning with two large glasses of lemonade, he sets one down in front of me and then takes a seat.

"Work stuff," he says when I'm still waiting for an answer.

"That's all I get? What about no secrets between us?"

"I will try my best to keep you as informed as possible, but I see no reason to worry you with unnecessary details."

"Maybe I should be the judge of what's unnecessary."

He laughs and pushes a fork towards me. "Eat, *zaika*. You need the protein."

When I don't eat, he sighs and says, "I'm going to need to take care of Ivan soon, probably in a day or two."

"By take care of you mean kill?"

"Yes."

"Does it ever bother you?"

I watch his face, looking for any trace of guilt or remorse, but there's nothing. We might as well be discussing the weather.

"No, *zaika*, it doesn't. We all have our talents. Mine just happens to be killing people."

"What kind of future do you expect us to have?"

He puts his fork down and leans back in his chair, knowing lunch is going to have to wait. "I have more money than we could ever spend, and I have fake IDs. We will get married, and we will live wherever you want. We'll have a family, and every day you'll walk around with an ache between your legs because you're mine, little bunny, and I will always remind you of that."

This time he leans across the table and puts the fork in my hand. "Eat your damn lunch. You haven't had enough calories today."

I bite back the smile at how damn bossy he is and stab a forkful of salad. Stuffing my mouth, I give him a grin and say, "Happy?" The word comes out muffled, but he groans, and I know he understood me.

"God, you're going to be a handful," he mutters before taking a bite of his own salad.

Chapter 9

Kirill

I wait until Lydia finishes every bite of her lunch. Only when her bowl is empty do I allow her to get up, not that she tried to get up before then. She may like to make a fuss about my healthy meals, but she sure devours them in a hurry. I've never cooked for anyone else before, and I'm surprised by how much I like it. I enjoy taking care of her. She brings out things in me that I never knew existed. I didn't think I was capable of love, and I sure as fuck never thought I would be the kind of guy who likes to cuddle in bed, but here I am, already looking forward to tonight when she'll curl her body up against mine and dance her fingers along my chest as she falls asleep. She's turned my world completely upside down, and I'm oddly okay with it.

Instead of leading her inside, I hold my hand out to her and say, "Do you want me to show you around?"

She smiles and threads her fingers through mine. "I would love that."

I walk with her beyond the veranda, wanting to see her reaction when the yard opens up on the side and she sees all the flowers. I know the second the notices the purple irises by the way her whole face lights up.

"Those look just like the ones at my house," she says, pointing at the line of flowers. I don't say anything, just watch her when she notices the yellow dahlias and purple hyacinths. She looks up at me, her brow furrowed in thought.

"Did you have these planted because you know I like them?"

"I asked Vadim to start transplanting them last year. You told me the flowers were important to you, that you and your mom planted them together, so I wanted you to have them here. No matter where we move to, this house will always be ours. We can come back whenever you want, and they'll always be here waiting."

"That's insanely sweet, Kirill."

"Insane, I've been called, but never insanely sweet."

She laughs and kisses the back of my hand, and before I can do something really embarrassing like get down on one knee and beg her to marry me, I gently lead her to the path behind the house, the one that leads to our private beach. Because the house is on a hill, it takes a few minutes to get to the beach, but once we're there, she laughs and takes off running. My dogs are on duty, but Peanut scampers down the hill, running after Lydia. I watch the two of them with a smile on my face. Partly the smile is because I just genuinely enjoy seeing her so happy, and partly it's because she's braless and I know she's not wearing panties. She drives me fucking crazy. I'd nearly lost it when she'd dropped the towel in the closet, showing me her newly shaved pussy. If Vadim hadn't showed up, I'd probably still have my head buried between her legs.

"Kirill," she shouts, cutting into the oral fantasy that's taking shape.

She waves me over, and when I start walking towards her, she laughs and takes off running. I go from being semi-hard to full-on hard as soon as she takes off, looking over her shoulder with a smile on her face.

Oh, little bunny, you should never run from the hunter.

When she sees me chasing her, she lets out a squeal and speeds up, but she's no match for me, and within seconds, I've wrapped an arm around her waist and I'm pulling her tightly against me.

"Fuck," I groan when she starts to squirm. I tighten my grip on her, stilling her body. Bringing my face to her neck, I flick my tongue against her pulse before biting down. God, this woman does something to me. She takes the feral part of me and magnifies it by a million. I've never wanted to possess and dominate a woman like I want to with her. I want to own every damn inch of her. I want to brand myself on her skin so deeply that she'll never be free of me.

The feel of her body softly shaking against mine pulls a deep groan from my chest. A nice man would see that as a sign to let up, but all it does is make me hold her tighter as I bite down harder and run my hand up her body, cupping one of her perfect tits in my hand.

"Kirill."

The sound of her whimpering my name has me pinching her pert nipple, twisting and pulling on it until she's panting and her knees start to buckle.

"Yes, *zaika*?"

Her fingers dig into my forearms, trying to find her balance and use me as leverage. "I think I'm ready to beg."

I laugh and scoop her into my arms, already headed back towards the house. She thinks she's ready to beg, but she has no idea. My little bunny isn't even close. Peanut scampers along at my feet, clearly enjoying his new home, and when we step inside, he runs for his water dish and then jumps up on the couch, sprawling out with an exhausted little huff. Perfect. While he takes his nap, I'm going to have some fun with Lydia.

Her fingers stroke my face and neck while I carry her up the stairs. When I meet her eyes, they're already glazed over with lust, but that's not what I'm looking for. I expected the lust. She's drawn to me just like I'm drawn to her. There's something magnetic between us, making it obvious that sexual arousal will never be an issue for either one of us. What I want to see in her eyes goes beyond that. Her blue eyes soften when I study her, and I know she's getting there. She's not fighting her feelings for me as much as she was, but she hasn't fully opened her heart up to me yet, and that's what I really want.

I set her down and slowly peel her shirt off. She raises her arms, not even attempting to stop me. Hell, she's the one who reaches down and starts unbuttoning her pants as soon as her shirt hits the floor.

"Please," she begs, and I have to grit my teeth to not give in to her pleas. This is going to test me far more than it's going to test her. She thinks I'm about to fuck her, and when I lift her onto the bed, she lifts her ass so I can pull her jeans off and then spreads her thighs for me. She grabs her knees, widening her legs even more, and when her outer lips gently part, I let out a pained groan. She's soaking wet, so fucking ready for me, but instead of slamming into her like I want to, I lean closer and press my lips to hers.

She moans and opens her mouth to me, running her tongue along mine as she tugs on my shirt, wanting me naked. I break the kiss long enough to yank my shirt off and then cup the back of her head, kissing her harder when she wraps her arms and legs around me. While I suck her tongue, I run my other hand down her chest, resting it on her heart, feeling her rapid pulse beneath my fingers, reminding her that this is the part I want to be let inside.

My lips move down her jaw, kissing a path along her skin as she whispers, "Please, Kirill. I'm ready. I want this."

I tap her heart again and nip at the tender skin of her neck, making her whimper and arch her hips up to me. Kissing and licking my way down, I capture one of her hard nipples between my teeth and give her a soft bite. Her hands run through my hair, but it's still too short for her to fist like she wants as I worship the perky tit in my mouth. When I'm satisfied, I kiss a line to the other and flick her nipple with my tongue before sucking her in. Her body shakes beneath me while her breathing picks up, the soft pants mixing with her moans and driving me wild with need.

"Please," she begs again, but I ignore her, kissing and sucking her skin until I've had my fill.

I release her with a wet pop, admiring how fucking sexy she looks with my spit on her skin before kissing a line down her stomach. The lower my mouth travels, the more my cock strains against my jeans, and by the time my head is between her legs, I'm toeing the line between pain and arousal. I nuzzle her pretty cunt, dragging my nose along her smooth skin and breathing her in. Her jasmine lotion mixes with her natural scent, and it's one hell of a heady mix that's threatening to make me lose all control.

"So fucking perfect," I murmur against her pussy before dipping lower and allowing myself my first taste of her. My tongue swipes along her slit, pulling a growl from me and a delicate whimper from her.

"Kirill," she moans, gripping my head even tighter. "Please, god, please. I need to come."

I laugh and flick her pink, swollen clit. "You might want to get comfortable, little bunny. I'm going to be here awhile."

Before she can respond, I slide my tongue into her, parting her wet lips and delving inside like a fucking starving man. Each stroke has her gasping and moaning, and when I know she's close, I slow down, guiding her body back where I want it—right on the cusp of her release, but not crossing over. I'm giving my girl a lesson, and soon she'll understand that I own her body. It's mine now. Pain and pleasure are mine to give. Her job is to accept that and take it.

I suck her pussy lips one at a time, giving her a soft bite before running my tongue over her clit. She bucks up against me, desperate for the release I'm denying her. I rim her bundle of nerves until her whole body is quivering.

"Fucking hell," she gasps, and I smile at the ragged sound of her voice. She'll be hoarse by the time I'm done with her. "Kirill, please."

I look at her and slowly lick her clit, lapping at it like a kitten to milk. Her blue eyes narrow, all that frustration turning into rage as she digs her fingers in harder, trying to force my face against her pussy so she can grind her way to her release. I laugh and give her another lick.

"You really are a monster," she hisses at me.

"*Zaika*, you have no idea." I latch onto her, sucking her hard, letting her taste the beginnings of her orgasm before killing it with a soft bite. Keeping her clit locked between my teeth, I watch her face morph from anger to shock to fear. It's fucking beautiful.

"I'm sorry," she whispers, too afraid to move for fear that I might bite down even harder.

My mouth is full, so I don't answer, just keep her between my teeth and reward her with a soft lick when she takes a deep, calming breath. When she brings her eyes back to mine, I give her a wink and another lick.

"Please let me come," she begs.

My answer is to keep her tightly gripped between my teeth as I slide one finger into her dripping pussy. As soon as she feels me, her body's instincts take over. She tightens around me, pulling me further in, and it's nearly my undoing. It takes every ounce of willpower I possess to stay where I'm at. I slowly finger her as pre-cum drips down my cock, soaking through my boxers and making it damn near impossible to think about anything except my need to be inside her.

She falls back onto the mattress, moaning my name and begging for what only I can give her. With her clit still locked between my teeth, my spit drips onto her already soaked pussy, mixing with her arousal as I finger her faster. I watch her body, the way her skin has bloomed with a beautiful red flush, the rosy nipples that are hard and tender from my bites, and her parted pouty lips as she gasps for air. I memorize every fucking detail of this moment, and when I know she's close, I replace my teeth with my lips and suck her hard, sending her over the edge with no warning.

Her screams fill the room. First it's my name, then it's a few *oh gods* and then finally it's just incoherent mewling sounds. I drag her pleasure out, making it last until she's whimpering and fisting the blanket because she's getting too sensitive. I don't give her a chance to rest. I throw her right into another orgasm, and then I do it again and again. I don't stop until her voice is nothing but a throaty hoarse rasp and she's too weak to even lift her head.

Grabbing the backs of her thighs, I spread her wider and then slowly, gently lick her clean. I cover her in kisses and soft swipes of my tongue, showing her a tenderness I've never shown to anyone else, but when I lift my head, tender is the last thing I have in mind. Standing back up, I pop the button on my jeans and yank my zipper down, desperate to get some relief. As soon as I free my cock, I let out a sigh of pure relief at being freed from the constraints of my pants. A soft whimper brings my attention back to the beautiful woman lying naked in my bed, my little bunny, the love of my life, the woman I would burn the whole fucking world down for.

"Hands and knees, sweetheart," I tell her, fisting the base of my shaft and stepping closer.

Her eyes widen at the sight of me, but she doesn't move. Her body is still sluggish from her orgasms, her mind still hazy.

"*Zaika*," I say, and when she hears the warning in my tone, she musters the strength to turn over. Her eyes lock onto my hand as I lazily work myself. "Isn't this what you were just begging me for?"

She nods without moving her eyes, the hunger in them is enough to send me over the edge, but I refuse to give in. "Are you going to fuck me?" she asks.

I step closer, guiding the head of my cock to her lips. "I'm going to claim your mouth, sweetheart." I hiss out a breath when she looks up at me and darts her tongue out, running it over my head. "I'm going to fuck this sweet mouth and make it mine."

She meets my eyes and nods her head, already opening her mouth for me. I cup her face and caress her cheek with my thumb.

"So fucking perfect," I say before sliding my head between her full lips. "Now show me what a good girl you are and suck my cock, baby."

The moan she gives at my words coupled with the feel of her sucking me in even deeper has me letting out a long string of Russian and fisting her hair in my hands as I try like hell to not come. She sucks and licks my head while I slowly thrust into her a little bit more. My eyes run over the sexy dip in her lower back and the curve of her round ass before going back to her mouth, not wanting to miss what's about to happen.

When I thrust in harder, she gags and moans around me, sending vibrations straight down to my balls as I let out another groan.

"Fuck, you're beautiful," I growl, watching her tears spill over. "I've thought about fucking your mouth so many times, *zaika*. Jerked off to it until I swear I could feel your mouth wrapped around me, but nothing compares to this." I slide in another inch, making her gag again. "Fucking hell," I groan, pulling back out a bit. "Just breathe, baby."

She sucks in a big breath through her nose while I go easy on her, letting her catch her breath. When I slide back in again, she fists the bedding beneath her hands and gags again. Fresh tears drip down her cheeks, and the sight of it nearly sends me into a frenzy.

"Relax, little bunny." I run a finger along her stretched-out lips. "This is my mouth, and I'm going to fuck it."

"Mm-hmm," she moans, her eyes wide and shining with an innocence that I'm about to obliterate.

With a growl, I thrust into her mouth, sliding deeper into the wet heat. I don't stop when she gags. I give her everything I have. Her round ass is too much of a temptation, and when I'm almost all the way in, I slide one hand down her spine, giving one cheek a hard enough smack to push her down that last inch.

"Jesus fucking Christ," I growl, looking down at her stuffed mouth and tear-streaked face.

She can't breathe, but she's not panicking. She's my submissive little bunny, waiting for instructions.

"Good girl, baby," I praise her, running my fingers over her sore ass before giving her another hard spank. "That's my good fucking girl."

Fisting her hair, I slowly slide out of her, allowing her to take in a lungful of air. I tease her with just the head of my cock, groaning when she licks and sucks and begs me with her eyes for more.

"I'm not going to go easy on you," I warn her.

She gives my head one more suck before letting go so she can say, "I don't want you to," before quickly wrapping her lips around me again.

Unable to hold back any longer, I slam into her, fucking her mouth in a brutal rhythm. Instead of tensing up, I feel her relax, giving herself over to me completely to use as I please. It's the kind of trust that can't be faked. Words are nice, but having a woman fully submit when you're ramming a cock down her throat is something I've never experienced before. She trusts me completely, and she knows that I'll never push her beyond what she can take. She's mine to ruin, but everything I do to her is mixed with the overwhelming love I feel for her.

Tears and spit drip down her beautiful face, and her tits bounce with every hard thrust I'm giving her. I'm not going to last much longer. I tighten my grip on her hair and growl, "Swallow," as I finally give in to my release. The force of it nearly makes my goddamn knees buckle. My vision darkens around the edges and blood roars through my ears as my cock pulses in her mouth, shooting my seed down her eager little throat. She moans and sucks me harder, and when she's able to, she swallows, the sensation sending another rush of pleasure through me.

When I'm finally empty, I loosen my grip on her hair, massaging away the sting. She stays wrapped around me as I grow soft in her mouth. Looking up at me, she slowly lets me go, and then surprises me by giving me the sweetest damn smile I've ever seen. Her lips are swollen, her face a mess of tears and spit, and I've never seen anything so gorgeous in my life.

I gently lift her so she's on her knees and then pull her against me and cup her face, wiping away the wetness from her cheeks. Brushing my lips over hers, I kiss her slowly, loving that she tastes like me. When I give her tongue a suck, she moans and wraps her arms around me, cupping the back of my neck and pulling me closer. By the time I stand up, she's breathless and panting again. She's a hungry little thing, and it's going to be a lot of fun keeping her satisfied.

"That's one hole I've claimed, little bunny. I'll be taking the other two soon enough."

Her eyes widen at my words, making me laugh as I give her ass a squeeze. She rests her head against my shoulder as I cup the back of her head and kiss her temple. I hold her for several minutes, not wanting to let her go, but finally I force myself to pull away. Picking up our discarded clothes, I help her get dressed and then zip my pants back up and put my shirt on. I'd like nothing more than to stay in bed with Lydia all day, every day, but I need to get some work done.

Grabbing her hand, I thread my fingers through hers and lead her out of the room and down to my home office. As soon as I let her hand go, she starts exploring. I watch her run her fingers over the bookshelf in the corner while I grab one of my laptops.

"What about my job?" she asks over her shoulder, pulling out one of the books to look at it. It's in Russian, but she still flips through it. "This looks like a crazy complicated language."

I smile and type in the password to unlock the laptop before handing it to her. "You already sent a very nice email to Chris, telling him that you were offered a job in another city and that you thought the change would be good for you. You apologized for not being able to give any more notice and thanked him for all he's done for you over the last couple of years."

"Well, that was awfully nice of me."

"It was," I say with a wink.

She holds up the computer. "What am I supposed to do with this?"

I pull my wallet out of my back pocket and hand her a credit card. "You're going shopping, sweetheart."

She reads the name on the card. "Who's Thomas Skylar?"

I raise my arms, gesturing to the house around us. "He's the man who owns this house. One of my many aliases. Order whatever you want or need."

"I need underwear," she says. "Lots of it."

"Go ahead, but just know I'm going to be ordering a few things for you as well." I eye her tits and smile. "There's a no-bra rule for you in the house, though."

"There is?"

"Yes," I say with a laugh. "Unless Vadim is here, then you can wear one."

"How nice of you."

"I thought so."

She tries to hide her smile, but I see it. Walking over to the leather chair by the windows, she sits down, laughing when Peanut comes charging in and jumps on her lap.

"Mind if I get him a few things too?"

"Baby, you can get whatever you want. You don't need to ask me. What's mine is yours."

She smiles and gets to work while I sit behind my desk and type in my password. First, I check the security footage, making sure everything looks okay. I see all four of my dogs, each of them sniffing around their sections of the property, and when I'm satisfied everything is as it should be, I switch to the monitor in front of me and pull up the file that Vadim sent me earlier. I slowly go through the information, reading up on what exactly has been going on between Ivan and Enzo. It doesn't look good. I watch the footage Vadim filmed from the night they had their meeting, and seeing Ivan's smug, smiling face is enough to irritate the fuck out of me. He's clearly sold me out, and he's going to pay for it with his life.

Movement from Lydia has me turning my focus to her, not that my focus is ever really off her. Even when I'm thinking about something else, she's still very present in my mind. There's never a moment when I'm not thinking about her. I watch as she sets the laptop down and stands up, raising her arms in a stretch that gives me a quick glimpse of her lower stomach before she puts her arms down. She gives Peanut a pet and then slowly starts to walk over to me. Her steps are cautious, like she's afraid she doesn't have the right to just come over and sit in my lap any damn time she wants to. I don't like her hesitancy, but I'm curious to see what she does, so I don't do anything. I keep scrolling through the file as she steps a bit closer. When she comes around the corner of my desk and stops, I wait for her to say something. She doesn't speak.

I want to tell her that I just came down her throat so why in the hell would I have a problem with her sitting in my lap, but that reasoning isn't accurate. I've been given lots of blowjobs over the years, and I never would've allowed a single one of those women into my lap for a cuddle. No fucking way. I've always had a strict no-touch policy. That is until I met Lydia. She's changed everything.

"All finished, *zaika*?" I finally ask when I can't take the silence anymore.

"Yeah." She fiddles with a pen that's sitting at the edge of my desk and looks at my monitors. If she's trying to be subtle about being nosy, she's failing miserably. Her blue eyes dart around, trying to take in all the information on each of the three monitors. I scoot my chair out a bit and pat my thigh, letting her know where I want her ass. She sucks in her bottom lip to try and hide the smile as she steps closer and sits in my lap.

I cup her cheek, pulling her face to mine while my other hand squeezes her hip. Her lips are still swollen from my cock, and god do I love that. "Don't be shy around me, little bunny. If I was doing something I didn't want you to see, then I wouldn't have invited you into my office while I was doing it."

My lips brush lightly along hers, just enough to cause my heart to race and a shiver to run down my spine. "You're always allowed in my lap. And unless I tie you up," I say with a wink, "you're always allowed to touch me."

"Okay," she whispers, the heat of her breath hitting my lips and causing my body to start to wake up again.

Unable to resist when she's this close, I capture her bottom lip between my teeth and give a soft bite before parting her lips with my tongue and delving inside for another taste. The kiss is slow and sweet and deep, and I have to force myself to break contact. I could spend the rest of my life kissing her and never grow tired of it. I rest my forehead against hers, tracing a line along her lower back with my thumb.

"I need to go out for a little bit tonight," I tell her.

She immediately pulls back to look at me, searching my face for information, her brow scrunched in worry. I've never had anyone worry about me before, and instead of it being the annoyance I always feared it would be, I find it oddly comforting.

"Relax, little bunny. I just need to take a look around and see what's going on."

"Because of them?" she asks, pointing at the monitor with the photo of Ivan and Enzo shaking hands.

"Yes. The man on the left is Ivan Teterev, and the one on the right is Enzo Faretti, the man whose son I killed."

"I'm going with you."

I laugh, and when I realize she's serious, I laugh even harder. "Yeah, I don't fucking think so."

"Why not?"

"Because it could be dangerous."

"Are you just going to drive around?"

"Yes."

"Perfect, no one will see me if I'm in your car."

"This is not happening," I say. "Someone could see you through the windows, and I'm not risking it."

Instead of just taking my words as law, which is what I'd like her to do, she thinks for a minute. "Do you have a motorcycle?"

"Yes."

She smiles, and I know I'm in trouble. "It's the perfect cover. We'll wear helmets so no one can identify us, and one lone guy on a motorcycle might draw attention, but we'll just look like a couple out on the town. No one is expecting scary hitman Kirill to be with a woman, am I right?"

I don't say anything because she already knows the answer. I have a notorious reputation for not trusting anyone. Vadim is the only man I've ever let get close and that trust took years to build. As far as women go, no one ever saw me with anyone because there was nothing to see. I had meaningless quickies. Everyone knows my opinion on having weaknesses. The last thing anyone would expect is for me to have a woman at my side.

Goddammit, she's right, and she sees it on my face because hers lights up in a huge smile.

"Told you," she whispers.

I laugh and squeeze her hip. "Don't get too cocky, sweetheart. We're still going to do it my way."

She pats my chest. "Whatever you say, babe."

It's ridiculous how much my heart swells at the term of endearment. God, she's turning me into a giant fucking softie. I switch off my computer and stand up, taking her with me. If she's going to be on the back of my motorcycle, then she's going to need more protection than the thin shirt she has on. Setting her down in the closet, I start going through her things, pulling down the leather jacket I asked Vadim to get her. I hold it out to her and then grab a pair of black boots.

"Put these on, little bunny."

While she steps into the boots, I grab my own leather jacket and boots and get myself ready. She looks sexy as fuck. Part badass, part innocent virgin who's eager to get defiled. Fucking hell. Shaking my head to clear it, I grab her hand and lead her downstairs. It's time to find out what the hell's been going on in my absence.

Chapter 10

Lydia

It's obvious Kirill isn't thrilled about taking me along tonight, but I wasn't wrong about being his perfect cover. I can't help the thrill it gives me to know that I'm the only woman he's let get close to him, that the mere idea of a woman being on the back of his bike is so out of character for Kirill that no one will think for one second it's him.

Before we leave, I give Peanut some love and make sure he has plenty of food and water and then slip him a dog treat, laughing when he quickly scampers off to fill his new home with half-eaten treasures. He's adapted well, and I'm thrilled to see it. It's only natural that he would since he's an animal, but it worries me a bit at how easily I've slipped into this new life. When I look at the man in front of me, I no longer see a monster. I no longer see the man who murdered my father. I see the man I'm falling in love with, the man that I'm starting to believe was framed and that I helped put in prison. I never saw his face that night, a detail I've yet to admit, and the guilt eats at me a little more with each passing second.

When he hands me a black helmet, I'm more than ready to cover my face, not wanting him to see the war going on inside me. I slip it on and wait as he helps me with the buckle before slipping his own helmet on. Kirill always looks sexy, it's just his natural state of being, but when he puts that dark helmet on and gets on his black motorcycle, it takes everything to a whole new level. He motions for me to get on, and when I awkwardly hike a leg over and then just sort of hang there because I haven't the slightest clue as to what the fuck I'm doing, I hear his deep laugh before he guides my feet to where they need to be.

"Hang on, little bunny," I hear him yell as he starts the motorcycle and it roars to life.

I wrap my arms around his tight waist, pressing my body up against his, surprised when I feel what has to be a gun at the small of his back. He must've grabbed it at some point, or it's just been there all damn day and I never noticed. Either way, it's there now, and knowing there's a deadly weapon between us and only inches from my pussy should scare the hell out of me, but instead it has me squeezing him tighter and running my fingers under his shirt so I can feel his skin beneath my touch.

He brings his hand to mine, giving me a gentle squeeze before revving the engine and taking off down the long driveway. I let out a squeal of pure joy that earns me another one of his deep laughs and a pat on my hand. He slows down when we get closer to the gate, but as soon as it's opened enough, he zips through, looking over his shoulder to make sure it shuts properly before speeding up even faster, racing us down the dark road.

Aside from having Kirill's head buried between my legs, being on the back of his motorcycle is the most fun I've ever had. When he takes a curve, he reaches back and gives my thigh a reassuring squeeze, and my heart does some sort of weird flip-flop while my pussy clenches, reminding me that I'm still not wearing any goddamn panties. The friction from my jeans mixed with the closeness of his body and the vibrations from the motorcycle I'm straddling make this the most enjoyable ride I've ever been on. I'm grinning like an idiot behind my helmet, grateful that he can't see me.

As we get closer to downtown, he slows the bike so we don't attract unwanted attention and then heads for the north side of the city, the rich part that I never had much use for. We pass high-rise apartment buildings with rooftop penthouses and restaurants that regular people will never be able to get reservations to, and when Kirill slows the bike down, I look around, trying to figure out where we are. He parks alongside the curb behind a big truck and lets the motorcycle idle while he scans the area. Pulling his phone out, he holds it in his hand so it looks like he's doing something with it, but all he's done is go to his home screen.

"Where are we?" I ask, raising my voice just enough so he can hear me.

"See the restaurant up ahead?"

The truck is hiding us, so I have to tilt my head a bit to see down the street. "The really fancy one that would never serve me in a million years?"

He turns his dark helmet to me. "If anyone ever treats you less than you deserve, you let me know, *zaika*. I'll take care of it."

I'm not sure if that means he'll kill them or it'll be more of a *hey, don't you dare treat my woman like that* kind of thing, and I'm scared to ask because I'm pretty sure I know what the answer is, so instead I drag my nails along his abs and say, "Down, killer. What about the restaurant?"

He shakes his head like he can't believe I just did that. "It's Ivan's favorite place. One of his mistresses owns it, and he likes to spend his evenings here."

One of his mistresses. The phrase rings through my head, but I file it away, intending to have a talk with Kirill about it later. I don't know much about the mafia life, but I've seen enough movies to know they all have women on the side. The thought of Kirill fucking someone else makes me feel sick to my stomach.

I push the nauseating thought aside and ask, "Do you want me to go in and like scope the place out or something?"

He barks out a disbelieving laugh and turns his dark helmet to face me again. "No way in hell, *zaika*."

"But they won't be paying any attention to me. I could go in and spy on him for you and then tell you what all I see."

"There's nothing you can say that will convince me to put your life in danger, so you might as well stop trying. If I wanted to go in there, I'd be in there, and none of those fuckers would see me. I'm just watching them from afar tonight."

That's probably the wisest choice, but I don't tell him that. I've never spied on anyone before, and I'm guessing I wouldn't be too stealthy. Plus, that place looks like you need to be wearing half-a-million dollars to even be let in the front door. The hostess would probably turn me away within seconds, and god that would be embarrassing. I'm pulled from my thoughts when I feel his body tense as all his attention turns to a group of men leaving the restaurant. We're too far away for me to see details, but the group of men in dark suits and neck tattoos is hard to miss.

"Is that the Teterev Bratva?" I ask.

"Yes, with some of the Faretti men."

I can tell by the sound of his voice that he's less than pleased to see the two groups mingling. We watch the men talk as they wait for the valets to bring around their expensive cars. Their numbers slowly dwindle until only two men remain. One of them lights a cigarette while the other checks his phone. When the valet brings a red Ferrari around, they shake hands before the one with the cigarette gets in and drives off. Kirill puts his phone away and gives my thigh a squeeze before following after him.

He stays far behind, keeping several cars between us, and when the Ferrari takes a right at the next stoplight, we do the same. Kirill slows down when the traffic thins out, putting even more distance between us until the Ferrari's headlights are barely visible ahead of us. Mansions surround us on either side now, and when the car pulls up to a black, iron gate, Kirill keeps going straight. We pass the red car right as the gates start to swing shut behind it, locking him inside his property. The enormous mansion that sits several hundred feet beyond the security fence is lit up, and I can see several men walking the property.

I'm guessing this is Ivan Teterev's house, and those are his armed guards.

I relax against Kirill's body as he loops around and heads us back towards downtown. He drives around for what feels like forever, but we don't stop again. I trace the lines of his abs, and when I dip a finger into his jeans, I hear his deep laugh again. He gives my thigh a squeeze and takes the road that will lead us back home. It scares me that I already think of it as home. Kirill's been a constant in my life for two years. His presence may have been terrifying at first, but that changed a long time ago. It morphed into comfort and desire, and now it's changing into something much, much deeper.

When Kirill pulls into his garage, I slip off the bike as soon as the engine stops, stretching out my legs before pulling my helmet off. I hand it to him and ask, "Learn anything?"

"Confirmed more like." He scrubs a hand over his stubbled jaw and sets our helmets on one of the shelves. "I'll need to take care of this soon."

I reach for his hand, surprised by the worry that immediately hits me at his words. I'm not so sure I want him going out there and doing hitman stuff again.

"Can't you just let it go?" When he raises a dark brow at me, I add, "I mean, can't we just leave and forget about all this?"

"No."

There's a finality in that one word, and I know that I will never be able to talk him into letting this go and walking away. Kirill wants vengeance, and he's going to make damn sure he gets it. Whatever he sees on my face makes his soften. He steps closer and cups my face, running his thumb over my cheek in the way that I've come to crave.

"You worrying about me, little bunny?"

"No," I say, and then roll my eyes and whisper, "Maybe."

He smiles and kisses my forehead. "I've never had anyone worry about me. I like it."

Before I can ask him to let this all go again, he grabs my hand and leads me inside.

"You haven't had supper yet," he says, because the man is obsessed with my caloric needs.

I let the Ivan thing go for now and instead watch him grill a couple of steaks. We spend the rest of the evening together, laughing and eating and then watching a movie, and it's so normal and perfect that it almost has me forgetting about everything else. I could get lost in this life with him so easily. I could forget about the other side of him, forget about how we met, forget everything, as long as he keeps looking at me like the way he is right now, like I'm the most important thing in the world to him.

When we fall asleep later, he doesn't have to ask me to cuddle up with him this time. I do it on my own because I want to, because I crave the comfort of his body, and because I want to be close to him. Peanut finds his spot on Kirill, and I smile while he groans good-naturedly and gives my dog a pet on the head.

For the first time in two years, I don't wake up screaming. At first I think it's a fluke, but then it happens again the next night and the night after that. After only three days with Kirill, I'm fully decided on what I want, and it's him. He hasn't taken care of Ivan yet, and I know it's eating at him, but he seems reluctant to leave me to go do it. He's also been avoiding my attempts at taking things further. Whenever I try, he buries his head between my legs, not letting up until I can barely utter my own name, let alone beg for his cock.

I woke up this morning and decided I've had enough. He's already downstairs making breakfast, so I take a shower and then slip on some of the lingerie that arrived yesterday. He'd ordered me way more than I thought, and when I'd offered to try some on, he'd told me not yet. I don't think he trusts himself. I smile and grab a pink, lacy thong with an attached garter belt and a pair of nude thigh highs. Unable to resist being a bit of an ass, I ignore the no-bra rule and put on the matching bra. It takes me a second to figure it all out, but once I've got the thigh highs hooked to the ribbon straps of the garter belt, I grab the dress that Kirill told me he loved in his letters. Sliding the sundress on, I look in the mirror, hoping like hell this works. The dress in itself is simple but cute with a square neckline and slender straps along my shoulders and a pink floral print that covers all of it.

After I've brushed my hair and put on a little bit of makeup, I take a deep breath and head down the stairs. His back is to me when I walk into the kitchen, and the sight of his broad shoulders has me more nervous than I've ever been in my life. I'm about to chicken out and bolt back up the stairs when he turns and sees me. The look on his face makes it impossible to move. His chiseled jaw is clenched tightly as he sets our plates on the counter and curls a finger at me, beckoning me closer. Every step has my bravery dwindling until I'm nearly shaking with nerves by the time I'm standing in front of him. He towers over me, and when I tilt my head to meet his eyes, the hunger in them has me taking a step back.

"Not so fast, little bunny," he says, grabbing onto my hip and digging his fingers in hard enough to ensure I can't leave. "You're wearing my favorite dress." He slides his other hand up my bare arm, leaving a trail of goosebumps on my skin. His fingers drag along my shoulder before hooking under the top of my dress and pulling it down enough to reveal a tiny bit of the pink, lacy bra. He makes a *tsk-tsk* noise and shakes his head slowly. "You're breaking rule number one, baby."

"You bought it for me," I whisper.

"I did, but I said you aren't allowed to wear them when we're home alone."

Grabbing the bottom of my dress, he lifts it up and takes a step back, letting out a slow breath when he sees what I'm wearing underneath. When his eyes meet mine, his pupils are blown and the vein in his neck is throbbing. I'm expecting a lot of things to happen, but I'm not prepared for what he says next.

"Time to eat breakfast, sweetheart."

He drops my dress and grabs our plates, motioning for me to follow him to the dining room table. I'm starting to second-guess the hunger I saw in his eyes. I feel like an idiot, an overdressed moron. I thought he'd take one look at me and carry me back to bed, finally giving me what I've been begging for, but instead he just wants to eat.

"Do you not want to have sex with me?" I ask, feeling my face turn a deep shade of red. He sets our plates down and laughs as he turns around to face me. Grabbing my wrist, he pulls me closer and presses my hand against his fully hard cock.

"Does it feel like I don't want to fuck you, *zaika*."

He presses me harder against him, and when I grip him as best I can, he lets out a low groan.

"Then why aren't you?" I whisper.

He smiles and gives me a wink. "You're not quite there yet. Plus, you need to eat."

Without waiting for my response, he scoots a chair out and sits down, but when I go to do the same, he grabs my waist and pulls me onto his lap. His eyes run over me as he traces his fingers along one of my thighs.

"You look amazing, baby. I thought about you in this dress so many times, but no fantasy could compare to this."

The hard length of him presses against my ass, but he makes no move to do anything about it. He just slowly strokes my thigh for a few more seconds and then calmly cuts off a piece of the blueberry pancake, spearing the piece on the end his fork and bringing it to my mouth.

"You made me pancakes?" I ask.

He smiles. "They're whole wheat with organic blueberries."

"Of course they are," I say, making him give a soft laugh.

"And it's organic maple syrup." He presses the fork gently against my lips. "Open, *zaika*."

The corner of his mouth lifts up in a small smile when I open my mouth and obey him. I let out an appreciative moan when the sugary syrup hits my tongue. He feeds me while his other hand never stops touching me, squeezing my hip, lightly stroking my arm and the nape of my neck, until every part of me is strung so tight I'm starting to shake. Only when the plate is empty does he push it away and reach for his own. Before he takes a bite, he brings his hands to the straps of my dress. Hooking his fingers under the thin straps, he keeps his stormy grey eyes on mine and slowly peels them down, pulling until the dress comes down below my breasts. Brushing the backs of his fingers over one lace-covered nipple, he gives me a heated look before reaching behind me. He unclasps the bra and slowly takes it off me, dropping it on the table without a second thought.

"Much better," he murmurs, running his eyes over me.

Satisfied, he picks his fork back up and starts to eat his breakfast. His fingers trace circles along my back as he eats, and it's the most exquisite torture I've ever experienced. He takes his time, running his eyes over me as he slowly chews and drinks his coffee. When I can't hold out any longer and I start to squirm against the hard cock beneath me, a smile tugs at his lips and he finally pushes his plate aside.

"Stand," he says, and that one word has me hopping to my feet. Part of me feels like one of his well-trained dogs, but a bigger part of me is too horny to give a fuck. He scoots his chair back a bit more and says, "Bend over the table and lift your dress up."

I hesitate, and he raises a dark brow, waiting to see what I'll do. Turning around, I bend my body over the hardwood table and reach back to grip the bottom of my dress. Taking a deep breath, I flip the fabric up, exposing my ass to him. I feel completely on display and kind of wishing I hadn't chosen the garter belt with the built-in thong.

He lets out a deep groan and drags his fingers over my bare ass cheeks. "You are mouthwatering, little bunny."

"Are you going to fuck me now?" I ask.

His fingers slide down the backs of my thighs, caressing the ribbons connecting my thigh highs to the garter belt before dipping between my legs. That one stroke of his finger along my slit is enough to make me moan his name and rock my hips back.

"You're soaking wet, sweetheart. Such a dirty girl." He presses harder, giving my clit a firm rub. "So hungry for my cock."

"Yes," I whimper, because fuck trying to be coy. I'm dick hungry, and we both know it.

"Beg me, little bunny."

One more swipe of his finger over my clit has me opening my mouth. "Please fuck me, Kirill," I say in a breathy rush. "Oh god, please," I whimper when he slips a finger under the lace of my panties and slowly parts my lips, sliding in deep.

"What do you need?" he taunts while he finger fucks me at an excruciatingly slow pace. My hips rock, meeting the thrusts of his finger as I clench around him, desperate for more.

"You," I moan. "I need you, Kirill."

"What part of me?"

He adds in a second finger, and my mind goes blank. It takes me several seconds before I can sputter, "Your cock." He keeps going until I'm so frustrated I lose my temper. "Fuck, I need your cock inside me right fucking now," I yell, slamming my hand down on the table hard enough to make the plates jump.

He laughs and pulls his fingers out while I give a pained whimper at the loss of contact. I hear his chair being pushed back before both his hands are on my hips, holding me in place as he presses against me, letting me feel how hard he is. I try to rock against him like a fucking dog in heat, desperate for release, but all he does is take a step back.

"Hands and knees, *zaika*."

"Huh?" I manage to say, looking over my shoulder at him.

"Hands and knees, little bunny. Don't make me ask again."

His grey eyes meet mine, brow raised and jaw tense. My eyes run down his body, and when I see the outline of his hard length pressing against his jeans, I drop to the ground without a second thought and look up at him. The proud look he gives me probably shouldn't make me as wet as it does, but there's no denying how much I enjoy it. I stay on my hands and knees, not knowing what I'm supposed to be doing. The hard floor digs into my knees, but I don't move. I do look back up at him when he just turns and walks away, though. Before I can ask what the hell is going on, he turns his head to the side, not even bothering to fully turn around.

"Follow me, *zaika*."

He walks off without another word, leaving me confused and

feeling stupid, but also more turned on than I've ever been. Grateful that at least Peanut is outside playing so I won't have him scampering around me thinking it's playtime, I start the slow process of crawling behind Kirill. When I leave the dining room, he's waiting for me, and as soon as I'm next to his legs, he squats down and hooks a finger under my chin, lifting my face up to him while his other hand strokes my hair. I realize it's like I'm being petted, and I definitely realize that I should probably be offended and pissed about this, but all it does is send a shiver of pleasure straight down my spine until it lands right between my legs. He smiles at the soft moan I give.

"That's my good girl," he murmurs, running his hand along the top of head. "Keep crawling, baby. You look sexy as fuck."

His thumb caresses my cheek and then drifts lower to circle one of my nipples. He cups my bare breast, giving me a squeeze before he stands and starts walking again. I follow him through the kitchen, letting out a sigh of relief when we hit the carpeted stairs. I'm all set to follow him up when he stops by the bottom step. I look up at him, waiting for him to go up. He reaches down and pulls my dress up until my entire lower body is exposed.

"Crawl, little bunny." His fingers trail along my spine and my bare ass. "Show me what's about to be mine."

I give a soft nod and rest my hands on the next step before lifting one knee. It's a slow process, and as I maneuver the stairs, it's his soft groans that have me slowing down even more. The sound of his pleasure make me feel wanted and beautiful and sexy. It makes me want to do more, to take my time and really give him a show. When I arch my hips even more, giving him a better view of the lace-covered pussy that's dripping for him, he lets out a string of Russian in a strained, rough voice. I keep going, teasing him with each slow step, and when I'm almost at the top, he surprises the hell out of me by giving one of my ass cheeks a hard spank. The sharp sting of it has me letting out a surprised yelp as I turn back to look at him. I suck in a quick breath when I see the feral look in his eyes.

He drags his fingers over my stinging cheek before lowering himself down behind me. My fingers dig into the stair I'm clinging to when I feel the wet heat of his tongue run over the skin he just spanked. His teeth nip at me gently, and when he palms my cheeks, spreading them wide, I let out a mewling sound as soon as he pushes my panties aside and licks a line from my clit to my asshole.

"Fuck," I gasp, barely clinging to my sanity as his tongue rims the one place I thought for sure was off-limits, lighting up every single nerve ending that I'd been completely ignorant about until this very moment. I never thought I'd be into anything anal, but I get it now. I'm a believer, a full-on convert. He gives me one more lick before pulling away, letting my panties fall back into place and then spanking my other cheek hard enough to send a mix of pain and pleasure straight through me.

"Keep going, *zaika*," he groans, giving my ass one last kiss before standing back up.

I crawl up the last few stairs and start down the hallway. I'm back on hardwood floors now, but the pain in my knees is worth hearing the heavy sound of his breathing behind me. Once I cross into our room, he walks ahead of me, sitting in one of the leather chairs by the French doors. His thighs are spread, elbows resting on the arms of the chair as he steeples his fingers and watches me with heavy-lidded eyes.

"Crawl to me, little bunny."

The way he's looking at me makes me feel like I'm the most important thing in the world to him and like I'm about to be ravaged in the best possible way, especially with the way his grey eyes are locked on my bare breasts and the way they lightly bounce with each step I take.

When I'm right between his legs, he says, "Take out what you want, sweetheart."

I smile and sit up on my knees, reaching forward to undo his jeans. I make quick work of the button and then slowly unzip his pants, the anticipation making my heart race and my palms sweat. His eyes never leave mine as I reach in and wrap my hand around his thick shaft, carefully pulling him free. He's covered in pre-cum, and he's rock-hard, veins standing out, the lines of them easily visible along the length of him. He's fucking perfect.

"You crawled for me, *zaika*," he says, cupping my cheek with one hand. "You got on your hands and knees and crawled for me, so fucking desperate for my cock."

"Yes," I whisper.

"Now you know how I feel about you. I'd do anything for you. I'd do anything to get to you. The hungry need you feel right now, that willingness to do anything as long as it gets me inside you, I've felt nothing but that since I first saw you. You are everything to me, and you consume every goddamn part of me."

His words send a rush of warmth through me, a slow burn that's about to light me on fire. Leaning forward, he runs his hands down my body, gripping my dress and pulling it slowly off. He tosses it aside, leaving me in nothing but the lingerie he bought.

"God, you're beautiful," he murmurs, trailing his fingers up my side and along the rounded side of my breast.

I grab his hand and scoot it over so his palm is resting against my heart. "You told me that you wanted in here, that you wouldn't sleep with me until you were in here and in here," I say, tapping on the side of my head. "You're already in my head, Kirill. You have been since I first saw you."

"And here?" he asks, pressing harder against my chest. "Am I in here too, *zaika*?"

"I don't want to get hurt," I whisper.

"I would never hurt you."

"Maybe not physically, but it would hurt me if you can't be faithful. You mentioned mistresses the other night, and I know that's common for men in your line of work, men who are involved in the mafia."

I'm fumbling over my words while he just keeps staring at me, looking sexy as hell. Finally, he says, "It would bother you if I had a mistress?"

"Yes," I say, and just the idea of it has my blood pressure rising. He feels my heart speed up, sees the red flush of my skin, and grins.

"I'm very happy to hear that."

"I'm glad you're so thrilled, but you didn't answer my question."

He laughs at my tone, but then his face turns serious when he leans closer. Keeping his hand pressed against my heart, he uses his other hand to grab mine and bring it to the cock that's still jutting out between us.

"This belongs to you, little bunny, and only you. No other woman will ever have it. I promise I will always be faithful to you. Every single part of me is yours."

He grips my hand, forcing me to hold him tighter as he slowly works himself. I feel the strength in him, the way my thumb can't reach my fingers because he's too damn big, and I start to feel a pinprick of fear. There's no way in fuck he's going to fit inside me. He's just too damn big, and why the hell I ever thought otherwise is a complete mystery to me.

"You feel what you do to me?" He uses my hand to stroke himself even harder. "You feel how hard you make me?"

I look down and stare as another bead of pre-cum forms before spilling out and dripping down his length, wetting my fingers even more. He's covered in his own arousal, and knowing that I'm the cause of this, that I'm the one who made his body react so strongly is making me downright giddy. It's a rush of power, knowing that a man as dangerous and sexy as Kirill wants me and only me. He already looks like he's about to lose control at any second, and when I start to lower my head, he lifts a dark brow at me as he tightens that chiseled jaw again.

"I always thought of myself as a man who has excellent control over himself, but you test me like no one else ever has, little bunny."

I keep my eyes on his and run my tongue over the head of his cock, lapping and probing at his slit. He hisses out a breath and runs his fingers through my hair, fisting it tight enough to force me off him.

"You never answered my question," he reminds me. Releasing the tight grip on my hair, he brings one hand down, cupping my breast and grazing his fingers over where my heart is beating a fast, crazed rhythm. "Am I in here, *zaika*?"

"Yes," I whisper.

He widens his fingers, pinching my nipple between them and squeezing it hard enough to make me gasp.

"Are you sure about that, sweetheart?"

"Yes." It comes out in a breathy rush, and when he fists my hair tighter with his other hand, and lowers me back to his cock, I lick my lips and meet his eyes.

Pupils blown with one dark brow raised, he says, "Show me," and squeezes my nipple even tighter between his fingers.

He's not asking me to tell him I love him. He's asking me to show him with my body how I feel about him, and that's exactly what I do. Gripping his shaft, I angle him where I want him and then close the distance between us. Instead of just taking him in, I kiss his slit, slowly working my way around his head, nipping and licking and running my tongue along the ridge of skin that connects to his shaft. When I flick my tongue against him, he groans and fists my hair tighter, trying to keep himself under control.

"Fuck, baby," he growls when I run my tongue down his length, moving my hand so I can get all of him.

I take my time, moaning my own pleasure as I savor every damn inch of him, covering him in my spit and letting him feel how much I love him with every kiss, every nip, every swipe of my tongue. By the time I wrap my lips around his head and suck him into the wet heat of my mouth, the poor guy is practically panting. He's switched to Russian, growling out god knows what as I take him in some more and run my fingers over his heavy, full balls. When I gag, I don't stop. I keep going, letting my tears and spit fall, degrading myself in the best possible way for him.

He rolls my nipple between his fingers, causing a dizzying wave of pleasure to run through me as I moan and push past the uncomfortableness of having him so deep in my throat. When I'm satisfied, I stop and wait. I can't meet his eyes from this angle, but he knows I can't breathe and that I'm putting myself completely in his hands. Spit puddles at the base of his cock as my lungs start to burn. He gives my nipple one last pinch before threading his fingers through my hair again, lifting up the strands so there's nothing obscuring his view.

"So fucking beautiful," he murmurs when another tear slips free. "My little bunny willingly choking on my cock for me. Such a good fucking girl, baby."

When my lungs start screaming for air and I let out a whimper, he lazily caresses my forehead with his thumb as if we have all the time in the world.

"You have no idea how badly I want to keep you here until you pass out, *zaika*."

My heart races at his words, because surely he wouldn't do that. A tiny voice in the back of my head says, *He's a power-hungry killer, of course he'd fucking do it!*

"I love you more than life itself, but that doesn't mean I wouldn't enjoy fucking your sweet face while you're unconscious."

I moan again, and truth be told, it's not because I'm upset. Part of me likes the idea of him using my body however he wants, even if I'm not awake to witness it. God, that's all kinds of fucked up, and I promise myself I'll examine it later, possibly in a therapy setting, but for now, I'm too busy drooling shamelessly and trying to ignore the light-headed feeling that's getting stronger with each passing second.

When I let out another whimper and dig my nails into his abs, he finally lifts me off his cock by my hair. The sharp sting mixes with the lust running through me, and when I get that first lungful of air, it becomes a potent cocktail of pure need. My eyes are heavy-lidded and glazed over when I look up and meet his.

He runs his thumb over my swollen lips and says, "I think you're finally ready, little bunny."

Chapter 11

Kirill

Her eyes widen at my words as she sucks in a quick breath. I've never seen anything as beautiful as Lydia, the woman who crawled on her hands and knees for me and almost made herself pass out on my cock because she didn't want to move without my permission. She's perfect, absolutely fucking perfect, and she's about to become all mine.

Wrapping my arms around her, I pick her up and carry her to the bed. She sits and watches me as I undress, worrying her bottom lip, unable to take her eyes off the cock that's hard as fucking steel and more than ready to be inside her. Wanting to keep her in the thigh highs and garter belt, I run my hands up her legs and snake my fingers under the soaking wet lace of her thong. In one quick motion, I rip the lace, exposing the pussy that I'll never be able to get my fill of. I toss the pieces aside, groaning at the sight of her.

"Your little cunt is dripping for me, little bunny." I run a finger up her slit, coating my finger and bringing it to my mouth so I can taste her again. "My girl's a sloppy wet mess."

Her lips part at my words, and the feral look in her eyes has me nearly losing control. She parts her thighs wider for me, but when she meets my eyes again, I see the worry in them.

"What's wrong?" I cup her face and lean closer. "We can stop, baby. If you don't want to do any more, I need you to tell me."

"No, I want to," she says in a quick rush, but then her eyes dart back to my cock. "I don't think you're going to fit," she whispers, and I can't help but smile at her innocence.

"I'll fit, little bunny, don't worry about that." I run my hand down her stomach and press the palm of my hand against her pussy as I slide my thumb into her. She moans and clamps down on me, nearly making my eyes roll back in my head. "You're going to spread so goddamn good for me."

I run a slippery finger over her clit, smiling when she throws her head back on a moan and fists the bedding. Switching my fingers, I bring my thumb to her swollen bundle of nerves and slide two fingers into her tight, wet pussy, working her until her whole body is shaking and the room is filled with her sexy moans and the erotic wet sounds of her arousal. When she starts to come, she clenches around me even tighter, sucking my fingers in even deeper and moaning my name as she comes undone. My dick swells even more, desperate to get inside her, and as soon as I feel her body start to relax, I slide my fingers out and hover my body on top of hers.

Fisting my cock, I guide my head to her drenched slit and meet her beautiful blue eyes. "Are you sure?" I ask her. "Because once I get inside you, I may never leave."

She smiles like I'm joking, and nods her head. "I'm sure." She rests her palms on my face, pulling me closer. "I love you, Kirill, and I want this."

My heart nearly breaks at her words. No one's ever told me they love me, never given themselves to me in the way that Lydia has. I'm completely lost to her. She owns every damn part of me, and I will never want anyone but her.

"I love you too," I tell her and then slowly slide in.

She winces when I push past her body's natural resistance, filling her with my thick head and making her mine.

"You're doing so good, *zaika*." I cup her face and kiss her gently, knowing there's a hell of lot more cock she needs to take before this is over. "Just relax, baby. I need you to be a good girl and take all of me."

"I will," she whispers, even as her eyes start to water when I give her another inch.

"Fuck," I groan, running my tongue up her cheeks, licking the salty tears from her as I give her more.

"Kirill," she gasps, clinging to me so tightly that her whole body is tense and shaking. "It's too big."

I can't help but smile against her lips.

"Are you smiling?"

I laugh at her tone and lift my head enough so I can see her face. "I'm sorry, baby, but you telling me my cock is huge and that you don't think your pussy can take it will always make me smile." I give a soft shrug. "I'm happy to prove to you that your pussy can in fact take it, but I still love hearing it."

"I'm not so sure it can. You're almost all the way in, right?"

She frowns at my big smile. "About halfway," I tell her.

"Holy shit," she whispers.

I give her a wink and slowly slide out, fucking her with half my dick. She moans and digs her nails into my shoulders, eyes widening in surprise at the sensations running through her.

"Not so bad, is it?" I tease.

"No," she pants. "Not bad at all."

"Ready for more?"

She nods and bites her bottom lip.

"Deep breath, baby."

When she exhales, I bring my mouth to hers, gently nipping and licking her lips before sliding my tongue in. I kiss her slowly and deeply and rock my hips, easing into her the rest of the way until I'm buried inside her and she's gripping my cock so goddamn good. I groan at the feel of her tight, wet heat, feeling a sense of peace wash over me unlike anything I've ever experienced. Being inside her feels *right*, like I was always supposed to end up right here between her legs with her small body clinging to me and her hungry tongue in my mouth. My little bunny sets me on fire, and I'll gladly burn for her. I kiss her harder, knowing I'll never be able to get enough.

She moans and runs her nails down my back, digging her heels into my ass as she rocks up against me, meeting my thrusts with her own until we've settled into the perfect rhythm. Her nipples scrape my chest, pulling another groan from me, and when I cup the back of her head, she gives my bottom lip a hard enough bite to surprise me.

I pull back and watch her take my cock. She's clenched so fucking tightly around me, and the sight of her arousal coating me as I slam into her nearly pushes me over the edge, but there's no way in hell I'm giving in before she comes again. She lets out a soft gasp when I bring a hand between us and drag my thumb over her swollen clit.

"You going to come for me, baby?"

"Yes," she moans, and then widens her eyes in surprise when I use my other hand to hike her leg up onto my shoulder, giving me the freedom to go even deeper. She runs her nails down my chest hard enough to sting and mark my skin with thin, red trails that extend from my neck to abs.

"I knew my little bunny would like it rough," I tell her, thrusting in even harder as I roll her clit between my fingers. "You look so sweet and innocent, but I knew you'd be feral in bed, a wild, untamed woman who'd do anything for my cock." I circle my hips and give her clit another firm rub.

"Yes," she whimpers, nodding her head in agreement.

"You want my cum, sweetheart? You want me to fill this tight pussy up until you're dripping my seed?"

"Yes, fuck yes," she begs. "Please, Kirill."

Her begging is my undoing, just like it always has been. My one weakness that I will never be able to resist.

"If you want it, then come around my cock, *zaika*. Let your greedy little cunt take it from my body."

All it takes is one more firm rub and she's moaning my name, her whole body tensing as the orgasm consumes her. Closing the distance, I bring my mouth to hers, wanting to taste her when I find my own release. It doesn't take long. Her pussy grips me hard, and when I feel a tremor run along my cock from base to tip as another rush of pleasure runs through her, I'm a fucking goner. With a growl, I slam into her, giving in to the euphoria. Everything else fades away. Noting else exists outside of this woman who means more to me than my next breath. I lose myself completely in her wet, willing body, never wanting to be free of her. Each pulse of my cock is staking my claim on her, and just like I promised, I fill her to the fucking brim.

By the time I come down, my heart is racing, my ears are ringing, and I have fucking goosebumps. Sex with Lydia isn't just a good fuck. It's a goddamn religious experience. I slow the kiss down, savoring the taste and feel of her, breathing in the soft jasmine scent from her lotion, and memorizing every detail of this moment. Her fingers trail gently along my back, no longer trying to claw through my skin. She's relaxed, her body sated for the moment, and when I pull back, the sex-drunk look on her face makes me laugh.

"Don't laugh at me," she says, and even her voice is slow and lazy and a bit raspy.

"I'm not laughing at you, sweetheart. You just look very satisfied right now. It's adorable."

"I am satisfied." She reaches her arms up in a stretch and smiles at me. "That was amazing."

"It was," I agree, because it definitely fucking was. I cup her face, running my thumb over her smooth cheek. I'm in no hurry to slide out of her, but when my hips move as I reposition myself, she winces, and while part of me wants to beat my chest and grunt like a fucking proud animal, the other part of me hates that she's in pain and wants to take it away. I'm always amazed at the instincts she's managed to unearth from my cold heart. Caring, sensitive, considerate—these are not words that anyone from my past would ever use to describe me. It's easy with Lydia, though. It just feels natural.

Giving her one last kiss, I slowly slide out of her, immediately missing her once I'm free of her body. I look down at my semi-hard cock and groan. Blood and our joined release coat me, and I grip my shaft, running my hand up my length, wetting my hand with the evidence of what we just did. Placing my palm on her stomach, I smear her skin with it, right over the faint word still marking her skin. *Mine.* Every goddamn inch of her is mine, and I'm never letting her go. My eyes run over her swollen, used pussy, dripping my seed just like I promised her it would be.

"You look so beautiful after being taken by me, little bunny. Marked and used and wet with my cum—you're stunning, baby."

She smiles up at me, and the love I see in her eyes freezes me in place. I'm completely and utterly unworthy of it, and if I was a good man at all, I never would've allowed it to come to this, but I couldn't just leave her alone and let her live her life in peace. I needed her to become mine, because from the moment I saw her, that's how she felt. Mine to love and protect and worship, and I plan on doing all three of those things for as long as I live. My life is hers, every damn bit of it.

"Come on, *zaika*," I say, peeling off the garter belt and thigh highs before scooping her into my arms and carrying her into the bathroom. She rests her head against my shoulder while I get the bath started. Her fingers run along the tattoos on my neck, whisper-soft touches that have goosebumps forming on my skin.

"I never thought we'd end up here. I saw you in that courtroom, and you were so beautiful, but so goddamn scary, and I hated you so much, but I was so wrong."

My chest tightens at her words, but I refuse to dissect it. I don't want to bring all my feelings to light. I just want to feel her body against mine as I take care of her. I get into the tub and sink under the hot water, keeping her cradled against my chest.

"Shh, baby," I whisper, giving her forehead a kiss. "None of that matters anymore. The only thing that matters is that we're together now."

"Thanks for watching over me, Kirill. The truth is I'm not sure how

I would've made it through those two years without you. The idea of you having someone watch me was scary at first, but then it became a comfort. I'd hear my car make a new noise, and instead of feeling stressed and worried about what the hell I was going to do about it, I knew someone would take care of it for me. The same thing with problems around the house. It was a comfort to know I wasn't alone, but it was your letters that I loved most."

"I loved yours too, *zaika*." I give a soft laugh and add, "Once I convinced you to start writing me instead of just telling me to fuck off."

"I'm glad you didn't listen to that."

"That was never going to happen."

I run my fingers along her wet skin and hold her until the water starts to grow cold and Peanut comes racing in, wondering what in the hell we're doing. He puts his small paws on the edge of the tub and barks at us. She laughs and reaches over to pet his head. He does a cute wiggly, excited dance, giving us puppy-dog eyes that he knows she'll be unable to resist.

"Okay," she laughs. "We're getting out." She looks back at me and gives me a kiss. "I think he wants some attention."

"He's not used to sharing your affection." I give him a quick pet. "Better get him a dog treat before he starts to feel really neglected. It's been a while since he had one. I'd hate for him to get his first ever hunger pain."

She laughs at my teasing tone and returns my kiss before I stand up to get us some towels. Tying one around my waist, I hold the other out to her. She smiles at my need to take care of her but doesn't try to push me away. I slowly pat her perfect body dry, planting kisses on her shoulders and the nape of her neck before wrapping the towel around her. She leans closer and kisses my chest, nuzzling her nose against my chest hair.

"How do you always smell so damn good?"

I cup the back of her head and kiss the top of it. "I was wondering the same thing about you. The jasmine smell drives me crazy, but what

I really crave is what's underneath it, your unique scent, the one I'll never be able to get enough of."

When Peanut gives another bark, she kisses my chest and smiles up at me. I reach a hand down and gently squeeze her ass.

"How sore are you?"

"I'm still sore," she admits. "You're fucking huge, Kirill. I think I'm going to be sore for a while." She points a finger at me when I can't hold back the smile, her eyes lit up with amusement even though she's trying to look stern. "You don't have to look so damn proud about it."

I lean down and give her bottom lip a soft bite. "But I am proud, *zaika*, and I feel like it's my duty to always make sure you're walking around with an ache between your legs."

She gives my lips a quick lick and steps back. "You have to give me time to recover from this first time, though."

I smile and watch her walk to the closet, getting a new pair of panties since I ruined the last pair. She obeys my no-bra rule this time and pulls on a T-shirt before grabbing a pair of jeans. Once she's dressed, I manage to take my eyes off her long enough to pull my own clothes back on. Even though I know we're safe here, old habits die hard, so when Lydia looks away for a second, I tuck my gun into the waistband of my jeans, letting it rest against the small of my back. We head back downstairs together with Peanut yapping at our heels. She gets him his treat while I start on lunch, and when she's done, she comes over and hops up on the counter, watching me cook like we've been doing this for years.

"So what about my house?" she asks.

"I've already taken over the mortgage payments with one of my other bank accounts. I don't want to draw attention by paying it off all at once, so the monthly payments will continue as usual. You can either keep it or sell it or rent it, whatever you want to do."

She thinks about it while watching me check the pasta. "I think I want to hang onto it for now, but eventually I think I'd like to sell it."

"Whatever you want, baby." I give her a wink and start chopping everything else I need for the pasta salad.

After lunch, we take a walk down by the beach, staying out until the sun begins to set. It's a perfect day, one I never thought in a million years I'd ever have, and I have a gnawing feeling that nothing this good can last. I shove the thought aside and tighten my grip on Lydia as we walk back to the house. I cook supper for her, loving the way she always cleans her plate, even though she still likes to snack on the licorice that I pretend I don't see. I've almost convinced myself that everything's going to be okay, that a guy like me can get a happy ending, when the alarm sounds on my phone. I recognize the sound, and it's not the one that lets me know someone is at the gate. The annoying beep emanating from my back pocket is the one that lets me know someone has breached the fence.

Lydia's body tenses in fear when I grip her upper arms and say, "Stay here. Do not leave this house," right before I run for the door.

Pulling my gun, I wait in the shadows and pull up the security camera feed while listening for my dogs. I see one man dropping down from the fence, not noticing the four large shapes closing in on him. As soon as I hear the first angry bark, I run in the direction of it, sprinting across the yard and into the woods. It's not pitch black dark yet, but it's getting close. I dodge a few low-hanging limbs, and when I hear a deep growl right before a man's pained scream, I speed up and close the last of the distance.

Stepping into the small clearing, I keep my gun trained on the man who's now laying on the ground with Pyotr's jaws locked around his throat. He's too afraid to move and make the dog bite down harder, but his body is anything but relaxed. His heels dig into the ground, and when he tries to scoot his hand to his pocket, Boris steps closer and bares his teeth, letting him know that if he keeps moving, he's going to lose the hand.

When I look down at him, I shake my head in disgust. I know this fucker. Hitmen typically work alone, and we sure as hell don't trust easily, but we know of each other. It's a small world, after all, and the guy who's just broken onto my property is Jay Winslow, an American hitman with an impressive reputation, although not nearly as good as mine.

"What the fuck are you doing, Jay?"

"Get him off me," he grits out between clenched teeth.

Before I give the command, I search his body, collecting the guns and knives he has on him. Stepping back, I point my gun at him and tell Pyotr to release him. The dog immediately lets go and takes a step back. His muzzle is bloody, and he's still on full alert. They all are. Jay looks at the four dogs and then at the gun I'm holding and lets out a sigh. He knows it's over. I'm just about to ask him how the hell he knew where I lived when I hear footsteps crashing through the woods. I look up just in time to see Lydia break through the trees.

Oh, little bunny, we're going to have a serious discussion about obedience later.

"Are you okay?" she gasps, running up to me and looking for any injuries.

I cup her face and kiss her forehead, because as pissed as I am that she's put herself in danger, I can't be mad at her. "I'm fine, baby. Go back inside. I'll be there in a few minutes."

She ignores me and looks at Jay. "Who's that?"

Jay's been silently watching our exchange, and when I meet his eyes, he lifts a brow at me in a *what the fuck?* kind of way. When I kiss Lydia again and angle her behind me so I'm in between them, Jay understands how badly he's fucked up.

"I didn't know anyone else was here," he quickly says. "I wouldn't have come after you if I'd known she was here."

I ignore him and ask, "How did you know where I lived?"

"I saw you the other night on your motorcycle."

"I was wearing a helmet," I remind him.

He groans when he moves his neck and reaches up to see how bad the wound is. He's bleeding, but it's superficial because my dogs are really fucking well trained.

"I memorized your license plate when I saw you at Ivan's a couple years ago. I figured it might come in handy."

I'm not surprised he's remembered a license plate from that long ago. To stay alive in this business means you do crazy shit like that.

"I followed you," he continues. "I watched you drive past Ivan's, and then I followed you here."

"You saw her on the back of my bike."

"Yeah, but I didn't know she would be here. Kirill doesn't do relationships. Everybody fucking knows that."

His eyes dart to where Lydia is peeking out from behind me because the girl just can't seem to help herself, but he quickly looks away when I say, "Take your fucking eyes off her."

"I didn't know," he says again, keeping his eyes on mine.

"You may not have known before you came here, but you and I both know that if you'd managed to get your ass inside my house, and that's a big fucking if, she would've been there with me. We don't leave witnesses in this line of work, do we, Jay?"

I can see it on his face that he's thinking about lying, trying to come up with some way to bullshit his way out of this, but in the end he knows it's pointless, so he says, "No, we don't."

"So why are you here? Who put the hit out on me?"

He sighs and looks up at the night sky. "Ivan did."

That stupid motherfucker!

"I got greedy," he admits with a sigh. "I went to him and told him you must've escaped. He told me he'd pay three million if I would take you out. Everyone's looking for you now, man, but no one else knows where you live. I sure as hell didn't tell anyone. I wanted the money for myself."

"Anything else I need to know?"

He runs a hand through his dark blond hair and closes his eyes, no doubt cursing his own stupidity for attempting this. "Ivan's hired more bodyguards. He's scared to death now that you're out."

"He should be." I look down at Jay, knowing I can't let him live, but also knowing I'm going to take zero pleasure in his death. "Anything you want me to do?"

He knows what I'm asking, so I'm not surprised when he gives me the address to an apartment and then says, "The key is in my front right pocket. Push aside the bed in the spare room and pull up the wood flooring. There's a bag of money and instructions on who to give it to."

"I'll make sure it's done," I tell him, giving him my word.

"What's going on?" Lydia whispers from right next to me.

I look down at her, knowing she's not going to like what I'm about to say. "Go inside, baby."

Proving me right, she shakes her head and says, "No, I'm not going anywhere."

I sigh and raise a brow at her. Leaning closer so only she can hear me, I press my lips against her ear and whisper, "You and I are going to have a serious discussion about your complete lack of obedience, little bunny. See how well-trained my dogs are?"

She sucks in an angry gasp at my comparison, and I can't help but smile.

"Go inside, *zaika*."

"What are you going to do?"

"You know what I'm going to do."

She steps back and looks at me. "Can't you just let him go?"

"No." I don't give her any more of an explanation, and she's not pleased about it.

"I'm not leaving." She crosses her arms over her chest and juts her chin out at me.

I let out a heavy sigh and take a step closer to Jay while I tell Boris in Russian to go and stand by her. When the dog is sitting by her side, she reaches down to pet him just like I knew she would. I tighten my grip on the knife I took from Jay and give the command for Boris to grab her arm and pull her towards the house. It's a gentle bite, nothing that will hurt her. I just need her to look away, and as soon as she does, I plunge the knife into Jay's heart. I can't resist giving it a twist because he would've killed Lydia without a second thought, even if she doesn't realize that right now. Jay's eyes widen in pain and shock while Lydia lets out a horrified gasp. I watch Jay die, only looking away when I'm sure his heart has stopped.

Not wanting to see the look on Lydia's face, but also knowing I can't avoid it, I stand and turn around to face her. One of her hands is covering her mouth, the other still held gently between Boris's jaws. I tell him to let her go, and he quickly does. He drops her arm and goes to stand by his brothers. Lydia's eyes are wide with fright and horror, and when I take a step closer, she takes a step back.

Fuck me.

"He came here to kill us," I gently remind her. I point back at Jay's dead body. "He would have killed you."

"Maybe he wouldn't have," she whispers. "Maybe if you'd let him go, we would've never seen him again."

I sigh and swipe a hand over my face. "He would have killed us if given the chance, and if I'd let him go, he would've seen that as a sign of weakness and tried again."

"How do you know that? You're just guessing, trying to make his death seem justifiable."

"I know this, because he and I are the same. This is what we do. We have a target, and we don't stop until they're dead. I'm sorry you had to see this, but you wouldn't have if you'd listened to me and kept your ass inside."

"I was afraid you might get hurt." Her voice is nothing but a shaky whisper, and the sound of it has me closing the distance and pulling her into my arms.

"You thought I might get hurt, so you decided to run outside after me without a weapon?"

She gives a small shrug. "I didn't have a plan. I was just worried about you. I left Peanut inside."

"Well, I'm glad you did, baby, but next time keep your perfect little ass in there with him. Do not ever put yourself at risk for me." I tilt her face up to mine. "Ever. Do you understand?"

"I understand what you're saying."

"That's an evasive answer, *zaika*." I run a finger down her cheek, knowing I'd never survive it if something happened to her. "Any man who would come after me is not a nice man, baby. They would kill you, some of them would make a point of doing it slowly, and some would do other things to you before finally putting you out of your misery."

I see the fear in her eyes, and I'm glad she's finally taking this seriously, but then I see her mind working, and I don't like where it's going. The suspicion in her blue eyes has me slowly shaking my head.

"Don't insult me, sweetheart. I may be a cold-blooded killer, but I'm not a fucking rapist or a torturer. I kill people quickly, and I've never forced myself on a woman."

Guilt washes over her face before she drops her head, resting her forehead against my chest. "I'm sorry," she whispers. "I know you'd never do that. I don't know why I questioned it."

I cup the back of her head. "I understand why you'd wonder about it, baby. I'm not upset because you did. I just need you to know that I'm not that kind of monster."

"I know you aren't."

She grips me in a tight hug, and I try not to think about how close a deadly killer got to her tonight. I kiss her head and squeeze her again before letting her go.

"Please go inside, baby, and let me take care of this."

She avoids looking at Jay's body and keeps her eyes on mine. "Need some help?"

I let out a soft laugh at the idea of asking her to help me dig a grave. "No, baby, I've got this. Go take care of Peanut. He's probably worried about you."

She nods and when she turns to leave, I tell Boris and Grisha to go with her. They walk on either side of her, guiding her back to the house and making sure she's safe. I hear her talking to them, but it's too low for me to catch what she's saying. Once they're out of sight, I turn my attention back to Jay. I grab the key from his front pocket and then search his body again, not at all surprised that he came here with nothing but weapons and the clothes he's wearing.

After a quick trip to the garage for a shovel, I toss his body over my shoulder and walk with Pyotr and Igor further into the woods. I find a nice spot and start the long process of digging a grave. By the time it's as deep as I want, I'm coated in sweat and cursing Jay's stupid greedy ass for attempting to come after me. Tossing his body in, I shovel the dirt back in and tamp it down. It's after midnight by the time I finish. When the sun rises, this will actually be a pretty spot that's close to the edge of the hill, overlooking the ocean. It's a professional courtesy that I buried him here instead of chopping him up and letting the sharks finish him off.

I give a low whistle for the dogs to follow me as I walk back. Stopping at the hose by the side of the house, I rinse off the worst of the dirt and then clean the blood from Pyotr's muzzle. Making sure they have food and water, I spend a few minutes praising them on a job well done, and when I realize I'm stalling, I force myself to leave them and go inside.

Peanut runs up to me as soon as I enter. I scoop him up because it's easier to pet him in my arms than for me to stay bent over to reach him. He gives a happy yip and licks my hand. Lydia watches me from the couch. She's curled up at one end with a soft blanket draped over her. A movie plays on the TV, but the volume is so low that I know she just put it on for some background noise and not because she's actually watching it.

"Everything okay?" she asks.

"Yeah, it's all done." I set Peanut down and he runs to her.

"I'm going to take a quick shower. We can talk when I get out if you want."

She nods and watches me leave. I hate the distance I feel between us right now. I hate that she caught a glimpse of my darker side, the part that I'd hoped would remain as hidden from her as possible. My fear is that the distance will just grow, that she'll close herself off to me. I shake my head at the thought, knowing I couldn't bear it, not after everything we shared today.

Stepping under the hot spray of water, I wash the blood and dirt off me while the hurt look in her eyes replays over and over again in my mind. When I'm as clean as a man like me can get, I step out and dry off before pulling on a pair of grey joggers. Walking into the bedroom,

I'm surprised to find Lydia already under the covers and waiting for me. I lay down, letting out the breath I hadn't realized I'd been holding when she immediately closes the distance and snuggles up against me. She doesn't say anything, just kisses my chest and drapes an arm and leg over me while Peanut makes himself comfortable on my stomach. If someone had described this sleeping position to me a couple of weeks ago, I would've said it sounded like a claustrophobic hell, but when I run my hand through her hair and listen to the soft sound of her breathing, it doesn't feel like hell; it feels like pure heaven.

Chapter 12

Lydia

I have no idea what to expect when I go downstairs the next morning. Our routine seems to be that he wakes up first and goes downstairs to make breakfast with Peanut while I sleep in and then shower and meet him in the kitchen. This morning isn't any different. After I'm showered and dressed, I find him by the stove, flipping an omelet and looking sexy as hell while doing it. He's still in nothing but that pair of grey joggers, and the sight of him makes my damn head spin. He does not look like a man who just committed murder and buried the body on his own land. He looks like I should be slipping money into the waistband of his joggers and begging for a private dance in the back room.

When his grey eyes meet mine, I can tell he's worried about what he'll find, but his shoulders visibly relax as I step closer and wrap my arms around his waist. Closing my eyes, I hug him tightly, hearing the steady beat of his heart and savoring the feel of his strong arms as they wrap around me. I'm still sore from yesterday, but not even that ache between my legs can stop the warm flush from running through my body at the memory of how damn good he'd felt inside me.

I rest my chin on his warm chest and look up at him. "What the hell are you doing with me?" I ask.

He smiles and gives a soft laugh. Reaching over to turn the oven off, he keeps his other arm around me and asks, "What do you mean?"

"You could have anyone. You should have some gorgeous six-foot-tall woman with legs that never end and the kind of big tits that make men drool when they see them." I shake my head in confusion. "I don't get it."

He studies me for a second, brow furrowed in confusion, and then he picks me up. I wrap my legs around him and rest my hands on his muscled shoulders.

"What the hell made you think that?"

I shrug and wave one hand at the gorgeous chest and face in front of me. "It's just kind of obvious," I say.

He lifts a dark brow at that. "You think so, little bunny?"

"Yes," I whisper.

"Well, I feel the same way about you."

I laugh before I can stop it.

"I'm serious," he says. "The only difference is that I don't look at you and wonder why you're with me. I'll never understand that, so I've given up trying. I look at you and think that I would kill any motherfucker who tried to take you from me."

He leans closer and very lightly licks my lips, sending an immediate rush of pleasure straight through me. "You're the only woman I want, and you're the only woman I'll ever want. You're so beautiful, *zaika*, so goddamn beautiful it takes my breath away every time I look at you." He rests his forehead against mine. "I think I fell in love with you the first second I saw you."

"When I was trying my hardest to not throw up on the witness stand? Yeah, that must've been hot as hell," I say, but he doesn't smile or give a soft laugh like I'm expecting. His eyes fill with a deep pain that takes me by complete surprise. I guess me trying to make a joke of wrongly accusing him of murdering my dad isn't in the best taste, but I've always hidden behind sarcastic humor.

"I'm sorry," I say. "I guess I shouldn't joke about that."

"You have nothing to apologize for. I was just thinking how much better you deserve and how I'm a selfish jackass because I'll never let you go so you can find an honest man."

"I don't want anyone else," I remind him. I cup his face and stroke his stubbled cheeks. "I don't ever want you to let me go."

He tightens his grip on me and says, "I never will, little bunny." He holds me for several more seconds before setting me down and giving my ass a soft smack. "You need to eat breakfast."

I look down at him in those grey joggers and sigh. He's not fully hard, but he's getting there, and I can easily see the outline of his cock stretching against the fabric of his left thigh.

"House rule number two: You should always wear grey joggers without boxers," I tell him, and this time he lets out a deep laugh that makes me smile.

"Making house rules now, are we?"

"Yes," I say, grabbing the plate he offers me. "I'll let you know when I come up with another."

He laughs and takes his own plate, joining me at the island. We talk while we eat, but neither one of us brings up the murder I witnessed him commit last night. Instead of it being awkward, it's surprisingly peaceful, and when we finish eating and he tells me he needs to go take care of something, my first thought is that I don't want him to leave. He gives me a kiss and runs upstairs to shower. I watch him go and then pick Peanut up to cuddle with him. He's been spending more time outdoors than usual, and I think he's convinced himself that he's one of Kirill's guard dogs. I don't have the heart to tell him otherwise, so I just scratch behind his ears and give him a kiss, letting him down when he whines so he can run out the doggy door and go back on patrol.

Kirill comes down wearing jeans, a long-sleeve black tee, and his usual black, steel-toe boots. He looks like the sexiest damn killer I've ever seen.

"Already breaking house rule number two," I tell him.

He looks down at my shirt, smiling at my obvious lack of bra. "It's nice to see you're being obedient." He pauses and adds, "For once."

Laughing at the look I give him, he steps closer, and I lift my face to see him. With his boots on, our height difference is more noticeable than ever. He smiles and runs his fingers through my hair.

"I love how short you are, baby."

"Well, that's good, because I'm pretty sure I'm done growing. This is as good as it's going to get."

"Good." He smiles again and kisses my forehead. "I need to go, but I'll be back as soon as I can."

"You're going to his house, aren't you? To Jay's?"

"I am." He meets my eyes and waits. "Promise me you'll stay inside the house while I'm gone."

"I thought you said I was safe here."

"You are. I'm just being overly cautious after what happened last night."

"Can I go with you?"

"No."

His answer is immediate, and the tone is firm.

"Don't you even want to think about it?"

His lip quirks up the tiniest bit. "No, *zaika*, I don't. You're staying here, and that's final."

When I start to argue, he presses a finger against my lips and says, "If I think for one second you're going to disobey me on this, little bunny, then I'm going to tie you to the bed before I leave."

"You wouldn't," I say around his finger.

He gives me a wink. "Try me."

I think about arguing, but the determined look in his eyes tells me that this is not just an idle threat. He really would tie me to the bed, and a part of me doesn't hate the idea. I just don't want to be left there alone for hours. He lets out a soft laugh and runs his finger over my lips.

"Be a good girl and stay inside, and maybe I'll tie you up later. It can be part of your punishment for disobeying me last night."

"Huh?"

He laughs and brings his mouth close to mine. "You didn't think I forgot, did you? You disobeyed me, *zaika*. I can't just let that go. You could've been killed. I need to know that when I tell you to do something, you'll do it."

"I'm going to stay inside the house," I mutter.

"We'll see."

"What if I come with you and just wait in the car?" I ask, knowing it's a long shot, but trying all the same.

He taps the tip of my nose. "No."

When I go to say something else, he cups the back of my head and cuts my words off with a kiss. I can't argue with him when he's running his tongue along mine and making my brain freeze at the burst of lust that consumes me, and he knows it. I wrap my hands around his neck and pull him closer, but instead of bending down even more, he picks me up and brings me to his level. I lock my legs around his waist and tighten one arm around him, bringing my other hand to rest against his cheek. His hand squeezes my ass when I give his tongue a suck, and I'm more than ready for him to just bend me over the couch when he pulls back with a groan.

"Goddamn, you make it hard to leave, baby."

He laughs when I say, "You give the best goodbye kisses, Kirill. You sure you don't want to just stay?"

"I would if I could, but I promise I won't be long. Keep your phone close and call me if you need me." He gives me one more kiss, pulling back way quicker than I'd like, and then smiling at the frustrated look I give him. "Please stay inside, baby."

"I will. I promise."

"Good girl." He gives my ass a playful smack before setting me back down. Before walking away, he cups my face and gives me the sweetest smile. "I love you, little bunny."

My heart speeds up at his words, and I'm smiling like an idiot when I say, "I love you too."

He's still grinning when he gives me one last kiss and then turns to leave. I watch him walk away, and a few seconds later, Peanut comes barreling back through the doggy door, no doubt sent to watch over me by Kirill. I scoop him up and bring him over to the couch with me. Flipping through the channels, I pet him and try not to worry. It's still not safe for Kirill to leave the house, and I can't help but fear that maybe this is some sort of trap, but I know he isn't stupid. He won't do anything to get himself caught.

Keeping my phone next to me, I try to watch a movie, but my mind keeps wandering. When I get so antsy that I can't sit still, I get up and start to pace. Peanut follows me, but eventually grows bored and goes to lay down on his dog bed. Since the house is empty, I decide to take the opportunity to do a little exploring. As I head down the hall, I shove my phone in my back pocket and remind myself that I'm not snooping, just exploring. There is a difference, damn it.

The first room I walk into is one of the downstairs spare rooms. I look in the closet and dresser, pleased to find them both empty. I didn't expect to find anything, but there was still an irrational fear in the back of my mind that maybe I'd find another woman's clothes or some evidence that he'd brought women here. The room and connecting bathroom are completely empty, though. I give the other spare rooms a quick sweep before standing in the doorway to his office. I'm not about to touch his computer setup. One look at all that expensive equipment has me giving it a wide berth. I know myself and my complete lack of computer know-how. My guess is I'd do something to fuck up the entire system in just a few minutes of fiddling around on it. God, that would be an embarrassing conversation to have when he gets home.

Instead, I walk to the wall of bookshelves and start to snoop the old-fashioned way. Running my fingers along the spines, I examine the books, mainly in Russian, and then pick up a knickknack. It's a small statue of St. Basil's Cathedral, and judging by how damn sturdy it is, I'm guessing it's a paperweight. The sound of my phone chirping in my pocket nearly gives me a heart attack. I let out a soft gasp and set the cathedral back on the shelf before grabbing my phone and looking at the screen. I read the text from Kirill and groan.

Find anything interesting, little bunny?

I jerk my head up, looking around his office, but I don't see any obvious cameras. I shouldn't be surprised with the amount of security he has surrounding this place. I give a wave, turning around so he can see me from whatever direction he's spying on me from. When another text comes in, I read it and laugh.

Above the window.

I look, but I still don't see the damn camera. I still look in that direction though, and give him a big smile and wave. "Can you hear me?" I ask, wondering if he's got audio hooked up too.

Yes.

"I wasn't going to snoop on your computer," I clarify.

You wouldn't be able to even if you tried, sweetheart. ;)

Well, that hurts my pride a little bit, but I can't argue with his logic. He sends me the laughing emoji when he sees me roll my eyes at him.

"Where are you? Are you almost done?"

Yeah, I'm about to head back now. I'll be there in about twenty minutes.

I slowly walk back to the center of the room, standing in front of his desk and looking up at where I know the camera is hidden. An idea hits me, and he must see something in my eyes because his next text immediately comes in.

What are you up to, zaika?

I don't say anything, just smile and slowly pull my shirt off, letting it drop to his office floor.

Fuck, baby, what are you doing?

"What does it look like I'm doing?" I ask the empty room. This time when his text comes in I can't read it right away because I'm too busy stepping out of my pants. I'm wearing a red, lacy pair of panties today, and when I turn around and slowly peel them off, I make sure to drag it out so I'm bent over for several seconds while my phone chirps with all the incoming messages I'm getting. Picking my phone up, I laugh at the string of messages.

Goddamn, little bunny, you better not fucking get undressed without me there.

Oh, sweetheart, you're in so much trouble.

Fuck, you've got an amazing ass.

You have no idea how hard you're making me.

Enjoy sitting down without pain, baby, because I'm going to change that as soon as I get home.

The last message has me sucking in a quick breath at the thought of the spanking I'm going to get. I know I'm playing with fire, but this is too much fun to pass up. I like teasing him. I like pushing this dangerous man to the limit. I shouldn't. The smart thing would be to obey and become docile and just do whatever he wants, but I can't seem to manage that. I don't *want* to do that. I like seeing the wild look in his eyes, knowing that he's using all his willpower to keep himself in check. For *me*. That kind of power is my new weakness. I'm completely addicted to it, and I need my fix.

With a smirk, I walk around his desk and sit my bare ass in his nice leather chair. With an even bigger smile, I set my phone where I can easily read my messages and then hike my feet up onto his desk, bracing my heels against the edge as I spread my thighs wide.

Fucking hell, little bunny, you're in so much trouble. Don't you dare touch that sweet cunt without me.

"This sweet cunt?" I ask, trailing a hand down between my breasts and along my stomach before going lower. When I drag a finger along my wet slit, I say, "You're not here to stop me," before sliding a finger in.

No, but I'm going to be there soon. I think you're forgetting that, zaika.

I bring one hand up to cup my breast and give my nipple a soft pinch while I keep fingering myself.

God, you're such a disobedient, greedy girl. Don't come without me. Your ass is already in enough trouble.

Sliding in another finger, I moan and say, "But I really want to."

Tough fucking shit.

I laugh at his response and bring my wet fingers to my clit.

Lydia, he warns.

When I press harder and start to rub myself faster while I pinch my nipple again and let out a breathy moan, he texts, *You are sexy as fuck, but my god, sweetheart, am I going to make you regret this.*

I decide, perhaps naïvely and foolishly, that my impending orgasm is more important, so I ignore the dangerous hitman and keep rubbing my clit. Wet erotic sounds fill his office, and I know he can hear it because his next text says, *Such a filthy dirty girl. I can hear your sloppy wet cunt, baby. Your fingers will never be able to satisfy you. Not anymore. You want my big cock, don't you, little bunny?*

"Yes," I moan, knowing he can hear the frustration behind that one word, because he's right. Nothing will ever be able to satisfy me after having his dick. It's giant cock or nothing from here on out. That still doesn't stop me from embracing this orgasm, though. It may not be as enjoyable as the ones he gives me, but it's better than nothing. When it hits, it hits hard, and I moan his name into the empty room, feeling my pussy pulse with the sharp wave of pleasure as my release drips out of me and onto his chair. I keep working myself, gentling my hand, savoring the aftershocks until my limbs are loose and I'm feeling super relaxed and slightly giddy. All that bliss is quickly replaced with a sharp rush of adrenaline when I read his latest text.

I'm home, little bunny.

I jump from his chair and race from the room. He only mentioned seeing me in his office, so it's possible he doesn't have cameras in the rest of the house. Possible, but unlikely. I don't wait around to worry about it. I take off down the hall and run into one of the spare rooms, diving under the bed and hoping like hell he won't find me until his initial anger has worn off. I know I'm fucked when I hear the steady pounding of his boots on the hardwood floors. He's not slow or stopping to investigate possible hiding places. No, he's headed right towards me, no doubt having just watching my naked ass crawl under the bed.

I still hold my breath and turn my head to the side so I can see the open doorway. There is zero hesitancy when he steps into the room. I follow his steel-toe, black boots as they cross the room in his long strides, stopping right before the edge of the bed. I expected him to be a bit irritated at my complete disobedience, but I'll be honest, I hadn't expected quite this level of pissed-off. In one quick motion, he pushes the bed aside like it weighs nothing and looks down at me. His eyes are definitely stormy grey right now—a tempest building inside him and about to crash over me.

"Hi," I say, giving him a quick wave and an *I'm sorry* smile.

I don't even get so much as a lip twitch. His face is a mask of stony calm, and that's when I mentally kick my ass for thinking I could piss off the scary man and come out of it unscathed. Without taking his eyes off me, he slowly unbuckles his black belt. I have just enough time to think *oh fuck* before he's pulling it free of his belt loops. Once the leather strap is pulled free, he tightens his grip on it and flicks it out so it gives a sharp snap. Fear and lust wash over me. The sight before me is scary as fuck, yes, but it's also so goddamn delicious. His large hand gripping that belt, the smell of leather hitting my nose, the tattoos covering his forearms, and the look of pissed-off possessiveness that he's giving me—it all works together to quickly stir my body back to life.

"Kneel," he says, and his tone is hard and calm.

I quickly do as he says, but it's going to take more than my quick obedience to get back in his good graces.

"Clasp your hands and hold them out."

Again, I immediately do what he says. When my wrists are together, hands clasped and held out to him, he takes his belt and wraps it around them. It's the type of belt that has holes in it all the way through, so it's not hard for him to tightly secure it, leaving a long tail that he can grab onto. Satisfied with my bound hands, he reaches down and picks me up, hauling me over his shoulder so my ass is in the air.

"Kirill!" I shout in surprise.

He gives my ass one sharp smack that has me hissing out a curse. "You knew it would come to this, little bunny, and still you did it."

It's the only response I get before he starts carrying me upstairs. I mutter a low, "Caveman much?" but if I'm being honest, he's not wrong. I taunted and pushed him because I like it. I wanted to see what he would do, and I know if I told him to set me down and that I didn't want to do anything, he would let me go. We just both know I don't want that, and I sure as hell don't want him to stop whatever he has planned.

Once in the bedroom, he walks to the closet and grabs something from one of the drawers on his side before carrying me back to the center of the bedroom. He sets me down. It's not rough, but it's also not all that gentle.

"Kneel," he says again, and I fall to my knees.

When I see the black tie in his hand, I look up at him and meet the eyes that are still giving nothing away.

"Is this a formal occasion?" I deadpan, and I'm rewarded with the tiniest of smirks before the mask falls back into place and he grabs the end of the belt, giving it a hard tug that forces me to quickly scoot closer on my knees. I notice he didn't set me down on the soft, shaggy rug. The hardwood flooring digs into my knees, the sharp, aching pain a reminder that this is supposed to be a bit uncomfortable.

He cups my face, running his thumb over my cheek, giving me this moment of sweetness. I lean into his touch and close my eyes, but his voice has me opening them again. The hard look is back in his eyes when he says, "Try to take it like a good girl, *zaika*, but if it's too much, tap my thigh, and I'll stop."

I swallow and nod my head, wondering just what in the hell I've signed myself up for. Keeping the belt wrapped around one hand, he opens the tie and presses it against my eyes, tying it tightly behind my head, surrounding me in darkness. There's something about having your vision taken away that immediately throws you into panic mode. My breathing picks up, and I turn my head. Why? I'm not sure. It just feels right, like I'm trying to hear what the hell is about to happen. I remind myself that I'm not a goddamn bat, and echolocation is not a skill that's magically going to appear just because I've got a fucking tie around my eyes.

All my senses perk up when I hear his zipper being pulled down and then the sound of his jeans being peeled off before dropping to the floor. I hear him step closer, but he doesn't touch me. My wrists are still being held up at my chest, almost as if I'm kneeling and praying before my god, which I guess isn't all that far off. Religion hasn't ever done much for me, but this man who's just bound me and put me on my knees regularly gives me glimpses of heaven.

I sigh when I feel his fingers dancing along my collarbone, tracing the line of my neck before wrapping his long fingers around it and holding me in place.

"The next time I tell you to do something, are you going to do it?" he asks.

I lick my lips and debate lying, but decide there's no point in it. "Maybe."

"Maybe?" he repeats, the disbelief obvious in his tone. "What the fuck does that mean, little bunny?"

"It means that I will if I agree with it."

He lets out a harsh laugh. "So much to learn," he murmurs, tightening his grip on my throat, not enough to block the airflow, but enough to constrict the hell out of it.

"Open," he growls.

I open wide for him, waiting for what I know is coming. He keeps me waiting on my knees, hands bound and mouth hanging open until my jaw aches and spit is puddling under my tongue. I resist the urge to close my mouth and swallow. I hold still until the spit starts to drip down my chin. His deep groan when he sees it lets me know I made the right choice. The feel of his thick head brushing against my lips startles me enough to make me gasp. My head pulls back on instinct, but the tight grip on my neck makes it impossible for me to move. I know I can tap his thigh at any time and this will all stop, but there's no way in hell I'm doing that.

With my knees in agony and my vision gone, I run my tongue over his head before wrapping my lips around him and sucking him in deeper. He growls something in Russian and widens his stance so he can reach me easier. His thumb gently caresses my throat, and I know he's telling me to prepare myself for what's about to happen. I take in a deep, steadying breath, and as soon as I exhale, he slams into me, feeding me his cock in one hard thrust. I don't even get a chance to gag before he's down my throat, blocking my air and making my eyes water.

"So fucking beautiful," he growls, holding me in place, watching me choke on his cock.

I will my body to relax, giving myself over to him completely. My lungs burn right along with my jaw and my knees, but I don't tap his thigh. I don't want it to stop.

"I need to know you're going to listen to me, *zaika*," he growls. His accent is much thicker, his voice strained, his whole body radiating with tension. "I need to know you're safe. If I tell you to do something, it's because there's a reason for it. Last night you got lucky. You could've been killed."

His voice is laced with pain when he adds, "I couldn't go on without you. I have to keep you safe, and you have to let me."

My lungs are screaming for air, and I let out a soft moan when spots start to fill my vision. He waits a second longer before finally sliding out and allowing me a quick breath. The reprieve doesn't last long. Once I get that first sweet inhale, he slams back into me, and this time he doesn't stop. He fucks my mouth in a brutal, hard rhythm, and all I can do is take it. This isn't a sexy blowjob where I can tease him with my lips and tongue. This is purely about him using my mouth to get off. Spit drips down my chin, tears soak his tie and fall down my cheeks, and I love every goddamn second of it.

He tugs on the belt, bringing my hands further up, and when my fingers meet his balls, I know what he wants. I run my fingers over him, lightly dragging my nails along the underside of his heavy sack as he lets out another deep groan. I'm expecting to feel the pulse of his cock as he lets go, but at the last minute, he pulls from my aching mouth right before I feel the wet heat of him hit my face. He groans as more of his seed hits my parted lips and chin.

When he's empty, I run my tongue over my lips and fill my mouth with him while he lets out another groan at the sight of it. Letting go of the belt, my arms fall down, and before I can register what's happening, I'm in his arms and his mouth is on me. The kiss is hungry, demanding, and messy because I'm still covered in his release. There's always something feral right below the surface of Kirill, and when he unleashes that side of himself, it's overwhelming in the best possible way. Our tongues collide, each of us hungry and desperate for the other. I'm already soaking wet, dripping down my thighs as I moan and bring my hands up to rest on his chest.

"Fucking hell," he groans against my lips, cupping the back of my head and lowering me to the floor as he settles between my legs. "Do you feel what you do to me?"

He's already hard again, and when he presses against my wet slit, I moan his name and wrap my bound wrists behind his head while I spread my thighs wider. He nudges my slit, pressing in just enough to make me mewl at the feel of him and arch my hips, so fucking desperate to get him inside me.

"Promise me you're going to listen to me next time, *zaika*."

I let out a frustrated groan and wrap my legs around him, trying to force him into me.

"Promise me," he repeats, knowing there's no way in hell I'm going to be able to overpower him. He teases me with the head of his cock, gently pushing in just a little bit more before taking it away and leaving me feeling emptier than I ever thought possible.

"I promise," I gasp, digging my fingers into his back and wishing I could see his face. "I promise I'll listen next time, just please fuck me."

"I love you," he whispers against my lips as he slides into me.

"I love you," I whisper back right before his tongue finds mine again and everything else fades away.

He cups my face, spreading his cum across my cheeks as he pounds into me, marking me and claiming me again. His scent surrounds me, making me feel completely safe and loved and when the orgasm hits, I cling to him and whimper his name into our kiss. The pleasure seems magnified with my sight taken from me, or maybe it's just the way he's circling his hips, hitting me right where I need him and lighting up all those nerve endings that I never even knew existed before him.

With a growl he lets go, filling me for the second time and, I think, surprising even himself. He pulses inside me as I clench him tighter and take everything he has to give. When his body stills, he kisses me softly and pulls the tie from my eyes. I blink at the sudden light and look at the face that always makes my heart beat a little bit faster. He brushes back my sweaty hair and runs his thumb along my swollen, sore lips.

"You know," I tell him, "your punishments kind of make me want to just keep on disobeying."

He laughs and gives me a soft kiss. "Why the hell am I not surprised? You promised me, though, little bunny, and I'm trusting you at your word."

"I won't run out into danger, Kirill, don't worry. I never said anything about not making myself come in your office, though."

"God, that was the sexiest thing I've ever seen," he admits. "I can't believe a cop didn't pull me over for speeding."

"I didn't think of that," I say, a sudden wave of guilt hitting me. "I never would've forgiven myself if you'd been caught while I was fucking myself in your chair."

He laughs and kisses me again. "I would've just broken out again, *zaika*. I will always find my way back to you."

I smile and pull my arms from around his neck so I can touch his face. I run my fingers down his scar, noticing the way his eyes look calmer now, not so much a tempest and more of a beautiful overcast day.

"You're perfect," I tell him.

He throws his head back and gives a deep laugh that's as adorable as it is infectious. "God, my baby is so fucking sweet and compliant when she's drunk on post-orgasmic bliss."

"You should always keep me like this then."

He slides out of me and then scoops me up into his arms. Kissing my head, he carries me into the bathroom and says, "Good girls get orgasms, baby."

Apparently so do bad ones, but I don't say that. I just lean against him and let him baby the hell out of my sore body, feeling completely safe and loved.

Chapter 13

Kirill

While the bath runs, I undo the belt from her wrists and massage the pain away. She's still giving me a cute, loopy grin, and I can't help but return it, letting her bring out my soft side again. I enjoy babying her and taking care of her after she's been fucked good and hard and is dirty and sticky from my seed. I fucking love her like this, but I know she needs a good soak. She's going to be sore enough as it is.

I spend the next hour caring for her, holding her small body against mine in the hot water, washing her and massaging her tired muscles, and then helping her get into some of her favorite comfy clothes. When I'm satisfied, I carry her downstairs and start making her something to eat. It's been a long day, and I'm starving. Finding the duffel bag of money under the flooring of Jay's spare room had been easy, dropping it off at his sister's house, not so much. The note he'd left on top of the money had been simple enough, just a message asking whoever opened the bag to deliver it to his sister, and then he'd listed her address. There had been a sealed envelope inside, but I hadn't opened it. That's between Jay and his sister, none of my concern.

When I'd driven to her house, I'd set it by her front door and then rang the doorbell before hiding off to the side. I needed to make sure she got it, but I also didn't want her seeing my face. I'd just about convinced myself that she wasn't home when a short blonde had finally opened the door and stepped outside. As soon as she'd seen the bag, her face had crumpled and she'd clasped a hand over her mouth to stifle the scream. Looks like Jay had already prepared her for this outcome. I took no pleasure in her misery, but I also knew that given the choice between anyone and Lydia, I'd pick Lydia every damn time. He was a threat to her life, so he had to go. Simple as that.

I'd been in my car and about to head back when I'd stopped to check my security cameras. As soon as I'd pulled up the app and seen Lydia tiptoeing through the house, I'd laughed and couldn't resist sending her a text. I hadn't expected her to get naked and finger herself. She's full of surprises, my little bunny, and I fucking love it.

"Vadim's coming over in a few minutes," I tell her as I load up her plate, giving her extra chicken because she needs the protein. "He and I need to discuss a few things."

"You mean you need to discuss killing Ivan?" she asks, trying to appear casual, even though I can see her sneaking a hand into the drawer that holds her licorice.

I lift a brow at her, letting her know that I'm on to her game, and finish divvying up the Greek salad I made while she takes a big bite and tries to look innocent.

"I'm hungry," she says in her own defense. "And don't worry, I'll still clean my plate."

"You better," I tell her with a wink. "And, yes, he's coming here to discuss Ivan."

We sit at the table, the same one I bent her over, and eat until both our plates are empty. As soon as my phone alerts me to Vadim's arrival, I grab our plates and kiss her head before walking into the kitchen to clean up. Lydia gets the door when she hears the knock, and I can't help but smile at the domestic turn my life has taken. They walk into the kitchen, Lydia with her arms crossed casually across her chest because she's obeying rule number one while she offers him a drink. He greets me in Russian, and once he's got a soda in hand, we make our way to my office. My eyes quickly fall on the chair she'd had her bare ass in, and the memory has me fighting a smile. Vadim sees her discarded clothes on the floor and lets out a soft laugh.

"I take it things are going well?"

"They are," I say, not elaborating on what happened in here. No one gets to know about that side of her but me. I sit in my chair and type in the password for my computer. The monitors spark to life, and when I pull up the video feed of the cameras that I asked Vadim to set up earlier today, Ivan's house fills my screen. I study the footage. The cameras are all outside, but he's put up several along the security gate that surrounds the property so I can see every angle of the place.

"Anything new going on?" I ask.

Vadim takes the chair on the other side of the desk and shakes his head. "Not really. He's upped his security, obviously taken a hit out on you, and he's been sticking closer to home lately. He feels safe there. He even cancelled his visit with one of his mistresses last night, didn't want to venture off the property."

"He's a fucking idiot. He's forgetting that I've met him at his house many times. I know the layout of it as well as he does, probably better."

When I see Lydia hovering in the doorway, I stretch my arm out and motion for her to come closer. She gives me a shy smile, arms still crossed over her chest, but now she's fidgeting nervously with the cuffs of her sweatshirt.

"I'm sorry. I'm not trying to interrupt or anything."

As soon as she's close enough, I grab her waist and pull her onto my lap. I kiss her cheek and bring my lips close to her ear. "There's never a time when I don't want you near me, *zaika*."

She kisses my cheek and whispers, "Okay," and then relaxes against me while I switch back to Russian and talk to Vadim. I fill him in on exactly what happened last night with Jay, and then tell him what I'm planning to do tonight with Ivan.

"You sure you want to do it tonight?" he asks.

"Yes, there's no point in waiting, and things are just going to get worse. If Jay found me, then others will too. It's only a matter of time. I'm taking her out of the country, but I'd rather not do it with a hit out on me. I don't want to be worried about this for the rest of our lives. Besides," I say with a grin, "I'll be fine as long as I have some backup. You haven't let yourself get soft while I was locked up, have you?"

"Fuck you," he says with a soft laugh. "I may have been on babysitting duty, but I've kept up with my training. I'm still a good enough shot to cover your ass."

I smile at his modesty. One of the reasons I chose to work with Vadim is because of his background as a sniper in the Russian special forces. I want someone I can trust, but also someone who can keep my ass safe from afar should the need arise. We've made a pretty good team over the years, and I'm going to need his help tonight if this is going to work.

Looking back at the screen, I count twenty armed guards, five on each side of the large mansion, and it doesn't take a genius to know there are going to be more inside, but it's nothing I can't handle. If he thinks for one second he can keep me out, he's in for one hell of a surprise. He's made it harder for me, but not impossible—a decision that will cost him his life before the sun rises.

Vadim and I devise a plan while I run my hands through Lydia's hair and keep a tight grip on her thigh. She may not understand the words we're speaking, but she knows what we're talking about, and I know she's worrying about me. I'm still not used to having someone care about my safety. Most people actively want me dead, so for someone to worry about my life, and not just worry but actually put themselves at risk to try and keep me safe, well, it's unusual to say the least. I'm not sure I'll ever get used to it.

"She's gotten attached to you," Vadim says, switching topics and watching the way she's stroking my neck with her fingers.

"She has." I don't say anything else, but I'm not surprised it doesn't deter him. He's always ignored my gruff ways.

"What are you planning on doing after this?"

"We'll be leaving the country. Anywhere she wants to go."

He studies me for a second. "Is that all?"

I hold his gaze. "Yes," I say, making it clear it's the end of this particular line of questioning. Getting us back on topic, I watch the live feed and see Ivan's wife and kids drive through the large, iron gate that surrounds his property. "Is his family often there?"

"Yeah, especially at night, and like I said, he's been keeping close to home himself, no more late-night visits to his mistresses."

"Good." I smile and kiss Lydia's forehead. "Men are much more compliant when family is close by."

Vadim sighs and runs a hand through his hair. "I know you won't go that route if you don't have to."

"I won't," I agree, "but I'll do whatever the hell needs to be done to take care of this and end the threat on our lives. Ivan's a dick, but I don't think he'll risk his family to save his own ass." I give a soft shrug. "You never know, though. Some men don't handle death all that well."

We iron out the last of the details and agree to meet at Ivan's at midnight. Before he leaves, he switches to English and tells Lydia, "The house is doing good, and I just wanted you to know that you are missing out big time. I drove by to check on things earlier, and your neighbor has decided that sunbathing in a speedo is what everyone wants to see."

She laughs and says, "Mr. Henderson? Oh my god." She turns to me, filling me in on the details while her eyes light up in amusement. "He just got divorced last year, and he's in his late sixties. I don't think the man has ever even had so much as a light tan." She turns back to Vadim. "Did it almost blind you when you saw him?"

Vadim laughs. "Good thing I was wearing sunglasses."

I watch them and feel a pang of jealousy. There's not the slightest hint of anything flirtatious; I just hate that they share something I can't be a part of. Vadim may not have ever spoken to her, but in some ways he knows her better than I do, and god does that irritate the hell out of me. I tighten my grip on her, unable to help the possessive reaction. She must sense my frustration because she puts a hand on top of mine and gives me a gentle squeeze before turning her face and kissing my cheek.

"I love you," she whispers, and I melt at her words.

"I love you too, *zaika*." Cupping the back of her head, I hold her closer, not caring in the slightest that this tiny woman can turn me into a goddamn puddle in front of Vadim. When I look over at him, his mouth is parted in surprise, although he recovers quickly and tries to act like he's not shocked. Vadim has seen me do a lot of things over the years, but he's never seen me cuddle with a woman and tell her I love her. First time for everything, I guess.

"I'm going to get the fuck out of here before my head explodes," he tells me in Russian with a soft laugh. "I'll see you tonight." Giving Lydia a smile, he tells her in English, "Glad to see you're doing so well. I'm sure I'll see you again soon."

"Bye, Vadim," she tells him, giving him a smile and a wave.

"See you at midnight," I holler out to him as he walks down the hall. I hear Peanut scrambling along the floors. He must've just burst through the doggy door. Vadim laughs and judging by the happy little yips echoing down the hall, Peanut is thrilled to see him.

"He really isn't the greatest guard dog," Lydia says with a laugh.

"He has a very sweet personality," I say, "which means he's very trusting, but that's okay. He doesn't need to guard you. That's my job."

"But who's going to keep you safe?"

I smile and kiss the tip of her nose. "I'll keep myself safe, baby."

She motions to the video footage in front of us. "You're going there tonight?"

"Yes."

"With Vadim?"

"Yes."

"Don't suppose there's anything I can do to help?"

I smile and say, "Nope."

She sighs and leans back against me. "Can I at least watch it unfold?"

I think about it, and although it might upset her, I'm guessing she'll be more upset if I tell her no. "I'll leave the footage up for you, but you'll only be able to see the outside. It might be better if you don't, though," I add, even though I know it's pointless.

Proving me right she says, "I want to watch, but I swear if I see you get hurt on here, I'm going there myself."

I groan at her stubborn refusal to just fucking obey me and seriously debate whether it would be inhumane to tie her to the bed. I quickly decide that it would be. On the off chance that something happens to me and Vadim, she'd be trapped with no way to free herself and no one would even know she's here. I can't subject her to that sort of danger.

"That's not what we agreed," I remind her as calmly as I can and run my thumb over her still-swollen lips. "Or have you forgotten your lesson already?"

Her eyes go heavy-lidded at the memory. "I remember. I said I wouldn't run out and put myself in danger, and I won't, but I'm also not going to just sit here and watch you die." She turns to me and gives me a big smile. "Look on the bright side, if you're that hurt to where I feel like my only choice is to go to Ivan's, then we're both kind of fucked anyway, so we might as well go out together."

"That does not make me feel better," I groan. "I'd much rather have my last thought be that at least you're safe. Can't you at least give a dying man some peace?"

She looks so fucking sad when she cups my face and pulls me closer. "Don't you dare die, Kirill."

"I'm not planning on it, *zaika*." I kiss her gently, running my tongue over her sore lips, remembering how sexy she'd looked taking my cock with spit dripping down her chin. When I pull back, her pupils are blown and she's giving me that hungry look again. I love how insatiable she is, but my greedy girl is going to have to wait. She's sore and needs a rest. "You're the most important thing in the world to me, little bunny, and I need to know you're safe. After tonight, a big threat will be gone, but I still need to deal with Enzo. Once that's done, we can go anywhere you want. Have you decided where you want to live?"

"I don't know. Do you want someplace warm or cold?"

"I'll be happy anywhere as long as you're there with me."

She smiles and gives a soft laugh. "That's very sweet, but seriously, do you have a preference?"

I think about it and say, "I don't really like the extreme heat, but I also don't think I'd like a place where it never gets hot enough to swim. I like a mix."

"I'll do some digging around," she says with a grin. "I don't speak anything other than English, so that kind of sucks."

"You'll learn." I give her a wink. "You were almost valedictorian."

She laughs. "Yeah, that was a super good use of my time." I see the mischievous look in her eyes before she says, "I should've been out partying, had some fun, you know?"

I grab her and bring my mouth to her neck, giving her a not-so-gentle bite. She laughs harder and wraps her arms around me. I kiss and lick her neck until she's moaning and rocking her hips in my lap. "Only mine," I whisper against her skin. "No one else will ever have you."

"No one else," she says in a breathy moan, agreeing with me and then letting out an annoyed huff when I pull back.

"Sorry, baby," I say with a smile. "I need to make sure everything is ready for tonight."

"You owe me later."

I laugh and give her another kiss. "Deal."

She stays in my lap while I watch the camera feed on one computer monitor and read some files on Ivan's new bodyguards on another. They're all well trained, but I expected nothing less. None of them standout as being more than Vadim and I can handle, though. When peanut comes in wanting his supper, she gives me a kiss on the cheek before getting up to take care of him. I smile when I hear a drawer opening in the kitchen and the sound of her grabbing some licorice from the bag.

I spend the next hour going over the layout of the house and property to fully refresh my memory and then plan out exactly what I'm going to do, and when I feel confident that every detail is memorized and ingrained in my mind, I get up and stretch, rolling out the tension in my neck and shoulders before walking into the kitchen to start supper. Lydia and Peanut are on the couch watching a comedy, and when I start getting what I need for supper, she starts to get up to help.

"Keep watching, baby. I've got this."

She smiles and blows me a kiss. I give her a wink and start cooking. When it's done, I bring her a plate and sit down next to her. After we've eaten and the movie is over, I set an alarm on my phone and pull her into my lap as I lay back and rest my feet on the leather ottoman. I didn't get much sleep last night, and it's catching up to me. I can't afford to make any stupid mistakes tonight, so I'm forcing myself to take a nap. Lydia yawns and grabs the blanket she'd been using earlier, draping it over us and resting her head against my shoulder. I wrap my arms around her and kiss her head.

Her breathing evens out, and the soft, steady breaths quickly lull me to sleep. The next thing I know my alarm is beeping and it's time for me to start getting ready. Her body stirs at the sound of my alarm, and she gives a soft moan at the intrusion. I turn it off and gently scoot out from under her, letting her sleep some more. I pull the blanket up and kiss her cheek before going upstairs. Taking a quick shower to help fully wake myself up, I go over the plan again in my head. I'm still mentally reviewing everything as I dress in black tactical gear, and when I start to grab my weapons, Lydia walks in and wraps her arms around me from behind.

"Morning, little bunny," I say with a smile, reaching around to pull her in front of me so I can hug her back.

"It's close to midnight."

"True enough, but I'm guessing you're going to be up all night worrying about me."

"Maybe," she admits. Resting her chin on my chest, she looks up at me. "Are you sure you have to do this? We could just run."

I brush back a strand of her dark hair and shake my head. "I won't put you in danger like that. If there's a hit on me, we will never get a moment of peace. I'll be hunted no matter where we go." I slide my hand between us and splay my hand over her lower stomach. "We can't bring a child into a life as dangerous as that."

"A baby?"

I laugh at her wide-eyed expression. "It's only a matter of time, sweetheart, if it hasn't happened already. I can't wait to see you pregnant."

She looks at me like she thinks I'm joking but isn't quite sure, but when she feels my cock start to grow, she realizes just how serious I am. With a groan, I force the image of her naked, pregnant body from my mind so I can focus on work. Leaning down, I kiss her slowly, savoring the taste of her, and only pulling back when I know it's either that or fuck her in the closet and risk being late. I can't do that, not when there's so much riding on this plan.

"We'll finish this later, little bunny."

She nods and steps back while I sheathe knives on my forearm, waist, and one by my ankle. I put a gun against the small of my back and another one in the shoulder holster I'm wearing along with extra clips in the pockets of my black cargo pants. Excessive? Maybe, but better to have too much than not enough. The last thing I do is grab an earpiece with a mic so I can communicate with Vadim.

"Damn, you don't mess around," she whispers, running her eyes over me.

"No, sweetheart, I don't." I cup her face and kiss between her eyebrows where she's furrowed the skin in worry. "Stop looking so scared. I'm actually pretty damn good at my job."

"I know you are," she whispers. Locking her blue eyes on mine, she says, "Promise me you'll come back."

It's a dumb promise to make, but I can't deny her. I'd promise her anything. "I'll be back, *zaika*. I promise. I will always find my way back to you."

She lets out a soft sigh, taking comfort in my vow and wraps her arms around me when I pick her up and carry her back downstairs. I bring her into my office and sign back into my computer so she'll be able to see everything. On the other monitor, I pull up my own security cameras, zooming in on the one that shows the garage and driveway so she'll be able to watch me leave and return.

"Thank you," she whispers by my ear before kissing it.

"Try not to worry, baby. I'll be back as soon as I can."

She kisses a line along my cheek before finding my lips. Her tongue delves inside, and even though I know it means I'll be walking out of here hard and miserable, I can't resist cupping the back of her head and deepening the kiss. She opens wider for me, giving me what I need, and when I give her tongue a suck and she moans and starts to rock her hips, I know it's time for me to set her down. With a groan, I pull away and lower her into my office chair.

"I need to go, *zaika*. Stay inside and keep your phone close."

She nods and tries to hide how worried she is. I smile and give her one last quick kiss before whistling for Peanut. He comes barreling in, and as soon as he's close enough, I scoop him up and put him in Lydia's arms. Giving her a wink, I turn to leave, forcing myself to put all my focus on what's about to happen and not on the woman who I'm dangerously in love with.

I lock the door behind me, and before I get into my Porsche, I look up at the security camera and give her a wave goodbye. I know she's safe. Between the security at the house and the four well-trained, lethal dogs, she's as safe as she can get. Knowing that doesn't make it any easier to drive away, though. I speed down the road, being careful to not go too fast and draw attention to myself, and slowing down even more when I hit downtown.

"You hear me?" I ask when I'm almost there.

Vadim's voice is immediately in my ear. "Yeah, loud and clear. Everything's quiet where I'm at. Looks good."

I park a couple streets over and get out, slipping into the darkness of a side street and making my way to the back of Ivan's property. Vadim is already in position on the right side of the house, no doubt perfectly camouflaged and invisible to the naked eye. They won't know he's there until he starts firing, and even then the suppressor he's using will distort the sound enough to make it difficult for anyone to pinpoint his exact location.

"Guards are almost finished walking the grounds," Vadim whispers. "Ivan is inside with his family."

"I'm almost there," I whisper back.

As soon as I'm to the iron gate of his security fence, I follow it until I spot the large oak tree, the one I warned him to cut down three years ago. I'm not at all surprised that's he ignored me. He always did think he knew best about everything. It does't take much for me to pull myself onto the thick lower branch, and from there it's only a few minutes before I'm straddling the long branch that reaches over the fence. I look down onto the property, watching the last of the guards walk by. He's looking around, but he's not looking up, so he walks right by me being none the wiser.

As soon as he's far enough away, I whisper, "In position," to Vadim and grab my gun.

"Ready when you are," is his quick response.

I wait for the guards to make their way back to join the others near the side of the house and say, "Ready" right before I fire off three quick shots, taking out three guards before they've even realized they're under attack. I hear Vadim's suppressed shots, but I keep my focus on my own job. I take out one more before grabbing the branch and hanging down, dropping the last few feet, grateful that Ivan doesn't share my love of killer dogs. I run towards the house, stopping to shoot two more guards before leaning against the house to avoid their return fire. Everyone's using silencers, but it's a good thing he doesn't have any neighbors too close. Silencers suppress the sound, but they don't hide it completely.

"You're good on this side," Vadim says, and then calls out a quick, "On your right."

I turn and shoot the man who was sneaking up on me while Vadim uses his rifle scope to try and spot any more movement.

"Clear," he says after a few seconds. "But there's still more inside. Holler if you need me."

"Will do," I tell him, putting a new clip in my gun and grabbing the largest of my knives. Using the side entrance that's reserved for his guards, I slip into the large house without making a sound. The place is quiet and dark. It's well after midnight, and his family is already asleep. I hear footsteps headed my way, and when a man walks around the corner, I use my knife, quickly stabbing him in the throat so he can't scream. His eyes bug out in surprise, but then they widen even more in fear and pain. It doesn't last long. I'd made sure to hit the carotid artery, so he bleeds out fast. Stepping over him, I make my way up the wide staircase, knowing Ivan is most likely still awake and in his office. He's always been a night owl, and I doubt that's changed. Men like him are creatures of habit, and it's usually what gets them killed. They never alter their schedules, too stuck in the old way of doing things and not wanting to put forth the effort to change.

When I peek around the corner, I see the guard standing outside his office door. A quick glance down the other hallway makes it obvious that he didn't bother to put a man outside his kids' rooms or the bedroom his wife is sleeping in. What a dick. There's no way to sneak up on the armed guard, so I do the only thing I can do. I walk out in the open, and as soon as he sees me, I shoot him right between the eyes. I know Ivan's heard the suppressed shot, but I fling open the door with my gun raised and pointed right where I know he's sitting behind his desk, not giving him enough time to reach for a weapon. His face pales when he realizes who's just walked through his door.

"Kirill," he whispers, and then the motherfucker tries to cover it all with a smile. He spreads his arms like he's thrilled to see me. "I knew prison wouldn't be able to contain you, you sneaky bastard. Why didn't you come see me right away? We need to get you back in the game. I've got several jobs I need you on. I hope you're ready to make a lot of money."

I keep my gun trained on him and walk closer. I hear Vadim in my ear. *Is he seriously trying to play this off as normal?* I don't bother saying anything because the answer is painfully obvious.

"Hands on the fucking desk," I say when Ivan starts to lower them.

"What's going on?" He raises a brow at me. "I hope you haven't been listening to rumors, Kirill." The fake laugh he gives almost makes me cringe in embarrassment for him. "People are saying that Enzo and I have struck a deal, but I can promise you that's not the case. I'm just trying to get close to him, and then I'm going to take him out."

"Is that so?"

"Yes, of course it is. You didn't think I'd really betray you, did you?"

I sit in the chair across from him and study the man that I've worked for since I was fifteen. I've always been surprised at how many men fall for his bullshit. He has tells if you know what to look for, and right now he's screaming his guilt to me with the way his eyes are held a little too wide, the forced earnestness that makes me want to smack him, and the way he's lightly rubbing his thumb and forefinger together on his left hand. Easy signs to miss, most people do, but for me, it's impossible not to see them.

"Cut the bullshit, Ivan. I know you've made a deal with Enzo, I know you pinned all the blame on me for the death of his son, and I know that you've put a hit out on me. Jay's dead, by the way."

His face pales when he realizes how much trouble he's in. As expected the next reaction is pleading.

"My family is here. You can't do this, Kirill."

I give a harsh laugh. "You don't think so?"

"They're just kids, and my wife is innocent."

"They're safe as long as you don't scream like a fucking baby and wake them up. If they're not witnesses, I won't kill them. Their lives are in your hands."

He takes a deep breath and gives me a slight nod. I motion towards the phone that's lying on the desk near his right hand.

"Call off the hit on me." When he hesitates, I stand and put the muzzle of my gun against his forehead. "Right fucking now."

His hands shake as he grabs his phone. I watch everything he does, not trusting him for a second, but when I see the official message calling off the hit and canceling the bounty, I let out a relieved breath as the message is sent, making its way through the underground channels, and soon everyone will know it's over.

"I've worked for you a long time, Ivan, and you sold me out without a second thought."

"You were in prison," he says, no longer bothering to try and lie. "What the fuck was I supposed to do? Enzo would've destroyed me, everything I've spent my life building."

"I warned you about going after his son, and some fucking loyalty would've been nice after everything I've done for you." I remove the gun from his head, trying not to laugh at the spark of hope that fills his eyes. "You're not a very smart man, Ivan. I think most everyone would probably tell you that the one person you should never piss off is the hitman on your payroll. What the hell did you think I was going to do?"

"I didn't think you'd ever get out," he admits.

"You should know me better than that."

He surprises me by switching topics. "Rumor has it Lydia Moore has disappeared."

"Is that so?" Unlike Ivan, I don't have any tells. He's not going to be getting any information from my face or tone or body.

"Does she know the truth about you?" His lips curl up in a smug grin. "You think she'll still want you when she does?"

Easy, man. Just shoot him and get the fuck out. I hear Vadim's voice in my ear, and I know I need to be quick and get my ass out of here, but Ivan's gone and pissed me off, and I can't just walk away now that he's said that. When I slide my knife out of the sheath, he realizes his mistake.

"I'm sorry," he quickly says.

I ignore him. "Remember what I said about not waking your family." It's the only warning I give him before I reach between his lips and pull out his tongue, cutting it off in one quick swipe so he can't ever mention Lydia's name again. Plus, I need to send a message. Whoever finds his body will know who killed him and why. People need to stop fucking with my life, and if carving up Ivan is going to get me some peace, then so be it.

By the time I leave his office, I'm covered in blood, and he's missing a few body parts. I put his fingers, tongue, and dick in a nice little pile on his desk, but his balls are still shoved down his throat. I think it all sends a nice message of *Stay the fuck out of Kirill Chernikov's life or face the consequences.*

I hadn't lied to Lydia. I don't torture. My kills are quick and efficient, but drastic times call for drastic measures and all that. I lock the door behind me and smear blood on the door handle as a warning about what they're going to find on the other side. I don't want his kids walking in on that. I may be a monster, but not even I am that cruel.

Are you fucking done yet? Vadim growls in my ear. *All his guards are down, but others are going to show soon, and there's no way Enzo doesn't know about this already. I'm guessing he knew the second Ivan called off the hit.*

"I'm leaving now," I tell him, racing down the stairs and out the same door I came in at. I can't go out the same way I came in because the tree limb is too high for me to reach on this side, so I race across the yard to where I know Vadim is hiding. He's perched in a tall tree that gives him a clear view of the yard, and when he sees me, he throws a rope down. I grab it and start climbing. As soon as I hit the top of the fence, I swing over to the other side, but before I start my descent, I remember that Lydia is watching all this, so I turn to where I know the closest camera is and give her a smile and wave and then climb down. Vadim is only seconds behind me. He takes one look at my bloody appearance and groans.

"Fuck, man, you better hope like hell you don't get pulled over."

"I won't." I smack him on the back and grin. "Thanks for the backup."

"Anytime." He smiles back, because we both love the rush of adrenaline this job brings. He may not approve of every single decision I make, but Vadim loves this just as much as I do.

I run to my car while he disappears to his own. I'm more than ready to get back to my girl.

Chapter 14

Lydia

My eyes are glued to the separate video feeds being shown on the large monitor in front of me. I've stress eaten my way through half a bag of Twizzlers, and I'll be very surprised if Peanut doesn't develop a bald spot from my manic petting.

"Sorry, buddy," I tell him, forcing my hand to be still.

I look up just in time to see Kirill scaling the security fence, stopping just long enough to smile and wave directly at the camera. The footage might be black and white, but there's no denying he's covered in blood.

Holy fuck, the man is absolutely insane.

"That's who I've fallen in love with," I whisper to Peanut with a shake of my head. He gives a sympathetic heavy sigh that makes me smile. I keep my eyes on the cameras, making sure everything stays the same, and when it's obvious that Kirill's really gone and that the place isn't going to be immediately swamped with police, I decide to take advantage of the fact that the computer is unlocked. I know the drive back will be at least twenty minutes, so I quickly open a browser and type Kirill's name into the search engine. I've avoided looking at the news, but I know his escape from prison must be everywhere. I'm expecting every news channel to have his gorgeous face front and center, but when nothing comes up, I'm so stunned by it that all I can do is sit there and stare for a few seconds. I try different phrases and even go straight to several news websites. Nothing, not a single mention of an escape from prison.

I'm still wondering what the hell is going on when movement catches my eye. I look at the other monitor and watch the black Porsche pull up the driveway. Putting aside my confusion, I set Peanut down and run for the door. I'd been scared to death something was going to happen to him, and when he'd disappeared inside the house and didn't reappear for thirty goddamn minutes, I'd thought I was going to have a heart attack. That half-eaten Twizzlers bag is all on him. Throwing the door open, I run to him, catching him halfway to the house. I don't slow down, just jump into his arms, knowing he'll catch me and not giving a rat's ass that he's covered in another man's blood. It's not Kirill's, and that's all I care about right now.

"You scared the hell out of me," I tell him.

He tightens his arms around me and laughs. "I told you it might be best if you didn't watch."

I pull back, cupping his face and running my eyes over him, convincing myself that he's safe and unharmed. "He's dead?" I ask.

"He's dead."

I look down at all the dried blood. "What the hell happened in there?"

He gives a small shrug. "I needed to send a message. He called off the hit before he died, so now there's only Enzo to take care of."

His grey eyes are darker than usual, and I can almost feel the adrenaline coursing through him. One of his hands grips my ass as the other cups the back of my head, pulling me closer. The rage and bloodlust he'd just felt when ending Ivan's life is quickly turning into something else, and I'm at the center of it.

He nips at my bottom lip and whispers, "Don't fucking move, little bunny."

Even though my heart is racing, I try to lighten things by asking, "What if I do? You going to chase me?"

"Yes," he says, and the deadly tone of his voice makes two things abundantly clear: I will not make it far, and when he catches me, gentle is the last thing he's going to be. I know a sane person would go full submissive right now, anything to not draw the attention of the crazed guy who's barely hanging on, but that's the last thing I want to do. A grin is already pulling at my lips.

"*Zaika*," he warns while running his nose along my cheek, "don't push me too far."

"Let me down," I whisper against his cheek, running my tongue up his scar.

He tightens his grip on me. "No."

"Why not?"

"Because I don't trust myself."

I rest my forehead against his. "But I trust you."

His grey eyes look tortured with grief when he says in a low voice, "You shouldn't."

My first thought is cheating, so I rear back and grip his shoulders. "Is there someone else?"

He seems confused by my train of thought, but he quickly says, "Never, baby. I would never do that to you."

Relieved, I pat his shoulder and say, "Well, okay then. Now put me down. I feel like running."

He groans but gives me what I want. Slowly sliding me down his body, I let out a soft moan when I feel how hard he is. When I'm standing in front of him, he meets my eyes, and the security lights on the outside of the house are giving off enough light for me to see how dark his are becoming. He looks downright feral.

"Are you sure about this?"

"Yes." I eye the weapons he's still wearing and debate whether or not I should ask him to take them off but then quickly decide that I want them on. I don't question it. I've given up on trying to understand my reactions to him. "But you have to give me a head start. Your legs are way longer than mine, and it's only fair if you give me a fighting chance."

The corner of his lips quirk up the tiniest bit. "This is a dangerous game you're playing, little bunny."

"I told you I trust you."

He grabs my hand and presses it against the cock that's straining at his pants like a monster just waiting to be set free. "And I told you that you shouldn't." He leans down and squeezes my ass. "If I catch you, sweetheart, it's not your pussy I'm going to be fucking."

Holy shit. He sees the fear in my eyes and waits for me to back down, but I don't. When I stand up even straighter and say, "I want a full minute head start."

"Jesus fucking Christ," he groans, squeezing my ass even harder and nipping at the skin of my neck, already so close to losing control. "Run, *zaika*. You have sixty seconds, and then I'm coming for you."

With one last nip of my skin, this one sharp enough to sting, he pulls back and lets me go. Giving me a wink, he starts a timer on the large, black watch that looks like he could probably sail around the world with just that and a bottle of water. I don't stick around to see what he's planning, I turn and run as fast as my short legs can take me. I barrel around the side of the house, looking all kinds of things but graceful isn't one of them, and ignore the sound of his amused laughter. I bolt for the path that leads down to the ocean, hoping like hell I can manage it in the dark without breaking my neck. My heart races, my palms sweat, and the voice in my head is frantically screaming at me, *Are you out of your goddamn mind?!*, while my butt cheeks clench in fear. That doesn't stop the giddy, unhinged laugh from escaping as I slip and almost somersault my way to the beach.

"Ready or not, little bunny, here I come!"

Kirill's voice echoes around me, sending a shiver of fear and excitement straight down my spine. It sure as hell doesn't feel like a whole minute has passed, but I'm not about to wait here so I can argue with him about it. I run faster, feeling my bare feet hit the sand right as I hear his heavy footsteps behind me. I waste a few precious seconds looking back and trying to see him, but it's too dark, and I don't have time to wait. I face the ocean that I can hear but not see and take off.

My feet dig into the sand as I run faster than I ever have in my life. When I hit the water, I veer to the right, but I'm quickly running out of steam. I curse my lack of aerobic stamina and my love of red licorice candy as my pace slows and I gasp for air, hoping the waves will mask my heavy breathing. My legs feel rubbery when I start to slow down even more, and I'm just about to chance a look behind me when a strong arm wraps around my middle, pulling me off my feet and against a very large, very hard body.

"What the hell?" I gasp. "I didn't even hear you."

He lets out a deep, sexy chuckle, not sounding even slightly winded when he says, "Caught you, little bunny."

Sliding a hand up my body, he presses his palm against my rapidly beating heart and runs his tongue up my neck before biting my earlobe.

"Your heart is racing, baby." His teeth graze along my ear. "Ready to get that ass fucked?"

"Shit," I whimper, feeling my body start to shake as my mind gives a haughty *told you so* that I choose to ignore.

His other hand reaches down to cup my pussy, keeping my feet off the ground and completely at his mercy. "Kirill," I whisper, not sure what I want to say, but needing the connection anyway.

"I've got you, baby," he murmurs against my skin. "I'm going to fuck this sweet ass, but I will never hurt you, little bunny. I need you to trust me."

"I do," I whisper, feeling his erection digging into my ass. I push the fear aside and nod my head, more sure than ever. "I do trust you," I repeat.

"Good girl."

He sets me down in the dry sand, laying me on my back and hovering his body over mine. There's enough moonlight for me to make out vague details of his face, but not near enough for me to see him clearly. He's partially in shadows, and that just makes him look even sexier. Grabbing the bottom of my T-shirt, he starts to pull it off me, tossing it aside once I'm free of it. He lets out a groan at the sight of my bare chest and runs a hand along my skin, cupping my breasts and grazing his fingers over my nipples.

"The sight of your body drives me crazy," he says in a low, raspy tone, his accent thicker than ever. When he leans closer, I slide my hands behind his neck and pull him closer, pressing my lips to his in a hungry kiss. He groans and settles more of his weight onto me, letting me feel the hard length of him between my legs. I arch up to him and suck his tongue into my mouth. The kiss is more feral than anything else, but I still feel the love in it, the way he cups the back of my head and makes sure to not put too much weight on me. Every swipe of his tongue, every suck and nibble he gives my lips—all of it is mixed with the all-consuming love he feels for me. He's dangerous and wild, more demon than angel, but he's gentle with me, never pushing me too hard or giving me more than I can take.

I run my hands down his body, freezing when I feel all his weapons. I'd forgotten how armed he is, and when my fingers meet the cold, hard metal of his gun, he breaks our kiss and reaches back to remove it.

"Careful, baby, don't hurt yourself."

I watch as he slowly removes his weapons, the ones I watched him use to end several lives tonight, and then sets them aside before pulling off his bloody shirt. Running his fingers down my stomach, he hooks them under my yoga pants and starts to pull them off. I put the soles of my feet to the night sky as he slowly peels my pants off. When I'm naked, he lifts my ass and tucks my shirt under me, protecting me from the sand, and then he grips my calves, keeping my legs straight up. He presses his lips to my ankle before slowly kissing his way down first one calf and then the other. When he licks the back of my knee, I let out a breathy sigh and reach down to run my hands through his hair. It's getting longer, but it's still too short to fist.

When he starts to kiss my inner thigh, I drop my ankles and spread my knees wide. He groans and digs his fingers into the soft flesh of my hips, holding me in place as he nips and kisses a line along my leg.

"Kirill," I moan when his face is hovering above my pussy, so close I can feel the heat of his breath on my sensitive skin.

"Yes, baby?" he says as if he has all the time in the world.

"Please," I beg, letting out a frustrated moan when he flicks his tongue over my clit, one quick motion that leaves me panting for more.

"Please what, *zaika*? Use your words, baby."

He gives me one more flick, and it's enough to push away my embarrassment. I grip his head tighter and moan, "Please lick my pussy."

"Like this?" he asks, giving me one slow lick that feels amazing but isn't enough to push me over the edge.

"More," I beg.

"You said lick, sweetheart. This is a lick." He gives me one more to prove his point, and then laughs when I let out a frustrated groan. "I'm just doing what I'm told," he reminds me, clearly enjoying every damn second of this.

"I need more."

"Then tell me what you want." He flicks my clit harder and then gives it a soft suck, urging me to communicate, to trust him enough to tell him what I need, so I take a deep breath and do exactly that.

"I want you to eat my pussy," I say, ignoring the way my face is heating up. "I want you to fuck me with your tongue. I want you to devour me, Kirill."

"Good fucking girl," he growls before sliding his tongue into my pussy, fucking me in long strokes that have me rocking up to him and moaning his name to the night sky. He feasts on me like a wild, starving animal. Licking, sucking, and biting until I'm tense with the need to come. When he wraps his lips around my clit and gives me a suck, I scream his name and buck up against him, consumed by a fierce pleasure that radiates through me, touching every damn part of my body. He keeps going, not letting up, not even when I become too sensitive and try to wriggle out of his firm grasp. He holds me in place, forcing another orgasm onto me, and only when I've screamed myself hoarse and my whole body is shaking does he let up. He gives my slit one last long lick before lifting his head.

"Fucking delicious," he murmurs, kissing a line along my stomach. "I crave the taste of you, baby. All goddamn day, I'm craving the taste of your pussy. Makes my fucking mouth water just thinking about it."

He unzips his pants and frees his cock, not even bothering to take them all the way off. Lining himself up, he slides into me, spreading me wide with one hard thrust. I whimper out something incomprehensible and wrap my arms around his shoulders as soon as he's close enough.

"I can't resist feeling your pussy wrapped tightly around me, baby, but I'm not coming until I'm in your ass."

The rough sound of his voice mixed with the hard thrusts he's giving me send my senses reeling as I struggle to not lose myself completely. I feel like I'm on the brink of exploding, of disappearing into the night sky, so I hold him even tighter, using him as my anchor to keep me in the here and now.

"I love you," I say in a breathy rush, feeling my pussy clench around him as my body reaches the breaking point again.

"I love you," he growls against my lips, fucking me into another orgasm. He doesn't stop until I'm gasping and weightless and drunk on pure ecstasy. I feel him smile against my lips before whispering, "Now you're ready to get your ass fucked, sweetheart. Roll over. Hands and knees."

I whimper when he slides out of me, missing the feel of him, and use the last of my strength to get in position. Digging my knees and hands into the sand, I look back at him, nervous and excited and not knowing what in the hell to expect. He drags his fingers along my soaking wet slit, coating his hand in my arousal before bringing it to his shaft. I can hear the wet sounds of our mixed arousal as he fists himself. Letting go, he runs his fingers over my asshole until I'm so wet it's easy for him to start to slide one finger in.

When I immediately tense, he grips my hip with one hand and says, "Easy, baby. Just relax. I promise this is going to feel so fucking good."

I nod my head and take a deep breath. He presses into me, pushing past my body's natural resistance, and when I take it, he groans and says, "That's my good girl. Let me see how filthy you like it, baby."

He slides his finger all the way in, surprising me with how good it feels. I rock back against him, digging my hands into the sand and moaning as I arch my lower back, giving him better access.

"Perfect, baby, just like that," he praises while sliding a second finger in. "You're going to spread so goddamn good for me."

"Mm-hmm," I moan, hoping like hell it's true. I know his fingers are nothing compared to the thick beast between his legs, and I really hope my body can take it.

He fingers my ass, working me until I'm whimpering his name and desperate to come again. Sliding his fingers out, he gives my cheek a soft pat. A second later I hear him spit right before I feel the warm saliva hit my asshole and then the thick head of his cock press against me.

"Kirill," I moan, suddenly terrified.

"Your body was made for me, *zaika*, and this tight ass is going to take my cock."

I have my doubts, but I nod my head and try like hell to relax. When he starts to press his head in, I tense at the burning sensation, but when I take another deep breath, he slides in some more, and it's not near as bad as I feared it would be. It feels wrong but in a good way, and there's something about giving him this part of myself, a part that I never in a million years ever thought I'd give a man, that makes me feel so damn close to him.

He slides in some more and leans over so his body is cocooning mine. His nose runs across my cheek, breathing me in with a light moan.

"You're doing so good, baby," he whispers against my skin. "Such a good girl."

One of his hands rests near mine, and when he nudges a finger under my palm, I lift my hand up and rest it on his, threading our fingers together while his other hand slides across my stomach and between my legs.

"Goddamn," he groans when he's fully inside me. "You okay, baby?"

I nod and let out a shaky breath. Truth is I'm more than okay. I feel like I should definitely get some sort of award for this, and in all honesty, I'm more proud about being able to take Kirill's cock in the ass than I am about any of the awards I got in school. I would happily hang this certificate of achievement on the wall. This makes me feel like a fucking queen, and when I start to rock my hips, I feel him smile against my cheek.

"I knew my girl would like it filthy." He slides out of me very slowly before sinking back into me. "Is this what you want? You want me to fuck your sweet little ass?"

"Yes," I moan. "God yes."

He pinches my clit between his fingers and starts to fuck me faster.

"Give me your mouth," he growls.

I turn and as soon as I'm close enough, he captures my lips in a hard kiss that takes away my ability to think. All I can do in this moment is take what he's giving me, and I'm more than happy to do just that. He slides three fingers into me, fucking both my holes while his tongue claims my mouth. Every part of me is his. He's put his mark on every part of me, claimed me in the most intimate ways, and I know there's no separating us after this. He's a part of me, embedded into my very core, and I feel so fucking grateful.

When he feels how close I am, he works me harder, bringing me to the edge so easily before toppling me over with his skilled fingers. He swallows my screams, slamming into me even harder before he groans and I feel his cock pulsing inside me, filling me with everything he has. I'm lost in bliss, surrounded by it, and even after I start to come down, I still feel it rushing through me with the aftershocks.

"God, I love you," he whispers against my lips. "So fucking much, baby."

"I love you too," I say, my voice raw and raspy. My whole body is sore, and I let out a soft laugh. "I don't think I can move."

He laughs and slowly slides out of me. "You don't need to. I'm carrying you back to the house. You need another hot soak, baby."

"I'm starting to see a pattern here. I think I'm always going to be a little bit sore because of your giant cock."

I can hear the amusement in his voice when he says, "No way in hell am I going to apologize for that. I'll always take care of you afterwards, though."

"Sounds like a good deal." I roll onto my back, watching him grab his weapons and our clothes before scooping me into his arms. He makes it seem so effortless to carry my weight, and it's one of my most favorite things. He makes me feel delicate, like I'm something to be cherished and cared for. I never thought that he'd be that kind of man, but Kirill constantly surprises me in the best possible ways.

Once we're back inside and soaking in a hot tub, the exhaustion catches up to me. My body is completely worn out, and it's impossible for me to keep my eyes open. His arms are wrapped around me, fingers gently caressing my skin, and I smile when he kisses my temple and whispers, "It's okay, baby. Get some sleep. I'll take care of you."

I'm not sure how much time passes, but when I wake, it's still dark outside and I'm in bed alone. Well, Peanut is snuggled up against me, but Kirill is missing. Giving my sweet dog a kiss, I gently scoot out of bed so he'll keep sleeping. I'm naked, so I grab my robe and am just about to go downstairs to look for him when I spot his broad shoulders on the balcony. He's sitting in one of the chairs with his back to me. I watch as he lifts a glass to his lips and takes a healthy drink. The clink of ice makes me nervous. This is the first time I've seen him with alcohol, and the way he's quickly downing it sends alarm bells all through me.

Stepping through the French doors, I walk to him and wrap my arms around his neck. "Are you okay?"

He squeezes my hand and pulls me around and into his lap. Burying his face against my neck, he breathes me in and lets out a soft sigh. "I never expected to fall so damn hard for you," he murmurs, and I begin to wonder just how many of these drinks he's had. "I shouldn't have let you fall for me, but I couldn't help it, *zaika*. I was lost to you the second I saw you. You were so beautiful," he sighs again, "so goddamn beautiful and so brave."

"Kirill, what's going on?"

His hands tighten around me, fingers digging into my flesh and when that's not enough, he slides a hand into my robe and grabs my hip, keeping me pinned in place.

"I never leave witnesses," he says, and his voice is so soft I have to strain to hear him.

"I know you don't." I say it slowly, feeling more nervous with each passing second, but it's what he says next that has me frozen in place.

"Except for one time."

"No," I whisper, already shaking my head in denial. He tightens his grip on me when my body starts to tremble.

"I turned around and saw you standing there, and it was like my heart stopped in that moment, or maybe it's more like it started beating for the first time. You were so beautiful and scared, but you didn't scream and you didn't run. You just looked at me and begged, and there was no way in hell I could shoot you. I could never hurt you, little bunny. I'm not capable of it."

A deep keening sound pierces the air around us, and it takes several seconds for my brain to realize that it's coming from me. I struggle against him, but he only holds me tighter.

"I'm sorry, baby. I'm so fucking sorry, but I didn't know you. I had no idea he had a daughter or that you were even home. The first time I knew of your existence is when you turned the corner and saw me."

"But why?" I yell at him. "Why did you kill him? He wasn't rich or powerful enough to even attract your attention. I don't understand."

"He owed a lot of money at the casino he liked to go to, the casino that's owned by one of Ivan's mistresses. One night he got drunk and made a big scene after losing ten grand on one hand of cards. When Carla came out to speak with him, he screamed at her and called her a cheating bitch. She complained to Ivan, and I was quickly brought onboard to take care of the problem. After I was arrested, I told Vadim to pay off his debt so they wouldn't come after you."

"Am I supposed to thank you for that?" I try to pull back, but when he won't let me go, I smack his chest, and then because it feels so damn good, I do it again and again. He lets me, doesn't even try to fend off my pathetic slaps, and the hurt in his eyes is almost enough to make me feel bad for him. Almost. But then I remember my dad, I remember that night and how it had felt walking into that room and seeing his lifeless body and the terror I'd felt when I'd seen the gunman just standing there, looking at me. I'd had nightmares for two fucking years because of him. I'd lost a dad because of him, the only parent I had left, and then he'd let me fall in love with him, knowing the whole goddamn time that he'd killed my dad. No, fuck this.

"Let me go," I holler at him.

"I can't."

I ignore the pain and sorrow in his voice.

"You can't just keep me here, Kirill. I don't want to be here with you anymore. I want to go."

He hugs me against him, and even though my body stiffens, he holds me so fucking gently, like he's scared I'm going to just disappear into thin air. Part of me wants so badly to just melt against him, to let him take care of me and comfort me, but I can't do that. I can't ignore the giant lie he's let me believe this whole fucking time.

"I love you," he groans. "I can't let you go, Lydia. I love you too fucking much."

I grit my teeth, ignoring the pain in my heart and force myself to lie and say, "But I don't love you. Not anymore, Kirill. You're a fucking lying monster, and I never want to see you again."

He takes in a shaky breath at my words and I nearly lose my resolve when I feel the wet heat of his tears hit my cheek.

He lets out a pained groan. "I can't take this, baby. Please don't hate me. I swear we can work through this. I'll spend the rest of my life making it up to you." His wet cheek presses against mine. "I've never begged for anything in my life, but I'm begging you now. Please don't do this."

I make my voice hard as steel when I say, "I didn't do this. You did." I push away from him again, and this time he doesn't stop me. With his shoulders slumped and the haunted look in his eyes, I can tell the fight has left him. He looks distraught, and I hate how much it hurts me to see it. "You broke my heart, Kirill," I tell him, feeling it break all over again when he raises his stormy grey eyes to mine. "Open up the gate. I don't want to be here anymore."

He gives a slow shake of his head. "I can't let you go."

Tears still run down his face, and seeing it has me crying even harder. I can't turn my heart on and off, no matter what he's just told me, but that doesn't mean I can stay here with him. I love him, and I know I will love him for the rest of my life, but I can't think straight when he's right in front of me. I don't know what to do or where to go. All I know is that if I don't get out of this fucking house right now, I'm going to lose it.

"Please, Kirill," I say, and he lets out a disbelieving laugh that I'm willing to use his weakness against him. "I just need some space. I need some time to think, and I need you to trust me enough to give it to me."

He reaches into his pocket and pulls his phone out, and when he punches in the code to open the gate, I let out the breath I'd been holding. "Take the Ferrari. It's an automatic, and the keys are hanging in the garage."

"Thank you," I whisper and then start to step back into the bedroom, but he grabs my wrist, holding me in place, and when I look down at him, the anguish in his eyes cuts me to the quick.

"I'm sorry," he says, his voice raw with emotion. "I'm so sorry I didn't tell you. I wanted to, but I was terrified of losing you."

"Why did you tell me now? Why not just keep it a secret?"

His thumb caresses my inner wrist, and just that one small touch has me wishing I could forget everything he just told me.

"Because I love you, and I couldn't bear to lie to you anymore. I want you to be with me while knowing the whole truth. I want your forgiveness, *zaika*. I want you, all of you." He brings my hand to his face, pressing the palm of it against his cheek. He lets out a breath and closes his eyes. "I can't live without you. I can't go back to a life that doesn't have you in it, right at the center of it."

I don't like seeing him like this, and even though I know he's responsible for my dad's death, I take no pleasure in seeing him hurting like this, and I know I can't just run away. If I can't forgive him, then I at least deserve some closure, but that will require a conversation that I don't have it in me to have right now.

"Peanut's sleeping, so if it's okay with you, I'm going to leave him here."

His eyes study mine. He knows what I'm offering, sees it as the olive branch it is. "Of course it's okay. I'll make sure he's taken care of."

I use every ounce of willpower I possess and pull my hand back. Before he lets me go, he kisses my palm and tells me he loves me again. I let out a sob as I turn and run back into the bedroom. I hurry up and pull on some clothes and sneakers and bolt out of the room before I can change my mind. I don't dare look back at him, knowing all my courage will leave me if I do and I'll just crumble into heap on the damn floor.

The black Ferrari is ready and waiting, and I know he's watching me on his security cameras as I peel out of the garage and race down his long driveway. As soon as I pass through the open gate, it starts to shut behind me, and the sight of those iron bars closing in my rearview mirror is enough to make me start sobbing again. He murdered my dad, and he lied to me about it, so why in the hell does it feel so damn wrong to be driving away? My heart feels like it's breaking in two, and my chest aches while my lungs struggle to fill with air. Unable to even see the damn road, I pull off to the side and cover my face with my hands, crying until my throat hurts, I feel weak, and my eyes are swollen and red. A little voice whispers in the back of my head that he never did actually lie to my face about this. He never flat-out said that he didn't kill my dad. He just very strongly hinted that he didn't do it. Is there a difference? Does it make it any better that he never looked me in the eyes and said *I didn't kill your dad*?

Maybe...kind of. God, I don't know.

I'm just about to start the car back up when there's a sharp tap on the window. I yelp in surprise, bringing my hand to my heart. My first thought is that Kirill followed me, but the man peering in the window is a complete stranger to me. He's older, but not by too much, probably mid-thirties, with dark eyes and a friendly smile on his face.

"Are you okay?" He speaks loud enough for me to hear through the window and looks at me with concern. No doubt I look like a crazy woman. I'm crying on the side of the road in the middle of the night, and looking down I realize that the clothes I grabbed don't even match. Well, that's just fucking perfect.

Trying like hell to appear sane, I smile and say, "Yes, I'm fine. Thank you."

"You don't look fine. Do you live around here? Would you like me to help you get home or call someone to come get you?"

He has an accent, but it's not the Russian one I've grown so used to. If I had to guess, I'd say Italian, and that's when alarm bells start ringing. I give him an *I'm completely harmless and clueless* smile while I slowly snake one hand up to start the car. That's when his grin turns wicked. I watch his face go from friendly stranger to deadly threat in less than two seconds. His lips curl up in a smirk as he brings one hand up and I see the gun he's holding. He taps the muzzle against the window.

"Get out of the fucking car, Lydia."

I try to come up with a plan that will save my ass, but my brain feels frozen, unable to process what's going on. The only thing running through my mind is that I'm so freaking glad I left Peanut at the house and that I wish Kirill was here. He'd know what to do. When I don't move, the man points the gun at me.

"I can shoot you in the thigh and drag you out of there if you want. Either way, you're coming with me. It's just that one way hurts a hell of a lot more than the other." He gives me another creepy smile. "Choose fast."

"I'm coming," I quickly say, because no way in hell am I actually going to choose to get shot if I don't have to. He's right. There's no way I'm getting out of this on my own. He'll shoot me before I can even get the car started. When I unlock the door, he wrenches it open and grabs onto my arm, squeezing tight enough to make me gasp. It's a cruel grip, one Kirill would never use on me, and the thought that I might never see him again, that I'm going to be killed and he'll never know that I lied when I said I didn't love him is enough to make me start crying again. I just left him, crying and alone and in complete anguish.

"Shut the fuck up," the man growls at me, pulling me to the car parked behind me that I hadn't even noticed was there. The lights are off, but when we get closer, someone turns them back on. The man opens the door and shoves me into the backseat, lowering himself in as he keeps his gun pointed at me. Two men are up front, both of them looking just as dangerous as the man sitting next to me.

"What's going on?" I ask, trying to sound brave and not like I'm seconds away from losing control of my bladder.

The man next to me says, "I told you to shut the fuck up." He switches to Italian and starts talking to the others. The driver turns to look back at me. His eyes run over me, and I quickly cross my arms over my chest, hiding the fact that I didn't put a bra on before I'd left the house. The grin he gives me terrifies me more than the gun pointed at me. A bullet to the head is at least a quick death, but this man is looking at me like I'd be begging for death by the time he's done with me. Without a word, he turns back around and starts driving.

I stare out the window, feeling the weight of my cell phone in my pocket but too scared to try and do anything with it. After a few minutes of silence, the men start speaking Italian again and I very slowly creep my fingers to my thigh. None of them seem to be on to me, so I slide my hand in my pocket, feeling the edge of my phone. I'm just about to use my fingerprint to unlock it when the sound of the cutesy ringtone I'd assigned to Kirill fills the inside of the car. I bite back my curse and clutch my phone.

"Give it to me," the man next to me yells. When I hesitate, he adds, "Give me the motherfucking phone or I will strip search you in the back of this car and you can ride the rest of the way naked. Your fucking choice."

I see Kirill's name when I start to hand the phone over, and before I can talk myself out of it, I swipe my finger across the screen and yell, "Help! Three Italians! I'm in their car!" It's all I can get out before I'm punched in the face, the force of it knocking my head against the window. My last thought is of Kirill before everything turns black.

Chapter 15

Kirill

Everything inside me freezes when I hear Lydia's panicked, terror-filled voice. Sober in an instant, I stand and grip my phone even tighter.

"Baby? What's going on? Are you okay?"

I hear a loud thud, a pained moan, and then silence. With the blood rushing through my ears and the fear that's etched its way into every cell in my body, it takes me a few seconds to realize that someone ended the call. I replay what she'd yelled out to me. Three Italians have her in their car. There's no way in hell Enzo isn't behind this. I killed his son, and now he has the woman I love more than anything in this world. When I call Vadim and explain what just happened, my voice is shaking, and I think that freaks him out more than anything else.

"I'm on my way," he quickly tells me. "We'll get her back, Kirill."

I don't bother agreeing with him. I just hang up and start putting all the weapons back on that I'd just taken off a few hours ago. Memories of my little bunny flood my brain, images of me fucking and holding her mixed with the look of absolute horror when I'd made my confession to her. I should've just kept my damn mouth shut, carried the burden and guilt around for the rest of my life, but I'd wanted to be honest with her.

I'd wanted her forgiveness. All it did was hurt her and now her life is in danger because of me.

I pull up the tracking sensor I have on my car and the tracking app I installed on her phone shortly after she came here. The information is just coming up when I hear the alarm go off, letting me know that Vadim's arrived. I open the gate for him and zoom in on the map that's filling my monitor. The car is only a couple of miles away, but the other dot on the screen is heading further south into Enzo's territory. The fact that they haven't disabled her phone yet doesn't sit well with me. They're either the stupidest kidnappers alive or they want me to know where she's at so I'll follow. I'm guessing it's the latter. Enzo doesn't just want her; he wants me too.

"Anything new?" Vadim asks, rushing into the room and looking at the monitor in front of me.

"No. They haven't disabled her phone."

"Fuck," he mutters. "It's going to be a trap."

"I know."

"I'm guessing you're still going?"

"I am."

He sighs and nods his head. "Okay, let's see where they stop so I can figure out the best place to set up with my rifle to give you some backup."

We wait in silence, each second feeling like a lifetime, and when I feel a soft nudge at my ankle, I look down and see Peanut looking up at me. I scoop him up without even thinking about it, petting him while he licks my hand. I don't know if I'm comforting him or he's comforting me. It feels like a mix, and I'll gladly take it because I'm very much at the end of my rope. I know what these men are capable of. I've seen what they do to women, and the thought of one of them putting their hands on my sweet girl makes me want to kill all of them as slowly and painfully as possible.

As soon as the dot stops, we both lean forward. I quickly pull up the address on another screen and zoom in. It's a warehouse right in the center of Enzo's territory.

"Fuck," Vadim mutters again.

"Yeah, fuck," I say, because this just turned into an even bigger nightmare. His men are going to be all over the place. No way in hell we'll be able to even sneak up on the building. No wonder they didn't care if the phone was still on. Only an absolute lunatic would venture that far into the Faretti family's domain. Lucky for me I'm more than a little unhinged after having my girl stolen. They're going to regret touching her. Every last one of them.

I give Peanut another pet before setting him down. "Come on," I tell Vadim. "We need more weapons."

"Fuck yeah we do."

He follows me into the garage where I unlock the door that leads to the small armory I've kept well stocked over the years. Vadim gives a low whistle. I've never let him in here before.

"Holy shit," he sighs, running his hands over the guns lining one of the walls.

"Take whatever you need and hurry up. I don't want her with them any longer than she has to be. I swear to god if they fucking touch her," I say, and then stop because I can't put words to the horror film running through my mind.

"They won't. They just took her to get to you." Vadim fills a duffle bag with guns and bullets, and I know he's just telling me what I need to hear, but I force myself to believe it because the alternative will leave me in a rage that I don't think I'll ever be able to come out of.

Once we have enough weapons to defend a small country, we toss them into my car. I give a sharp whistle and wait for the four large dogs to come running over. It doesn't take long. Opening the back door, I wait for them to get in. They barely fit, but they'll manage for the short drive we have.

"You're bringing the dogs?" Vadim asks, getting into the passenger side with his favorite rifle in hand.

"I am." I look back at my boys, already envisioning the bloody muzzles they're going to have when all is said and done. "You ready to kill some fuckers?" I ask them. They understand the Russian perfectly, and I'm not at all surprised when they each give a soft whine of excitement and Boris starts to drool.

"God, I'm so happy they see me as a friend," Vadim says. When I race down the driveway, he adds, "For fuck's sake, don't get pulled over. No way in hell would we be able to explain this."

I force myself to not drive too fast, but I don't take it slow either. I need to get to her. I can't stop thinking about how scared she must be. When we cross into Faretti's side of the city, I slow down even more, and as soon as we hit the side streets, I cut my lights. Two streets from the warehouse, I stop the car so Vadim and the dogs can get out. On the drive here, he'd been studying the map, finding the best place to hide himself.

"Try not to get your ass killed," he says before taking the earpiece I hand him and shutting the door.

I nod and tell the dogs, "Stay low, kill any threats."

I've never known exactly what they can understand, but I swear they get the gist of just about everything I say. They can read my body language and tone, both of those mixed with the Russian commands I've trained them with means they've never let me down. I'll be devastated if any of them get hurt, but I can't do this without them.

As soon as they're all gone, I start driving to the warehouse, bracing myself for whatever I might find. There are three cars parked out front, and the lights inside the building are on. They're making no attempt to hide, which just backs up what I already knew. They left a trail because they wanted me to find her. Before I get out of the car, I slip a switchblade into my boot so it rests snuggly against my ankle. I'm loaded with weapons because I know they're going to search me. My hope is that they'll miss one, because one is all I'll need.

"I'm going in," I mutter, giving Vadim a heads-up.

I'm in position. I've got a clear view through one of the windows. Brace yourself, man. You are not going to like what you find.

"Are they hurting her?" My jaw aches from how hard I'm gritting my teeth, but I need to know. I need to prepare myself for what I'm going to find because I can't let anything show on my face. Enzo can't know how much this is killing me. It'll only make things worse for Lydia.

They're not actively touching her, he says, and I can tell he's choosing his words very carefully.

"Vadim, I need you to tell me exactly what you fucking see so I can prepare myself."

He's not used to me having an emotional response to anything. It's new for me too, and I haven't quite gotten used to it. He lets out a sigh as I stare at the building in front of me.

"Fucking say it," I grit out.

She's naked, hands bound at the wrists and attached to a hook above her. Her toes are barely touching the ground. There's blood on her face, a few red marks on her body like they've hit her. She's conscious, and she looks scared to death.

While the image forms in my mind, he adds, *She's going to be okay. We're going to get her out of there. I count twenty men, Enzo included.*

"I'm going in," I repeat, feeling my mind start to close down. I have to become numb to everything. I have to force myself to not feel a damn thing. "If I don't survive this, tell her I had to do it this way, that there wasn't another option. Tell her I'm sorry for everything and that I love her."

You can tell her yourself, man.

When all he gets is silence, he sighs and says, *I'll tell her. You have my word.*

With that assurance in place, I get out of the car and walk to the door in front of me. I don't bother knocking. They already know I'm here anyway. Stepping inside, my eyes immediately dart to Lydia, and the sight nearly ruins my entire plan. She looks so small and fragile, so completely and utterly breakable. I see the humiliation and fear in her eyes, and as soon as she spots me, the rush of hope that mixes with it. I turn away, unable to watch it all change to hurt when she hears what I have to say.

I face Enzo instead and raise my arms in a *what the fuck* motion. "What the hell's going on, Enzo?"

Five suited men quickly rush over to me. Three keep their guns raised and pointed at me while the other two start to frisk me. I wink at the man kneeling in front of me, running his hands up my inner thighs. "Careful, that's not the weapon you're looking for." I laugh and add, "Or maybe it is. I'm not one to judge."

He doesn't share in my laugh, just glares at me and continues his search. They manage to find everything except the switchblade that's sitting snuggly in my boot. I try very hard to not gloat about that. Satisfied that I'm no longer a walking arsenal, they step back and I look over at Enzo again. The older man stands and walks over to where Lydia is hanging. He scrubs a hand over his neatly trimmed salt-and-pepper beard and then lets out a soft laugh that makes my skin crawl. When he runs the back of one hand along the side of her breast, I nearly lose the small grip on my sanity I have left.

"You killed my son," he says, lazily dragging a finger over her nipple as she tries like hell to get away from him and screams against the duct tape covering her mouth. "And his whore." He drops his hand and turns his eyes to me. They're cold and hard, devoid of any and all emotion. The same way mine used to look before I met Lydia. "So that's exactly what I'm going to do to you, except I'm going to make you watch me fuck her first, and then you're going to watch all my men fuck her." He runs a hand down her back, sliding it lower to cup one of her ass cheeks, and I bite my lip so hard I taste blood. "Have you taken her ass yet?" He laughs at the way her eyes widen in horror and gives her ass a sharp smack. "I'm going to kill her very slowly, and then I'll finally get to you." He gives another soft laugh. "Eventually."

Lydia lets out another muffled scream at what Enzo's just said and begs me with her eyes to do something, so I do the only thing I can do. I make myself as cold and empty as I used to be and let out a harsh laugh of my own.

"Have at it, Enzo. You think I give a fuck what you do to her?" I look around at the warehouse and his men. "If you wanted to hurt me, old man, you should've kidnapped one of my dogs." I let out a good-natured laugh. "I love those fuckers."

"I think you do care," Enzo says, gauging my reaction when he takes a knife out and brings the blade to her skin. He drags the blade along her stomach, and her breaths are so fast and erratic that I'm afraid she might make herself pass out. When he runs it along her bottom ribs, he presses in hard enough to cut a thin line of about four inches. Blood immediately beads and spills over.

It's a shallow cut, Vadim whispers in my ear, trying like hell to keep me calm.

I know this, but it doesn't make seeing it any easier. I raise a brow at Enzo as if I'm bored. "Ivan put a hit on your son, and I killed him." I smile and give a small shrug. "I'm a hitman, Enzo. It's what I do."

"He told me you did it on your own, that he knew nothing about it."

"Well, the two million he transferred to my account that night begs to differ. For the record, I did try to talk him out of it. It was a stupid move, and I knew it would start a war, one he would have a hard time winning. He ignored me, so I took out your son. The mistress just happened to be there."

"He was my only son," Enzo says, and I can hear the strain in his voice and how badly he's trying to keep himself under control. *You and me both, jackass.*

I smile and push him a bit further. "He died like a real pussy, but he should've been thanking me. He went out while fucking." I laugh and look at the armed man next to me like we're sharing a joke. "If only we could all go out like that, am I right?"

Just as predicted, that comment sends Enzo over the edge, and he puts all his focus on me instead of the woman I love.

Just tell me when, Vadim murmurs in my ear.

I face Enzo, keeping my chin held high, even when his men hold my arms back to give the old man a fighting chance. The punch to the jaw is almost hard enough to break it. Blood fills my mouth from where my teeth have shredded through my gums, and when I spit blood, I look back at him and laugh.

"I smothered him with a pillow while he lay beneath his whore. It was not a dignified death. I think he might've shit himself."

That earns me a rapid-fire round of punches, the last one hitting me in the gut and making my knees buckle. I run with it, letting myself become dead weight in their arms. They grunt at the effort to keep me up and Enzo barks, "Let him fucking fall. It'll still give him a front-row seat to the show."

As soon as they let go, I reach for the knife in my boot and say, "Now," just loud enough for Vadim. I hear several quick shots, and the men closest to me fall to the ground right before I hear another man scream and then the sound of one of my dogs ripping his throat out. Throwing my knife, I hit one of the other men in the chest while I take the gun from the closest dead man, barely noticing the way half his head is missing.

Alerted by the gunshots, more of Enzo's men come rushing in. The warehouse fills with the sounds of guns firing, snarling growls, and the pained screams of grown men. I start making my way closer to Lydia but keep some distance between us while I fire off several shots, not wanting her to get hit in the crossfire. I yell a quick command to my dogs to guard Lydia and then wait until Vadim's taken out the other men that I can't get a clear shot on.

Without anyone shooting, the silence is deafening. My ears ring, my heart races, and all I can think about is getting to Lydia. I scan the warehouse, looking for Enzo, hoping he's one of the dead men already on the ground. He isn't. I step closer to Lydia's hanging body, but I keep my eyes trained on the room around me.

"Do you see him?"

Vadim's reply is immediate. *No. I didn't shoot him.*

Neither did I, which means he's still very much alive. I'm almost to her when I spot him rounding the corner with his gun raised and aimed right at my precious *zaika*. I yell her name and lunge myself in front of her while I fire off a shot. Pain rips through me right as I see his head jerk back from the force of the bullet. He falls to the hard concrete floor at almost the same time as me.

Fuck! Vadim yells in my ear.

"Take care of her," I say, the Russian words sounding far away even to my own ears. "Keep her safe."

I barely register the sound of her muffled screams coming from somewhere above me. The bullet hit my chest, and already I can tell that I'm losing way too much blood. One of the dogs gives a whimper and licks my hand. I want to pet him, but my fingers refuse to move. When Vadim drops to his knees by my side and starts looking at the bullet hole, I let out an angry groan.

"Get her down," I grit out.

He sees the look in my eyes and lets out a frustrated sigh before jumping up to free Lydia from the hook she's been hanging from. He cuts through her bound hands and rips off his own shirt. I'm coherent enough to hate seeing her wearing another man's shirt, and that thought gives me a flicker of hope, but then my vision starts to darken, and I can tell I'm not going to be conscious much longer.

"Kirill," Lydia screams, dropping down next to me. She cups my face and presses her forehead against mine. "Please don't die," she whispers, and I want to tell her that I'm trying like hell not to, but I don't have the strength. Her tears hit my face, and when she presses her lips to mine, I think that this isn't a bad way to die at all. My baby's lips are on mine, her hands are on my face, and I'm surrounded by her love. Not a bad way to die at all.

Chapter 16

Lydia

"No, no, no, no, no!" I scream the word over and over again while I cup Kirill's beautiful, bloody face and will him to come back to me, but his eyes stay shut, and his body stays limp and unresponsive. Looking up at Vadim, I notice he's talking into his phone while keeping a hand pressed firmly against Kirill's chest. He's telling whoever's on the other end of that line the address to the warehouse and then describing where the gunshot wound is.

His eyes dart to mine before he says, "Hurry the fuck up. It doesn't look good." He hangs up and puts both hands on the wound that will not stop bleeding.

"We need to get him to a doctor." I look around at the dead men lying around us, the four dogs with bloody muzzles who are pacing nervously, and the weapons that I'm guessing are not legally registered. Calling the police is obviously out of the question, but we need an ambulance at least.

"Already on the way," Vadim says, making me feel a little bit better.

If they can get here in time, then maybe he can survive this. The thought of losing him sends a rush of pure terror through me. I'd been pissed at him earlier, so fucking pissed and angry and hurt, but I can't lose him. He threw himself in front of me. The only reason I'm breathing right now is because of him, and I will not let him die for me. I won't fucking allow it.

The door behind us bursts open, but I don't turn to look. I lean closer to Kirill, bringing my lips close to his ear. "Don't leave me," I beg. "I love you. Please don't leave me."

I have just enough time to kiss his cheek before a pair of strong arms are pulling me away. I try to fight my way out of the hold, but it's no use.

"It's okay," Vadim says, pulling me further away from Kirill and the two men who are quickly loading him onto a stretcher. "We need to let them do their job."

I watch them carry Kirill away, and it's only Vadim's arm around me that's keeping me upright. I sob until I can barely breathe, watching them put the man I love in the back of a makeshift ambulance.

"Who are they? Where are they taking him?" I manage to ask in a shaky, raw voice.

"They're doctors who don't mind earning money in a less than legal way." He picks me up, being careful to pull the shirt I'm wearing down so his arm isn't hitting my bare ass. There's nothing sexual about the hold, not even with me in nothing but a shirt and him without one. It's just comforting. He's watched over me for two years, and now he's just doing what he's been trained to do—taking care of me because Kirill isn't here to do it himself.

"I want to be with him," I say as he carries me to the car, giving a whistle for the dogs before opening the back door. Three of them jump in, but one stays right next to me. Vadim ignores him and carries me to the front passenger side. Once he's got me in and buckled up, the dog jumps in, sitting his large body between my legs. I see the bloody muzzle, but I don't care. I wrap my arms around him, burying my face in his neck because sometimes you just need a dog to make you feel better. Vadim runs back inside and comes back out a few minutes later carrying a couple of handguns, several knives, and a large gun slung across his back. He puts them in the trunk, and when he's behind the wheel, I ask, "Which one is this? I can't tell them apart yet."

"It's Grisha. Oddly enough, he's always had a soft spot for a hug." I know Vadim is trying to keep me calm, but I can hear the worry in his voice. We both know how much blood Kirill lost. I'm covered in it, and when they moved his body to the stretcher, there was a sizable puddle on the concrete. I stroke Grisha's fur and kiss the top of his head.

"Are you taking me to him?"

"No, I'm taking you home."

"What?" I ask, jerking my head up. I twist around in my seat, trying to find the black van they'd loaded Kirill into. "I don't want to go home. I want to be with him."

"Relax, Lydia. I'll take you to him, but first we need to drop the dogs off, and you need to get cleaned up."

I look down at the bloody shirt and the filthy body it's barely covering. I'd been so fucking scared when they'd grabbed me off the side of the road, and then when Enzo had introduced himself and told his men to strip me, I was so terrified that I could barely breathe. It had been so humiliating and scary, and I didn't think for one second that I was going to come out of it unscathed, but I had. Aside from a few hits and the cut Enzo gave me, I'd left that warehouse alive and breathing. All because of Kirill.

"Will they call you if anything changes with him?"

"They will."

"And you'll take me to him as soon as I get cleaned up?"

"I will."

"Okay then," I say, leaning back into the seat. The drive back seems to take forever. I can't stop imagining the worst-case scenario. By the time he pulls in front of the garage, I'm barely holding myself together.

Vadim squeezes my hand and says, "He's strong, Lydia. He's going to fight to stay here with you."

I nod, unable to speak because if I try, I'll just end up bawling again. He gives me another squeeze before getting out and freeing the dogs.

"I'm going to get them taken care of. I'll bring you to him as soon as you're ready."

"Thanks, Vadim," I tell him, before petting Grisha one last time and then running inside.

The empty house is like a slap to the face. Peanut runs up to me, sniffing and looking around for Kirill, and when he doesn't see him, he sniffs the blood I'm covered in and gives a soft whine. I pick him up and cry while I carry him upstairs. As soon as I cross into our bedroom, I force myself to block everything else out except the bathroom door. If I look at the bed or the balcony where I told him I didn't love him anymore, I will never be able to get through this.

Setting Peanut down, I start the shower and step in, peeling off the bloody shirt and tossing it aside before stepping under the hot spray. I scrub Kirill's blood off me, wondering if maybe I shouldn't. If he doesn't survive this, then I'm washing away the last piece of him I have. The morbid thought makes me cry even harder. I focus on how badly I need to be with him and scrub myself harder, not caring that it's causing me pain when I run over my bruises and scrapes. The slice along my ribs starts bleeding again, and instead of stopping, I press in even harder, welcoming the pain. I'd rather feel that than the all-consuming anguish that's threatening to rip me apart.

When I'm done, I hurry up and dry off and get dressed in yoga pants and a T-shirt. The last thing I grab is the hoodie Kirill wore the other day. It's going to be humongous on me, but I need to feel close to him. I need to feel like he's still with me. Before I leave the room, I pull on a pair of sneakers and grab Peanut because he's definitely coming with me. Vadim is waiting for me when I run back outside.

I get in the passenger seat and quickly ask, "Any news?"

"He's in surgery."

I can tell he's holding back. "What is it?"

He scratches at his beard as he drives us back out the gate and sighs. "They said to prepare for the worst. He lost a lot of blood, and the bullet did a lot of damage."

I bite my bottom lip, holding in the scream that's dying to come out.

"They don't know him, Lydia," Vadim reminds me. "They have no idea what a giant stubborn ass he is."

"Mm-hmm," I manage to mumble, hugging Peanut tighter and pressing my nose against the sweatshirt that still smells like him.

Vadim drives us away from the city until we're surrounded by woods. Sunrise is still a few hours away, and I don't see anything that looks even remotely familiar. When he turns down a desolate-looking side road, I finally ask, "Where are we?"

"Some place very hidden," he says. "It goes without saying that you can't ever tell anyone about this place or the doctors working here."

I look over at him and lift a brow. "Who in the hell would I tell? You've spied on my life. You know how boring it is."

He gives me a smile, even if it doesn't quite reach his eyes. "I thought you had a very interesting life."

"That's very generous of you, Vadim." I stare as we come around the bend and the whole place opens up, revealing a large, three-story house. "Well, it's definitely not boring now."

"No, it isn't. Welcome to the exciting world of crime."

"I think I'll be happy to go back to boring once Kirill is back home."

He smiles at me, and this time it reaches his eyes. "I think he would love that."

There's a tall privacy fence blocking us from getting any closer, and when Vadim stops the car, several armed men step out from the shadows, surrounding the car as my heart starts racing again. They're all in black with guns at their hips and even bigger ones in their hands. The rifles are clipped to slings that fit across their chests. They're holding them, but they don't aim them at us. It's only a small comfort, though, since I know that could change in a millisecond.

"Vadim," I whisper.

"It's okay. They have to keep this place guarded." He rolls down his window and says, "We're here to see Kirill Chernikov."

The man closest to Vadim, holds up his radio and speaks to someone inside, relaying what was just said. He turns back to us. "Any weapons?"

"No, none."

"Pop the trunk and step out of the car," the guy says, clearly not taking Vadim at his word.

"It's okay," Vadim tells me, motioning for me to open my door and get out. "They have to check."

I step out, clutching Peanut against my chest and eyeing the two large, armed men in front of me. The one on the left says, "Put the dog down and turn around, hands on the hood."

I hesitate, looking down at Peanut.

"He won't be harmed," the man says, "but you need to do as I say."

He's not mean about it, just no-nonsense, and when I set Peanut down, he motions for me to turn around, and I do. With my palms on the hood, he does a quick frisk, searching me for weapons but not lingering and making me feel like he's also coping a feel. He is thorough, though, and I know if I'd had a weapon hidden on me, he'd have found it.

The other men search the car, and when we're cleared, the man who'd frisked me, says, "Okay, you can get your dog and get back in."

I grab Peanut and quickly get in and shut the door. "God, that was intense," I say as Vadim drives us up to the house.

"Yeah, they don't fuck around. Anyone can use this place, but there are strict rules about it. Absolutely no fighting and no weapons. If Enzo had survived and his men had brought him here, there's nothing any of us could've done about it. They'd be here together, wishing they could kill each other, but unable to do anything about it."

The gate opens, and Vadim drives us the rest of the way, parking along the side of the garage. The white, three-story house doesn't look like a hospital, but I guess that's the point. I stay close to him as we walk up to the imposing house. Security lights have everything lit up enough so we can easily see where we're going. I'm not at all surprised to find that the front door is also locked and guarded. Evidently this guard's been in touch with the men at the gate because he gives us a nod and opens the door to let us through.

We step into an ornate foyer where a woman is sitting behind a desk with a big smile plastered across her face. This whole place is so surreal that all I can do is stand there and gawk while I hold Peanut and try to keep my shit together long enough to find out where Kirill is.

Vadim steps closer to the woman and says, "We're here for Kirill Chernikov." He looks in my direction and adds, "She's his, and should be treated like a spouse."

His tone offers no room for disagreement, but she's a pro and doesn't even bat an eye.

"Of course." Her voice is sickly sweet as she turns to me and gives me an even bigger smile. I don't think she's trying to be an ass. This has got to be a stressful job. She deals with the most dangerous men in the city, and it can't be easy doling out bad news to men who would have no problem killing you the second you step foot off this property. She seems like she's conditioned herself to be nothing but sweet and cheery, even if it is fake as hell. I would've done the same if I was in her position.

"Thank you," I tell her. "Can you tell us anything about him? About how he's doing?"

She types something into her computer and quickly reads the screen. "He's still in surgery. I'm sorry. I don't know anything more than that right now, but I can show you to his room. You can wait in there." She eyes Peanut and pinches her lips together when I tighten my grip on him, making it clear that I'm not letting him go. Finally, she relents and stands, motioning for us to follow her.

We take the wide staircase up to the second floor. I look around at all the closed doors, wondering what's behind them. The place is elegant, almost having the feel of a nice hotel, and I'm not at all surprised to see an elevator at the end of the hall.

"Where are the surgeries done?" I speak to the long, red hair in front of me since I'm still following her down the hall.

She turns slightly and says, "All surgeries take place downstairs."

"But what if he needs something else, something that can only be done in a hospital?" I look around and as nice as this place is, it's not an emergency room. It can't possibly have everything he might need.

The woman turns to face me. "We have two of the best doctors in the city here and the finest equipment. I would argue that what we have here is better than anything you could find in one of the downtown hospitals. The only difference is that here, Mr. Chernikov will have our undivided attention. He's not going to get lost in the shuffle or booted out before he's ready. He's in good hands, Mrs. Chernikov."

My eyes threaten to spill over again when she calls me that, but I don't correct her. I like the sound of it too much to do that. I just nod and give her a small smile before she leads us to the last door on the right. Using a keycard, she unlocks it and ushers us in. Instead of a king-size bed, there's an extra large hospital bed, a seating area with couch and chairs, a kitchenette along one wall with a small table and chairs, and a very large en suite bathroom. There's even a small balcony with French doors, and I'm guessing once the sun rises it's going to give a pretty amazing view of the forest around us. My first thought is that I can't wait to share it with Kirill, and then I remember that it's still a very real possibility that he'll never see it.

Sensing the collapse that's coming, Vadim squeezes my shoulder and tells the woman, "Thank you so much. Please let us know if you hear anything new."

She smiles and points toward the phone near the hospital bed. "If you need anything, just dial zero. We have room service 24/7 as well as laundry and maid services. I'm Mandy, by the way, the night receptionist. If I'm not working, then it'll be Rebecca."

"Thanks, Mandy," he says again. "We appreciate your help. Can you please send up a nurse to take a look at Lydia. She has a few cuts that need looking after."

"Of course. Someone will be up shortly." She hands Vadim the keycard for the room and then gives me one last smile before leaving. As soon as the doors shuts, my whole body starts to shake. Vadim leads me to one of the chairs and then goes to get me a glass of water.

"Try and drink this," he says, kneeling down and raising it to my lips.

I manage a few swallows and then push it aside. "What if he

doesn't make it?"

"He will."

He grabs my hand and pulls the other chair over so it's right in front of me, waiting until I've got myself a bit more under control.

"Lydia," he starts, and the soft, hesitant tone of his voice has me lifting my eyes to his. "You know he didn't mean anything he said in that warehouse, right? That was all done to protect you. He loves you so much."

"I know. Before he got there, that's all Enzo talked about. He said he was going to hurt me and make Kirill watch, that he wanted him to suffer like he's suffered." I give him a soft smile. "It wasn't pleasant to listen to, especially since Kirill can give one hell of a dead look, but I knew he was just saying whatever he thought he needed to say to keep me safe."

"He can give one hell of a dead look, can't he?" Vadim says with a laugh. "He used to scare the hell out of me, still does from time to time if I'm being honest."

"He told me he killed my dad." I hadn't planned on bringing it up, but now that it's out there, I realize how badly I need to talk about it. "We had a fight. He confessed, and we fought." I start crying again when I say, "I told him I didn't love him anymore, that I needed to leave so I could think about things. I just left him," I cry. "I just walked away and left him, even though he was devastated."

"Lydia, he knows you love him. I've known the man a long time, and I've never seen him like he is with you. I never would've believed it, but I see it with my own eyes every time he's near you. He took the job with your dad not having any clue who you were or that you even existed, and trust me when I say that it's completely out of character for him to have left you still breathing. I think he fell in love with you the second he saw you."

He squeezes my hand again. "He loves you, and he knows you love him, and he's going to stay alive for you. You know how damn stubborn he is."

I smile as best I can and nod my head. When there's a soft knock at the door, he looks at me, making sure I'm okay before he gets up to answer it.

"Hi, I'm here to see Mrs. Chernikov."

"She's over here," Vadim says, letting her in and leading her over to me.

The woman looks like she's in her mid-twenties, big brown eyes and one of those mouths that naturally turns down in a sexy pout. God, if they make tips here, I'm guessing she's getting her fair share.

"Hi," she says, squatting down near me. "I'm Jenny, one of the nurse's here." Her eyes run over my face. "Looks like you ran into a bit of trouble tonight." She smiles at Peanut and pets his head. "I love Yorkies."

"His name's Peanut." She pets him again while I ask, "How's Kirill doing?"

"Last I heard, he was stable, but he's still in surgery."

When she sees my face fall, she quickly says, "It's a good sign that he's stable at this point in the surgery." She waits until I meet her eyes again. "A very good sign. He's strong, and he's fighting."

"Thanks," I tell her, grateful for the seed of hope. I'll gladly clutch at it, because without that kernel of hope, I'll lose my fucking mind.

She rummages through the bag she brought and brings out some sterile bandages and ointment. She may look like she should be in a bikini photoshoot, but her confident, quick-working hands tell me she knows exactly what she's doing. Jenny is clearly not just a pretty face.

"That bastard got you good," she murmurs, running her fingers along my nose to make sure it isn't broken.

"Yeah, but he paid for it," I murmur.

She smiles and whispers, "Good."

When she's satisfied my face is okay, she runs her eyes over the rest of me, but the bulky sweatshirt I'm wearing isn't revealing anything.

"Did they hurt you anywhere else?"

I know what she's asking, so I quickly so, "No, nothing like that. I got very lucky. I do have a cut along my ribs, though."

Vadim steps closer so he can grab Peanut and then walks over to the kitchenette, busying himself with getting him some water while also giving me some privacy. I lift the hoodie and T-shirt up enough to show her the cut that I hadn't realized was bleeding again. It's already soaked through the T-shirt, and when she gently examines it, I hiss out a breath at the pain. I'd been so pumped full of adrenaline and then fear for Kirill, but now that I'm looking at the knife wound, it's starting to hurt like a son of a bitch.

"You need stitches," Jenny says. "Okay, hop on the bed for me. It won't take long."

"What about Kirill?"

"I'll be quick, and something tells me he'd want you to get taken care of."

"I can vouch for the truth of that statement," Vadim says from the kitchenette. "Kirill would kick my ass if you didn't get stitches when you needed them."

I know they're both right so I lay down and keep my shirt lifted enough for her to work. She disinfects the entire area and then starts gathering her supplies. Holding up a syringe, she says, "This is going to sting, but it'll be numb in just a few seconds."

I nod, not caring about the pain and welcoming it for the distraction it is. She sews up the cut, asking me questions about Peanut to distract me. Turns out she had a Yorkie growing up and is thinking about getting another but worried about the long hours she works and feeling like it wouldn't be fair to leave them alone for so long.

After she puts in the last stitch, she sighs and says, "Maybe one day."

"They're great dogs," I agree, "and I hated leaving Peanut alone when I worked long shifts, but he's a lot older and quickly learned that I'd always come back home to him. I'm guessing your shifts are a little longer than eight hours."

She laughs. "Yeah, sometimes way longer. The pay is pretty damn good, though."

"I bet." She's probably making way more than she would at a regular hospital, but I'm not about to ask for details.

"Okay, you're all set." She puts a bandage over my stitches and gives me some basic instructions and promises to come check on it tomorrow.

"Thanks, Jenny."

"Do you want me to leave you with something that'll help you sleep." She looks out at the sky that's just starting to lighten. "I'm guessing you've been up all night. A nap might help."

"No," I quickly say. "I want to be awake when he gets out of surgery."

"I thought you might say that." She holds up a small package of pills. "I'm leaving these anyway." She wags the package in Vadim's direction. "She can take these at any time. They'll help her sleep. I'm also leaving some mild pain pills."

"Okay, just leave them on the nightstand. I'll make sure she takes them if she needs it."

Setting the pills down, Jenny packs up her stuff and turns back to me. "I'll check on you tomorrow, and I really hope you get some good news about Kirill very soon."

"Thanks," I say, scooting up and getting off the bed. I feel nothing but a very mild sting from the stitches, but I'm guessing it'll get worse as the shots wear off. I don't want to take the pain pills. I want to be fully alert in case Kirill needs me. I walk Jenny to the door and thank her again before she leaves.

"Do you want me to order you something to eat?" Vadim asks, scanning the menu he found in one of the kitchen drawers. "Maybe some breakfast?"

"No, thanks."

"Lydia, you haven't eaten for hours. You need to keep your strength up. I don't see Twizzlers on the menu, but surely we can find something to substitute them with."

I smile, knowing how hard he's trying to keep me positive. I also know that agreeing to this will help him. He's just as scared as I am, and if making sure I'm getting food is helping him stay sane, then I'm not about to take that from him.

He looks so damn relieved when I say, "Maybe I should eat. Do they have anything light? Maybe a fruit salad and some toast?"

Running his finger down the menu, he gives me a big grin and goes over to the phone. He orders me the fruit salad, toast, and orange juice and gets himself the biscuits and gravy. The thought of food makes me feel nauseous, but I know I need to eat something to keep my strength up, and I know Kirill would be upset if I didn't. That alone is enough to get me to nibble at the food once it comes. Grabbing a piece of toast, I start to pace the floor. The sun's already risen, and I'm not sure how much more waiting I can take. I'm leaning against the balcony doors, watching the forest that stretches out as far as I can see when the phone rings. I jump at the loud noise and look over at Vadim.

"I can't do it," I tell him.

He nods and runs over to it without a second thought. I watch him, hugging my arms tightly across my chest while I bite my thumbnail. Kirill's cologne is faint but still clinging to the sweatshirt, and my heart physically aches at the reminder of him. When Vadim looks over and gives me a smile and a thumbs up, I let out a gasp and fall to my knees. I sob in pure gratitude as Peanut runs over to make sure I'm okay. Vadim hangs up and comes over to me, lifting me up and pulling me into a hug.

"He's okay." He rubs my back and kisses the top of my head. "He's going to make it. They're going to bring him up soon."

I have so many questions, but all I can do is nod and cling to him. He's alive. That's all I need to know right now. It feels like forever before there's finally a knock at the door. I throw it open, stepping aside as two men wheel Kirill into the room with two nurses pulling along machines and an IV. He's on a gurney, and as soon as I see him, I start crying again. He's still unconscious, and he looks like a man who's been to hell and back. He's paler than I've ever seen him, and for the first time, he doesn't look invincible. I very nearly lost him. My big, strong hitman is human after all, and he's in for one hell of a rude awakening when he opens his eyes, because I'm never allowing him to put himself in danger again.

It takes both men plus Vadim to transition Kirill's body to the hospital bed. The machines they've brought with him are beeping and showing a heart beat that's reassuringly steady. His entire chest is wrapped up, and as soon as the nurses step aside, I rush over to him and take his hand, kissing it and keeping it pressed against my cheek.

I barely register the people around us leaving, but when a man introduces himself as Dr. West, I quickly turn my head to see him. He's wearing dark blue scrubs and looks exhausted. His hair is mostly grey, but he's lean and fit and doesn't look a day past forty.

"How is he?" I ask. "When will he wake up?"

He walks over and eyes the monitor, checking Kirill's vitals and making sure everything is as it should be before he offers me his hand.

"You must be Lydia. When he was first brought here, that's all he kept saying, your name over and over again."

I nod but don't say anything, just squeeze Kirill's hand even tighter, letting his presence calm me as only he can.

"The surgery was a tough one, and I wasn't sure he was going to make it, but he's strong, and he wanted to live." He meets my eyes and says, "He fought damn hard to live, but his recovery is going to be slow. I want to keep him sedated for a few days. We'll watch him closely for infection, and he needs to rest as much as possible. This will allow him to do that."

"Okay." I look back at Kirill. "Is there anything I can do for him?"

Dr. West looks at me and smiles. "Just be here for him. Talk to him, let him know you're here." He gives me a friendly wink. "There's a reason we make sure the beds are big enough for two. Even the most badass of men heal faster when they have the woman they love next to them. Just be careful of his wound and the IV."

He sees Peanut and laughs. "Well, this is a first."

"Is it okay if he stays?" I ask.

"Yeah, it'll be fine." He bends down and pets the overexcited Yorkie at his feet. "Just don't let him chew on the bandages or anything."

I kiss Kirill's hand before setting it down and walking over to the doctor. "Luckily, Peanut is past the puppy chewing stage." When Dr.

West stands back up, I hold out my hand to him. "Thank you so much for saving him." He takes my hand in both of his and gives a soft nod. "I really can't thank you enough."

"I'm glad he's going to be okay. I don't often get bullet wounds of such a noble nature," he says with a small grin playing at his lips. "It's nice to treat one and see it end happy." He turns and shakes the hand Vadim offers, and then tells us both he'll be back to check on Kirill later today.

After he's gone, I give Vadim a hug, feeling the tension slowly leave my body and then turn all my attention back to Kirill. I don't waste any time, I climb into the large bed, pulling the blanket up over both of us, and being careful to avoid all the tubes coming out of him, I rest my head on his pillow and put my hand in his.

"I'm going to go get some sleep and get a few things from the house for you and Peanut," Vadim says before walking to stand on the other side of the bed. He leans close to Kirill and whispers something in Russian, then he gives his shoulder a very soft pat. He pulls a cell phone from his back pocket and puts it on the nightstand. "Text me if you think of anything you want me to bring."

"Thanks, Vadim." It's such a simple thing to say, but I hope he can hear how much I mean it, how very aware I am that I could not have survived this night without his help.

"Anytime, Lydia, but I do hope this was a one-time thing."

"Oh god, you and me both."

He smiles and lifts Peanut onto the bed before quietly leaving the room. I snuggle in closer to Kirill and whisper into his ear. I talk until my voice is hoarse. I tell him how sorry I am for what I said, how much I love and need him, and how he better not ever put himself in danger again because my heart can't take it. I fall asleep at some point, barely registering the nurses that come and go over the next few hours. None of that matters. All that matters is the feel of Kirill's body next to mine and the constant, steady heartbeat that keeps softly beeping on the machine behind me.

Chapter 17

Kirill

"Can you hear me, Mr. Chernikov?"

The voice is unfamiliar and sounds like it's a hell of a long way off. My brain struggles to make sense of what's going on, but then I hear the voice that every part of my being responds to.

"Kirill, come back to me. Open your eyes, baby. Please wake up."

God, that begging gets me every damn time. I push through the hazy mush that's become my brain and struggle to open my eyes. I feel her small hand in mine, and when I give it a weak squeeze, I hear the relieved laugh she gives.

"He just squeezed my hand." She kisses my cheek and whispers. "Open your eyes, baby. I miss you."

"Miss you too," I say, but my voice is barely more than a croak. I blink my eyes open, and the first thing I see is her beautiful face. I was convinced I'd never see it again. After I'd been shot, I knew I was dying. I could feel my body shutting down, and the only thing that had kept me fighting was her. I didn't want to leave her. It's as simple as that.

Tears run down her cheeks as she cups my face and kisses me. It's whisper soft because she's scared of hurting me, but it's heaven all the same. "I love you so much," she says, crying even harder.

"Love you too, little bunny."

She gives me a big smile and pulls back to take the glass of water from Vadim's hand. She puts the straw to my lips as Vadim says, "Good to see you awake, man."

I take a drink, closing my eyes at how damn good it tastes. I want to drink the whole damn cup, but the man whose voice I hadn't recognized pulls it away.

"Easy. Don't chug it." Now that I see him, it's obvious he's a doctor, most likely the man who saved my life. "I'm Dr. West," he says.

"Thanks for saving my life, Doc."

"I'm glad you made it through. You had me worried there for a second." He listens to my heart and looks in my eyes and then checks the bandages on my chest. The wound is starting to really throb. Noticing the way my jaw clenches, he holds up a button that's attached to a cord. "Press this for a dose of morphine. You still need to rest as much as possible, but we'll no longer need to keep you sedated."

"How long have I been here?"

"Close to a week."

"Holy shit," I say, looking at Lydia. God, she must've been scared to death. "I'm sorry," I tell her. She looks at me like I've lost my mind. "For making you worry," I clarify. I want to also say for killing your father and for the way we left things, but I figure I'll hold off on that until we're alone.

She kisses my hand and shakes her head. "You saved my life."

I give her a wink. "You're worth it."

She laughs and the sound of it does more for me than that hit of morphine I'm resisting. I don't want to fall asleep again so soon. I look back to the doctor. "When can I leave?"

"Told you," Vadim says with a laugh. "I told them it would be one of your first questions."

I smile at him, already making plans for the huge bonus he'll be getting for all this. "Thanks for looking after her."

He pats my foot and says in Russian, "Of course, man. She hasn't left your side since you got here. She even asked the nurses to teach her how to change the bandages." He gives a soft laugh. "And she insisted on being the one to give you your sponge baths. She was downright feral about making sure your dick remained unseen by any other female eyes."

I laugh and then groan when it sends a spark of pain through my body that's nearly blinding.

"It's going to go against your nature," Dr. West says, "but you're going to really need to baby yourself for a while."

"I'll make sure he does," Lydia says, and her no-nonsense tone lets me know that I'm in for an interesting few weeks. I wonder if she'll even allow me to get out of the damn bed.

"When can I go home?" I repeat. "If I agree to rest a ton," I add, giving Lydia a smile.

"Let's give it a couple of days," Dr. West says. "I want to see how you feel when all the sedatives wear off, make sure you can keep solid food down, all that fun stuff." He looks down at my bandaged chest. "That bullet was damn close to your heart, Mr. Chernikov. The fact that you're even here talking to us right now is kind of a one-in-a-million thing." He hesitates and darts a quick glance at Lydia. "Maybe you can get out of this particular line of work soon."

"I'm already out, Doc."

"Glad to hear it." He turns to leave and says, "I'll check on you again later. Try to get some rest and don't be afraid to use the morphine. There's no reason for you to be in pain if you don't have to be."

"Will do," I tell him, but I'm not hitting that button anytime soon. I want to spend time with Lydia.

After he's left, Peanut hops up onto the bed and licks my hand. I pet him while Lydia keeps looking at me like she can't believe I'm actually here in front of her. I feel the same way every time I look at her.

Vadim laughs and says in Russian, "I feel very much like a third wheel, so I'm going to get the hell out of here. Let me know if you want me to bring you anything. Their room service is crazy good. I can't imagine what your bill is going to be. I'm not going to lie. I ordered steak every night you were unconscious."

I smile but force myself to not laugh because I don't want the pain that comes with it. "Fucker," I tell him, but he knows I don't really care. "Thanks again, man."

"No worries. Your dogs miss you, by the way."

"They're all okay, right?"

"Yeah, but now they really have a taste for human blood," he says with a laugh. "Like more so than usual."

He gives me a wave and squeezes Lydia's shoulder before leaving the room. I hear the door shut, but I barely register the sound. All my focus is on the woman in front of me. I'm too weak to do much of anything, but I run my thumb over her hand and bring it to my face, kissing the palm and pressing it against my cheek, needing to feel some part of her against me.

"I was so scared," she whispers, leaning closer. "I was terrified that I'd lost you."

"I'm here, *zaika*. I'm not going anywhere."

Her fingers run over the light beard I've grown since I've been here before her eyes dart to my chest. "Do you need more morphine?"

"No, I don't want to fall asleep. I've gone long enough without seeing you." I reach up and run a finger along her jaw. "I'm sorry about what I had to say in front of Enzo. It took everything I had to not show how much seeing you hanging there was affecting me."

"I know," she whispers.

"How badly did they hurt you before I got there?"

"I'm fine," she says, not answering the question.

I remember the way Enzo had cut her, and when I reach down to lift the bottom of her T-shirt up, she grabs my hand to stop me.

"Really, Kirill, I'm fine."

"Let me see." When she hesitates, I say, "Please, baby. I need to see for myself."

She relents and lifts her shirt for me. I grit my teeth when I see the line of black stitches.

"They come out in a few days. It's really not a big deal. It doesn't hurt at all anymore," she says, trying to make me feel better.

I run my finger below the line, savoring the feel of her soft skin. "I'm so sorry," I whisper. "I'm sorry for so many damn things. I should never have let you go that night. Even if you hated me for the rest of your life, I shouldn't have let you leave."

She drops her shirt and grabs my hand. "No, you did the right thing. I wanted to leave, and you let me. I was angry and hurt and needed some space, and you gave that to me, even though you didn't want to." She kisses the back of my hand. "You came for me, Kirill. You saved my life and almost lost yours because of it."

"Always, baby. I will always find you, and your life is worth way more than mine."

She gives me a soft smile. "Agree to disagree."

I don't bother arguing because she brings the straw back to my lips, and the cool water on my tongue is damn near orgasmic. When I've had my fill, I smile and say, "You know I can hold a cup, right?"

"You're not going to be doing anything."

I smile even bigger at her bossy tone. "I heard you wouldn't let the nurses give me a sponge bath."

"Hell no, I wouldn't," she says, obviously not feeling the slightest bit bad about her decision to not let the nurses do what they're paid to do. "The only woman who gets near this dick is me."

I laugh and then grimace at the pain. When she scrunches up her brow in worry, I reach up and massage away the tension with the pad of my finger. "Relax, baby. I'm fine. Just a bit sore."

She nods and puts the cup aside before lying down next to me. Peanut's sprawled out by my legs, and I'm guessing he's recently been taught to not lay on me to sleep. Oddly enough, I kind of miss it. Lydia rests her head on the pillow next to me, and snuggles in close enough for me to feel the lines of her body against mine, but not so close that she's actually putting any weight on me.

"I can't wait to get out of here," I grumble, already feeling a bit claustrophobic.

She laughs and kisses my cheek. "I've got news for you, honey. Once you leave this place, I'm in charge, and you're not doing shit until you're feeling better."

"That's so cute, little bunny. You're giving orders like you actually think I'm going to obey them."

"Oh, you're going to all right, or I'll be the one tying you to the damn bed."

"You wouldn't dare."

"Try me."

Her voice is sweet, but I hear the warning in her words. I have no doubt she'll go through with it. To prove her point of being in charge of what's best for me, when she sees me grimace again when I make the mistake of trying to move my body closer to hers, she reaches over without a second thought and hits the morphine button.

"You did not just fucking do that," I say, already feeling a drowsy warmth wash over me. "I want to spend more time with you."

She kisses me softly and whispers against my lips. "I'll be here when you wake, baby. I promise. I love you."

I try to tell her I love her, but I'm not sure if the words actually make it out. I fall back asleep, even though I'm fighting like hell to stay awake. The next time I wake, the room is dark, and the first thing I do when my brain is coherent enough to think is shove the damn morphine button off the bed. I hear sweet, feminine laughter, and I know she's caught me.

"You're a stubborn man, Kirill."

"I am, little bunny, now get over here and give me a kiss or I might not forgive you for drugging my ass."

She laughs again and walks over to me, climbing onto the bed beside me. Her long, dark hair hangs down to brush my chest when she leans over and presses her lips to mine. It's a chaste kiss, and I'm having none of it. I bring my hand up and cup the back of her head, forcing her closer as my tongue parts her lips. She gives a soft moan of protest, but I ignore her because the taste and feel of her is far better than any medicine the doctors can give me. When she doesn't give me what I want, I give her bottom lip a soft bite and whisper, "Please don't keep yourself from me. Stop holding back, little bunny, and give me what I need."

This time when I slide my tongue back between her lips, she lets out a soft sigh and opens up to me. A sense of peace washes over me when she cups my face and moans. I can't resist sliding my hand down her body and digging my fingers into her hips, urging her even closer. My fingers graze the waistband of her yoga pants, and when they dip inside, she stills and tries to pull away.

"Don't even fucking think about it," I growl against her lips. "I need to feel you, *zaika*. I need it so fucking badly."

"But you're hurt, and someone could walk in."

I smile and drag a finger just under her waistband. "I am hurt, so be still or it's just going to make it more painful for me when I have to fight you to get what I want."

"That's so not fair," she mutters, but I can see the way her pupils are already blown and the way her breathing has picked up.

"It's been a long time since my girl's come," I say. "Unless there's something I don't know about." I tease my fingers even lower. "Have you been touching this pussy without me?"

"No," she pouts. "Of course not. I was scared to death for you."

I smile and very slowly slide my fingers into her panties. "Good girl, baby. Now it's time for your reward."

When I lower my hand and cup her bare, wet pussy, I let out a groan of pure pleasure at the feel of her. My cock is trying desperately to wake up, but thanks to the morphine, all I can manage is a semi-hard state that's more infuriating than anything else. It's not going to stop me from making my girl feel good, though.

"You're soaking my hand, sweetheart," I tell her, smiling at the way her hips are already slowly rocking. Yeah, it's been way too long since she's had an orgasm. She's on her knees, leaning over me, and when I slide two fingers in, her lips part in a gasp, and I'm mesmerized by the sight of it.

"You gonna come all over my hand, baby?"

"Yes," she moans, rocking her hips even harder.

Brushing my finger over her clit, she moans as her eyes roll back. "Show me how much you missed me. Grip my fingers." She clenches down on me, and I growl at how badly I need to be inside her. "Good fucking girl. Your greedy little cunt is sucking me in so good." I rub her clit harder, bringing her closer to the edge, and right before I push her over, I capture her lips with mine, kissing her hard and swallowing her screams. Even though my chest hurts like hell, I raise my arm and cup the back of her head, keeping her held tightly to me while I work her pussy. She clenches around me, feeling so damn tight, and I'd give anything to be able to fuck her right now. I think I'd sell my soul to the devil himself for one goddamn thrust inside this woman.

"Kirill," she whispers against my lips. Her voice shaky and raw, just how I like it.

I finger her lazily, letting her enjoy the aftershocks. "Yes, baby?"

"I should not have let you do that."

The guilt in her voice has me smiling. "It's cute that you think you had a choice."

She snorts out a laugh before she can stop it. "You're infuriating."

"I am," I agree, giving her clit one last rub before sliding my hand out and bringing the wet fingers to my mouth. "You have no idea how badly I needed this," I say before licking my fingers clean, filling my mouth with the taste of her delicious cunt. "When we get home, you will be sitting on my face daily."

She lifts a brow at me. "You think so?"

I suck my other finger clean and give her a wink. "I fucking know so."

With a satisfied sigh, I reach a hand out to cup one of her tits. "So what should we order for supper, baby?"

She smiles and gives a soft laugh before getting up to grab the menu. The next several days pass by in a blur of pain medicine and annoying visits from Dr. West and various nurses who keep poking and prodding. I know they're doing their job and that they saved my life, but damn it, I just want to go home.

When the doc comes in again to check on me, I ask, "Can I go home?"

He gives a soft laugh at my impatience and checks the chart he's holding. "You'll be thrilled to know that the answer is yes, Mr. Chernikov."

"Thank god."

"Are you sure?" Lydia asks, and I shoot her a *don't you dare* look. She ignores it of course. "He'll be okay at the house? What if the wound gets infected? Should he stay in bed?"

Dr. West smiles patiently and answers all her questions, addressing every single concern she has, and there are many. By the time he's handing me a bottle of antibiotics and more pain pills, Lydia's gone through a crash course of everything she could possibly need to know about signs of infection, how often the bandages should be changed, when they can come off, and when the stitches will need to come out. She still looks nervous and not fully convinced. Dr. West hands her a card with his cell number written on the back.

"Call me anytime, and if you feel like you should bring him back, don't hesitate to do so. We're always here if you need us."

She nods and takes the card, frowning at me when I start to get up. "What?" I ask her. "He said I can leave."

"We need a wheelchair."

"Like hell we do." I stand and walk over to the clothes Vadim brought me earlier. I'm a little lightheaded, but I'll be damned if I'm going to admit it. I send him a text, asking him to come get us and then pull on a pair of jeans. When I reach for a T-shirt, she grabs it from the hanger before I can.

"At least let me help."

I laugh because even stretching her arms up, she still can't easily put my shirt on me.

"It'll be easier like this anyway," she says, sliding my arms through the T-shirt before careful pulling it up and, when I bend down, over my head. "If I ask for a wheelchair, will you sit in it?"

I lean down and kiss her. "Not a chance in hell, sweetheart." I give her ass a soft smack, laughing at the way she blushes and darts her eyes to the doctor. Figuring I'll make it worse for her, I stand back up and ask him, "So when is sex okay?"

"Oh my god," Lydia whispers.

I give her a wink and clasp her hand in mine while I wait for the doctor to answer.

"The most important thing is to listen to your body," he says. "If you feel pain, you shouldn't do it. You'll want to take it easy and stick with positions that are comfortable. Don't go crazy and pick her up, that kind of thing."

She's blushing like a cute tomato by the time he says, "Oral sex is probably the best thing to start with and then go from there if it doesn't cause you pain."

I look down at Lydia and give her a wink. "Sounds good, Doc, thanks."

"Don't be freaked out if you have trouble sustaining an erection. It's a very common side effect of pain medications."

"Why do you think I've stopped using the damn morphine?"

He laughs and steps closer so he can shake my hand. "I've enjoyed having you here, but I hope to never see you again."

"Same here, Doc. Thanks for saving my life."

"My pleasure." He shakes Lydia's hand too and says, "A nurse will stop by in a few days to remove his stitches and check to make sure it's healing like it should. You need to make sure you're getting plenty of rest, too."

She nods and promises she will. We thank him again, and once he's gone, I lean down and kiss her before we start packing up the room. I've just finished transferring the money to cover the very hefty bill, proving that you can in fact put a price tag on a person's life, when Vadim comes in to help with the bags.

I'm more than ready to get the hell out of here. As we're making our way downstairs, one of the nurses comes out and gives Lydia a hug goodbye. The woman's been in to check on me many times, but I don't pay attention to other women, so I can't even remember her name.

She's obviously grown close to Lydia, though. They share another smile before we step outside and walk to Vadim's car. I sit in the back with Lydia and Peanut, and as soon as we're parked in front of our house, I get out and whistle for my dogs. They come running towards me, barking excitedly and wagging their tails. I laugh and kneel down, petting them and scratching behind their ears. I praise the hell out of them in Russian, knowing full well that night in the warehouse would've ended very differently without them. Vadim told me that everyone's been talking about how the Faretti family fucked up and messed with the wrong hitman. Rumor has it I'm completely unhinged and never travel anywhere without my pack of killer dogs. I'm more than okay with that.

While I was unconscious, Vadim also learned that Jay had been hired by Enzo's men and that they'd put a small tracker in his arm. He wasn't lying when he'd told me he'd gotten greedy. He was working for both Enzo and Ivan and planning on pocketing all the money. When Enzo and his men realized Jay had failed, they'd come up with a new plan. They were already watching the property, and that night when I let Lydia go, I gave them a perfect opportunity they weren't about to pass up. It's a choice that I'll regret for the rest of my life. I know she says that I did the right thing, but I'll never get the image of her hanging bound and naked from my mind. It'll haunt me till the day I die. Since she came into my life, my focus has solely been on keeping her safe, and I failed her that night.

After I send the dogs back to work, we say goodbye to Vadim and head inside with Peanut, who quickly runs off after he gets his dog treat. When Lydia immediately starts leading me upstairs, I don't resist. It's only when she leads me to the bed and tries to get me to lay down that I start to offer resistance.

"You need to rest," she says, and I smile at her bossy tone.

"What I need is you sitting on my face."

She has the nerve to laugh.

"Doctor's orders, baby. You heard him."

"I don't think this is exactly what he meant."

"Oh, I do." I lay back on the mattress and motion for her to come closer. "You'd better be naked and straddling my face in less than a minute, *zaika*, or I'm coming after you."

When she hesitates, I lift my wrist and set a timer for one minute on my watch.

"My god, you're stubborn," she says, but she's already unbuttoning her pants like a good girl.

When she's naked from the waist down, I say, "Shirt too. I want to see everything that belongs to me."

With a huff, she pulls her shirt off and unclasps her bra. Her stitches were removed, but the cut is still red and angry looking. Every time I see it, guilt rips through me, but the sight of it does nothing to detract from her beauty. She'll always be gorgeous to me, no matter what.

When she climbs onto the bed, she surprises me by turning around before straddling my face. I let out an appreciative groan when I see her ass hovering right above me. I run my hands over her plump cheeks, giving them a good hard squeeze. She braces her hands on either side of my waist and then uses one hand to unzip my pants.

"What are you doing?"

I hear the amusement in her voice when she says, "Following doctor's orders."

Smiling, I give her ass a hard enough smack to make her yelp. "It's my orders you need to follow, baby. Now take me out."

I can't see what she's doing, but I feel her fingers working my zipper before she reaches in and pulls me out. Thanks to the lack of morphine, I'm fully hard and more than ready to go.

"Good girl, baby. Now sit your pussy on my mouth and put your lips around my cock."

I feel like I've entered heaven when she lowers herself down, smothering me in the best way possible. She's holding back, not wanting to hurt me, but I want more. I want it all. Digging my fingers into her hips, I force her onto me as I slide my tongue inside her. My groan of pleasure joins hers when I feel the wet heat of her mouth wrap around my head before she slowly sucks me in. It's been too goddamn long since I've had my dick in her mouth.

Bringing a finger between us, I coat it in her arousal before pressing the tip against her tight little puckered hole. She moans and takes me in further, working me in a fast rhythm that's going to send me flying off the edge in just a minute. I lap up the taste of her, starved for every drop I can get, and when I flick her swollen clit with my tongue and slide my finger in her ass, she rocks her hips and lets out a deep groan that I feel in my fucking balls.

I lick and suck while she does the same to me, and it's nothing short of euphoric. She grinds against my face while I rock my hips, feeding her more of my cock, and when I feel her release hit my mouth, I growl against her pussy and let go, filling her sweet mouth with my seed. I'm lost to everything except the feel and taste of her, and I can't help but wonder if she has any idea how much I love her.

A shiver runs through her body when I give her clit another soft suck while I grow soft in her mouth. She licks and kisses me clean while I do the same to her. A soft moan escapes her when I slide my finger out of her ass and give her cheek a soft smack.

"Did I hurt you?" she asks, lifting up and quickly turning around, worry etched across her face now that her orgasm is over and she can think again.

"No, baby," I tell her, pulling her down to me and giving her a smile. "That felt amazing." I run my fingers through her hair as she lays her head on my shoulder, keeping clear of the healing wound on the other side of my chest. "I've missed your body so damn much."

As much as I don't want to admit it, the sixty-nine fun we just had has completely worn me out. I close my eyes, only expecting to rest for a second, but I fall into a deep sleep before I can stop it.

Chapter 18

Lydia

I watch Kirill sleep while I trace a line along his freshly shaved jaw. I can't believe I just rode this beautiful face. The memory of it has me letting out a soft sigh and snuggling in even closer. Even in sleep, he feels me move and tightens his grip on me. He has one hand splayed over my ass cheek, and I know if I try to move, those fingers are going to dig in and keep me close. There's no denying how much I love that.

The last couple of weeks, I haven't been sleeping all that well, and it's starting to catch up to me, but I don't want to close my eyes. While Kirill was still sedated, I'd started throwing up in the mornings, and when I told Jenny about it, she'd snuck me a pregnancy test. I look at the gorgeous man sleeping next to me, wondering how he's going to take the news of our baby. I'd wanted to tell him as soon as the doctor took him off the sedatives, but I didn't want to worry him or stress him out. Once I saw the positive test, I'd asked Dr. West about it, wanting to make sure that everything was okay. I hadn't been the one to get shot, but it had been scary as hell for me too, and I'd been afraid that the stress and worry might be dangerous. A quick ultrasound proved that everything was perfect. As soon as I'd heard the strong, fast heartbeat, I'd fallen completely in love.

I'm lost in the memory, running my fingers along Kirill's toned abs when he says, "What are you thinking about?"

I lift my head to look at him. "I'm sorry. Did I wake you?"

He smiles and runs a finger along my cheek while he grips my ass harder. "I didn't mean to fall asleep, and you can always wake me when you need me. What's going on?" His face softens when he says, "Is this about your dad? I know my getting shot doesn't change anything. I know you're still hurt that I didn't tell you." His finger runs along my jaw. "I'm so sorry I hurt you, baby. I'll regret it for the rest of my life."

I grab his hand and turn my head so I can kiss his palm. "I was hurt," I admit. "Really fucking hurt, but I lied when I said I didn't love you anymore. I can't stop loving you. When I thought I'd lost you, I wanted to stop breathing. I didn't want to stay in a world that didn't have you in it. I will always miss my dad, and maybe it makes me a horrible person for being able to look past it, but I love you and I want to be with you."

"You're not a horrible person. You're far too good for me, and I don't deserve you. I never will, but I will spend the rest of my life loving and taking care of you. I want to marry you, baby. I want you by my side, and I never want to see you walk out that damn door again, because my heart can't take it."

I smile and look into the grey eyes that are filled with love, and I know he meant every word of what he just said. "If that was a proposal, then I accept."

He laughs and pulls me closer, kissing me slowly and thoroughly before he pulls back and says, "That was an unofficial proposal. You'll get a real one, *zaika*. One where I'm on my knees before you, because you're the only woman on the planet that I would ever bow before, but I would do anything for you."

I smile against his lips as he slides a hand down and runs his fingers over my stomach. "Now we just need to get you swollen with my baby, sweetheart. God, I can't wait to see you pregnant."

"About that," I say, and his whole body stills. He studies me like a man who's trying really hard to not get his hopes up.

"Please finish that thought," he whispers.

"I'm pregnant."

As soon as the words are out, he's smiling bigger than I've ever seen and wrapping his arms around me. "When did you find out? Why didn't you tell me, baby?"

"I was throwing up in the mornings while you were still sedated. They gave me a test there and Dr. West did an ultrasound because I was worried about stress and all that. Everything is fine, though," I quickly say. "I wanted to tell you, but I didn't want to upset you while you were still recovering through the worst of it."

"I'm so sorry I wasn't awake to help you."

He looks so distraught, so I rest my hand on his chest and say, "Don't worry, babe. I'll try my best to throw up again."

He keeps a straight face when he says, "Please do."

I laugh and then feel my whole body light up from the way he's looking at me. He rolls onto his side, pushing me onto my back.

"Your wound," I tell him, but he ignores my concern and lowers his head to my stomach.

He whispers something in Russian, his lips tickling my skin, and kisses a line along my stomach. Looking up at me, his eyes are filled with love and there's a sweetness to them that I'm confident wasn't there before he met me, and that makes me feel so damn special.

"I can't believe we're going to have a baby."

I cup his face and gently push him onto his back again, because I know being on his side must be hurting him, whether he wants to admit it or not. He allows it. Too busy smiling to insist he's okay.

"Are you really happy about this?"

He grabs my hand and kisses it. "So fucking happy, baby." He smiles and presses the palm of my hand to his cheek. "I love you so much."

"I love you too."

When we head back downstairs, I laugh when I open the freezer and see it loaded with casseroles. Kirill comes up behind me and kisses the top of my head.

"I see you've learned Vadim's secret."

I tilt my head back and look up at him. "What secret?"

He laughs and says, "He cooks when he's nervous. He's probably been cooking all damn week for us."

I smile and reach in, seeing that all the containers have been clearly labeled. "Damn," I say, looking through all of them. "How about the eggplant parmesan?"

"Sounds good, baby." He gives my ass a soft smack and then says, "I'll be right back. I just want to make sure the security footage looks good and that nothing's changed."

"Okay." I preheat the oven and fill up the kettle so I can make some tea. "But don't be long. You're supposed to be resting."

He laughs as he walks away. "Yes, ma'am."

The casserole is in the oven, my tea is made, and I'm just about to go and hunt him down when he walks into the kitchen, looking so gorgeous I want to snap a photo just so I can frame it and see it anytime I want. The black of his T-shirt looks great against his tanned, tattooed skin, and it really makes the grey of his eyes stand out. The man is gorgeous, effortlessly handsome as hell. The small smile playing at his lips as he walks closer has me lifting a brow. I can tell he's up to something. I just have no idea what it is. Not until he stops in front of me and lowers down to one knee.

"Oh my god," I whisper, wondering if there's any way in hell I might be misreading what's about to happen, because god wouldn't that be embarrassing? I start screaming because I think he's about to propose when really he's just knelt down to tie his damn shoe. He lets me know exactly what's going on when he grabs my hand and reveals the black, velvet box he's holding.

"What? How did you?" I can barely get the words out. My voice is shaking, my eyes are threatening to spill over, and my heart is racing.

He smiles and squeezes my hand. "I've had this ring for a while," he admits.

"For how long?"

"A while," is all he says. "I've known I was going to propose to you for a long time. I knew that you were the only woman I'd ever want to be my wife."

He opens the box, and I let out a soft gasp. I had no idea they made diamonds this big in real life. There's a large, round, pink diamond in the center that's surrounded by smaller diamonds, and it's so beautiful and sparkly, and even though I've never been a real girly girl, this thing makes me want to squeal.

He gives me a wink, reading everything I'm thinking so easily. "I'm glad you like it."

"It's beautiful," I whisper.

"It's nothing compared to you."

I bite my bottom lip and try not to cry while he takes the ring out and slips it on my finger. It fits perfectly. I'm not at all surprised that this man knows my ring size. Even though I'd basically agreed to marry him already and the ring is already sparkling on my finger, he still looks up at me, those grey eyes calm instead of stormy, and says the words I'll never forget.

"I'm not a good man, sweetheart. I'm a bad man, the kind of man that shouldn't even be allowed in the same room as someone like you, but even with all my faults, I promise that I will always try to be the best possible husband to you. I will always protect you and love you and be faithful to you because no other woman will ever exist for me. You're all I want, and you're all I need. I will love you until the day I die."

He stops and gives a soft shake of his head. "No, that's not right. I will love you for eternity because how I feel for you isn't going to stop when my heart does. Whatever part of me continues on after death will be filled with love for you."

I'm crying hard enough to blur my vision now, but I still see the sweet smile he gives me. He leans closer and kisses my stomach. "And I will love our baby, all of our children, and be the best daddy in the world to them." He raises his eyes to mine and asks, "Will you marry me, baby?"

I rest my hands on his head and thread my fingers through his hair. Looking down, I don't see the man who killed my dad. I no longer see that when I look at him. The past can't be changed, and I'm not going to let it destroy our future. I know who Kirill is, the kind of man he is and what he's capable of, and I know he'd never hurt me and that he'll do everything he can to keep me and however many kids we have safe. I also know that I love him completely and that a life without him is not one I want. So when I say, "Yes," I mean it with everything I am. Every part of me is his, just like every part of him is mine.

The smile he gives me is one of pure joy, and when he stands and picks me up, I give him a wide-eyed look of horror. "You can't pick me up!"

He laughs and ignores me. "Don't worry, little bunny, I'm not putting any strain on the wound. I just want to hold my fiancée."

With my hands cupping his face, my beautiful engagement ring rests against his cheek as I lean closer for a kiss. I run my tongue along his bottom lip, pulling back when he tries to capture my lips with his. He lifts a dark brow at me.

"Someone's feeling ballsy." His eyes darken when he cups the back of my head and pulls me closer. "I think my little bunny has forgotten who's in charge here." He nips softly at my bottom lip. "I may be injured right now, but I'm a quick healer, sweetheart. I'll have you on your knees again in no time, kneeling at my feet like the good girl you are, blindfolded and bound."

When I let out a soft moan at his words, he gives me a sexy smirk right before he kisses me hard, making me forget about everything except the feel of his mouth on mine. He pulls back before I'm ready, and seeing the blatant hunger on my face makes him give me a wink before carrying me back to his office.

"You really need to put me down. I don't want you tearing the stitches or hurting yourself."

He smacks my ass. "Stop worrying about me, *zaika*. I worry about you, not the other way around."

"Oh, okay," I say, and he laughs at my sarcastic tone as he sets me down so he can grab the thick envelope from his desk drawer.

"Don't freak out," he says, giving me a crooked smile while his eyes stay lit up with amusement.

I take the envelope, not having any idea what in the hell I'm going to find in it. When I reach in, I pull out a stack of documents and passports. I look up at him in confusion, and when I open the first passport, my jaw drops open. It's an American passport, *my* passport apparently, but I've never gotten a passport, so I have no fucking clue what the hell this is or where he got it.

"Lydia Chernikov," I read, my eyebrows nearly hitting my hairline. "What the hell?" The other passport I grab is Russian, and when I open it, it's the same photo of me, but this time everything is written in Cyrillic with English beneath. "Lydia Chernikova."

"That's the female version of our last name in Russian," he clarifies when I'm still standing there dumbfounded.

I open up the other passports. An American and Russian one for Kirill, and then there's another set of American passports for us with the last name Johnson.

"Those are to get us out of the country. Way too common of a last name to draw attention."

I keep looking through everything. Driver's licenses, birth certificates, and when I see the marriage license, I hold it up to him. "When did we get married?"

He looks at the paper and grins. Pointing at the date that's been filled in, he says, "Two years ago. Happy anniversary, baby."

"This is insane. How? When?" I'm too stunned to do much more than stare and fumble around one-word questions.

"I had it all done when I was in prison. I knew we'd end up here, and I wanted to make sure we had what we needed when the time came." He waves a hand at what must have cost a small fortune. "They're all completely legit. We can fly out on a private plane, go anywhere you want, live wherever you want. No one's going to come for me."

"Yeah, why is that?" I ask. "I Googled you when you went to Ivan's that night and left me alone with your computer. There's nothing about you on the news."

He smiles at my admission. "I knew they'd do one of two things once they realized I'd escaped. They'd either have a worldwide manhunt, or they'd pretend it never happened."

He gives a soft laugh. "I'm still kind of surprised they went this route, but it makes sense. I mean, who the hell is going to know I'm not there? I was in solitary confinement. I never even saw the other prisoners. They can easily pretend I'm still there, and no one will be the wiser. Otherwise, they'll have one hell of a shitstorm to deal with. It's more important for them to pretend I'm still in prison, but that doesn't mean they'll be okay with me walking around and flaunting my freedom. Once we're out of the States, we can live our lives in peace." He steps closer and cups my face. "Where do you want our baby to be born?"

"Your mom's in Greece. I wouldn't mind meeting her. We could start there and explore, find a place we both like."

He smiles and leans down. "Whatever my fiancée wants."

Seven months later

"Oh my god, I can barely move. Just toss me in the water, I can float back to shore."

Kirill laughs and comes up behind me, wrapping his arms around my very large pregnant belly and burying his face in my neck.

"You look beautiful, baby."

I laugh and rest my hands on his. We've been in Greece for six months now, and it already feels like home. We bought a gorgeous house on the island of Corfu, and shortly after, Kirill surprised me with a yacht. In the earlier months of my pregnancy, we were on it all the time, traveling to the different islands, seeing so many things that I never thought I'd ever see. Every day I wake up grateful to be here, grateful to be with him and for the life we have together. Kirill's mom and stepdad live in Athens, and we've spent a lot of time with them, but we mostly keep to ourselves. We like it that way. Vadim flies over regularly, and I think we've just about convinced him to move here. It's hard not to fall in love with the gorgeous blue water and sandy beaches.

Shortly after coming here, Kirill had asked me if I wanted a wedding, and I didn't even have to think about my answer. I'd told him no. We already had the marriage certificate, and I had all the documents with my new last name. I was fine with that. I didn't need the white dress, and I don't regret my decision. One night after we'd eaten supper we'd taken a walk along the beach, and Kirill had surprised me by reciting vows to me under the moonlight. They were personal and from the heart, promises that were unique to him and our relationship, not just something he was reciting because a minster told him to. When he was finished, I did the same, and for the both of us, that's more meaningful than any marriage ceremony. It was perfect.

When our daughter lets out an especially hard kick, I groan while he gently rubs away the pain. He kisses my neck and asks, "You okay?"

"Yeah, she's just feisty today."

He gives a soft laugh. "Sounds just like her mommy."

"Oh yeah right," I say with a laugh. "If she's a little hellion, that's all on you."

"A hellion?" He turns me around and smiles down at me. "Our baby is going to be perfect. I have no doubt she's going to be beautiful just like you and give me more grey hairs than I want to think about, but she's going to be perfect."

"She will be," I agree, already so excited to meet her.

"Come on, baby, time to go back." He takes my hand and guides me to one of the comfy loungers. With my due date so close, Kirill doesn't feel comfortable staying out on the water all night. I watch him as he starts the motor and steers us back home. I lay back and close my eyes, enjoying the feel of the sun on my skin and the strong breeze that hits my face, smelling so strongly of the sea. When he guides us back into our boathouse, the sun is just starting to set.

"It's so beautiful here." I grab his hand as he helps me off the boat and then look out at the Ionian Sea we'd just been floating on. "It feels like a dream living here."

"It does," he agrees, "but that's only because I'm sharing it with you."

I rest my hand on his chest, running a finger over the scar, remembering the day he took a bullet for me and saved my life. "You're such a softie," I say, patting his hard chest.

He laughs and scoops me up in his arms, laughing again when I let out a yelp and throw my arms around his neck. "I'm too heavy for you to pick up!"

"You'll never be too heavy for me, sweetheart."

I know I'm heavy, but I fucking love that he still makes it look effortless to pick me up. He still makes me feel small and precious, even though I haven't seen my damn feet in months. As soon as we leave the boathouse, the dogs come running up to us, Peanut bringing up the rear while Boris prances around with him like they've been best friends since birth. They've taken very well to Greece. We don't have near as much land here, but our stretch of private beachfront property is enough to make them feel like they still have a job to do. They just get a lot more downtime too.

"They're getting lazy," Kirill says, laughing at the five doggie butts that are wiggling from all the excited tail wagging.

"They're happy," I say. "I'm sure they could still take down any threats. They're just in semi-retirement mode."

"Well, pretty soon they're going to be on baby guard duty, so they better stay on top of things."

"I'm sure they will."

They run off to play by the water while Kirill carries me up to the house. I smile at the veranda that's covered in flowers. Some are native to the island, but Kirill surprised me by bringing over some of my mom's irises, dahlias, and hyacinths. I kiss his shoulder. He smiles down at me, but he doesn't stop until we're in our bedroom. The floor-to-ceiling windows give an amazing view of the sun setting over the water.

"You like that view, little bunny?"

"Yes."

"Good, because I'm going to eat your pussy while you watch it."

His words send my heart racing. He sets me down and then gets on his back with his head near the windows and motions me closer. I'm still wearing my bikini. I'd been so embarrassed when I really started getting big to keep wearing one, but when I came outside in a one-piece one morning, he'd looked so damn devastated that I'd immediately gone inside and changed. He loves seeing my body, no matter how big it gets. I'd be an idiot to complain about that, so a bikini it is.

Standing over him, he looks up at me and sighs. "So fucking beautiful," he says, motioning me lower. When I less-than-gracefully get on my knees, he reaches up and starts to untie the triangle top. One of the perks of pregnancy are the bigger boobs, and we've both been living it up. For the first time in my life I have actual cleavage. It's been a fun few months.

"Goddamn," he breathes out when he pulls the strings and the fabric falls off, exposing my full breasts to him. "You look like a fucking goddess, baby, and I'm more than ready to worship you."

He cups my breasts in his hands, squeezing them gently as his thumbs caress my overly sensitive nipples. That touch alone is enough to make me gasp and rock my hips.

"You like that?" he asks, giving them a soft pinch and smiling at the whimper I give.

"Yes," I moan. "Do it again."

He gives me another pinch, this one hard enough to sting, and when he pulls his hands back, I give a soft whimper of protest.

"Patience, *zaika*." He runs his hands down my pregnant belly, lightly dancing his fingers over my skin. He stops to caress the scar from Enzo's knife. It's faint, but it's still there, and I know it pains him to see it. I grab his hand and kiss it, reminding him that I'm okay before he drops it lower and pulls at the ties on my hips. Tossing the bikini bottoms aside, he lets out a soft growl and grips my hips. "Your pussy is so fucking beautiful." He lovingly trails a finger along my slit, sending a rush of pleasure all through me with that one touch. "You're always so wet for me, baby."

He slowly slides a finger in, and I nearly come from how damn good it feels.

"So fucking tight," he murmurs, his accent growing thicker as his eyes darken to the stormy grey I love. "You hungry for my cock, little bunny?"

"Yes, god yes," I moan, clenching even tighter around his finger. He hisses out a breath when he feels it. "Don't you want me to do that to your cock?" I ask, teasing him while I cup my breasts, trying to get him to lose control so he'll fuck me like I need him to.

"Tongue first," he growls, sliding his finger out and then gripping my hips and helping me scoot up so I'm straddling his head. I can no longer see his gorgeous face because of my belly, but before he dives in, he asks, "Do you see any boats out there?"

I look out at the nearly dark water and scan the horizon. "No, we're good."

"Okay, if you see anyone, let me know. No one gets to see my baby naked but me."

I smile at his possessiveness and brace my hands against the window in front of me. I let out a whimper of pure bliss when I feel his tongue slide along my slit, hard enough to part my lips and dip inside.

"Goddamn," he growls. "I could eat you all damn day. Fucking delicious."

He nips and licks my pussy lips, taking his time, and only when my thighs start shaking does he finally slide his tongue into me. I rock my hips, grinding agains his talented mouth as he brings me closer to the edge. The view in front of me is breathtaking, but it's nothing compared to the pleasure Kirill is giving me. When he wraps his lips around my clit and gives me a hard suck, I look out at the night sky and scream his name with my release.

He growls and sucks me harder, and when I become too sensitive, he focuses on lapping up every drop of my release that he can get before returning his attention to my clit. He rims my sensitive skin, sending new aftershocks through me, and just when I think I can't take any more, he cups my tits in his hands, pinches my nipples, and gives my clit a hard flick of his tongue.

"Holy fuck!" I gasp, and I swear I hear a muffled laugh come from between my legs.

He does it again, pinching and flicking until I'm gasping and letting out raspy pleas for more. He finally takes pity on me and gives me the orgasm I'm so desperate for. The force of it is blinding. I smack my palms against the glass, grinding against my husband's gorgeous face, feeling completely loved and worshipped, just like he wanted me to feel.

When I start to come down, he gives my ass a soft pat and helps me scoot off him. I'm too spent to move, but he picks me up without so much as a strained grunt and carries me to bed. Lying on my side, he quickly strips out of his black swim trunks and spoons me from behind.

"Give me that mouth, baby," he says while hiking up one of my legs and getting himself into position. His thick head presses against my wet slit, and he slowly slides in when I turn my head and offer him my lips, covering my gasp of pure pleasure with a hungry kiss that steals my breath away.

He fucks me gently. Every slow thrust hitting me right where I need him. My tough, hitman husband fucks me like I'm the most precious thing in the world to him, and it makes my damn eyes water. His tongue runs along mine while his hand is splayed out across my belly in a possessive, protective gesture that always makes my heart melt when he does it.

"I love you," he whispers against my lips.

"I love you too," I say before sucking his tongue into my mouth.

He groans and slides his hand down. A few well-placed rubs and I'm screaming his name again. I clench him tighter as the orgasm thunders through me. He growls something in Russian and thrusts into me even harder while making sure to not be too rough. I cup his face as he pulses inside me and my body shakes as my muscles turn to mush. Completely sated, I let out a breathy sigh and smile up at him.

"Consider me worshipped," I say, making him laugh.

"I'll always worship you, baby. You're everything to me, and nothing else exists outside of you." He kisses the tip of my nose. "My beautiful goddess."

It's hard for me to believe that he's actually being serious, but the intense look in his eyes tells me he is. I pull him closer and run my tongue up the scar on the side of his face because I love how it always makes him laugh when I do it.

"I love you," I say. "My life is everything it is because of you. I'm so glad you didn't stop writing me when I told you to fuck off."

He laughs and kisses me. "Never, little bunny. I was already having our marriage certificate made."

I laugh and rest my head on the pillow while he curls his body around mine. His fingers dance along my stomach, and I feel him smile against me when our daughter gives another healthy kick. Yeah, she's going to be a wild thing, just like her daddy. The thought puts a smile on my face as I fall asleep surrounded by my husband and images of a grey-eyed, dark-haired little girl who isn't afraid of anything.

Epilogue

Kirill
One Month Later

Natalya wakes up from her nap and looks at me, and I'm lost all over again. Every time she turns those big, grey eyes on me, I turn into a giant puddle of emotion. Just like it was with her mom, it was love at first sight. As soon as I saw our daughter when they laid her naked little body on Lydia's stomach, that was it. I was a complete goner.

"Daddy loves you," I tell her in Russian, leaning down to kiss her small head. Her dark hair is silky soft, and I breathe in the scent of her while I run a finger along her chubby cheek. When she starts to root around, I laugh and kiss her head again. "I can't help you there, sweetheart. Let's go find mommy."

I stand up from the rocking chair in her nursery, about to go and find my beautiful wife when I turn and see her leaning against the doorframe watching me. Her face is lit up with a sweet smile, the same one she always gets on her face when she sees me with our daughter, and there's so much love in it that it always takes my damn breath away.

The way I love this woman shouldn't be allowed. It's too powerful, too all-consuming, but I don't know how to love her any other way. It's like asking a tsunami to become a spring shower. It's just not going to happen. My wife owns me, body and soul, and she's my everything. I wouldn't have it any other way.

Walking over, I lean down and kiss her, and it feels like coming home, just like it always does when my mouth touches hers. A peace washes over me, and with my wife in front of me and our daughter in my arms, I have everything I could ever need.

"Looks like someone's hungry," Lydia says, giving a soft laugh at the way our daughter is still rooting around in my arms.

The labor was only a couple of weeks ago, and as much as I try to help, I know my wife is exhausted, but she's still so breathtakingly beautiful that I can't help but just stare at her.

"What are you looking at?" She gives me a smile and reaches up to cup my face, running her fingers along my scar.

"My beautiful wife," I tell her.

"Yeah," she says, rolling her eyes at me. "It's the sweatpants and stained T-shirt, isn't it? So sexy."

"It is on you." She laughs like she thinks I'm joking. "Don't laugh at me, *zaika*. I think you're breathtaking." When Natalya gives a fussy whimper, I lean down and kiss her soft head. "Don't worry, little one. Your beautiful mommy is about to feed you."

Lydia leans in and kisses our daughter's head before stealing a quick kiss from me. After she sits in the rocker and gets situated, I put Natalya in her arms so she can breastfeed her. I watch, in awe yet again at how amazing my wife is. When she'd gone into labor, I'd never been more scared in my life. Dangling from roofs, being outnumbered and having to shoot myself out of a situation—no problem, but watching her in pain nearly broke me. I'd almost gotten my ass kicked out of the hospital. I was so worried that I ended up forgetting my English and what little Greek I know and had just started yelling at the nurses and doctor in Russian. It had taken all my willpower to calm the fuck down, well, that and the fact that there was no way in hell I was going to miss the birth of our baby. Lydia had been amazing, though. She knew I needed to do something, so she kept sending me out for ice chips and giving me other little jobs to do. She's never looked more like a queen than in that hospital bed, squeezing my hand while the contractions racked her body, taking it all like a goddamn champ.

"Have I told you today how amazing you are?"

Lydia looks up from our daughter and gives me a big smile. "Such a softie."

"I am for you two, yes."

When we hear the fast tapping of little dog nails on the floor in the hall, we both look to the door right before Peanut comes barreling in. I bend down and give him a pet before he jumps up, resting his front paws on Lydia's leg so he can see the baby. One of the first things we did after bringing her home was introduce her to the dogs. I swear they'd all immediately fallen in love with her. I know as soon as she starts crawling around, she's going to have five constant companions. I almost pity any future boyfriends. *Almost*. Vadim's quickly become like an uncle to her, which means he can guard the backdoor while I guard the front. Those boys don't stand a chance.

After Natalya's nursed herself to sleep, I pick her up and work on burping her while Lydia buttons her shirt back up. We're still on no-sex orders from the doc for a few more weeks, and I'd be lying if I said it wasn't killing me. I miss my wife. I miss the feel of her, of being inside her, but I'd wait forever for this woman.

I let out a soft laugh when I finally hear Natalya burp and kiss the side of her face. She burrows in closer to my neck, and I hold her for a few more minutes because I can't tolerate the thought of letting her go just yet. Lydia's right. I am a giant softie. I rub her small back and cup the back of her head before laying her down in her crib. When Lydia walks over, I wrap my arm around her as we watch our daughter sleep.

"Someday I guess it'll get old to just watch her sleep," she whispers. She looks up at me. "I mean, I hope so anyway. She'll hate it if she's sixteen and wakes up to find us both standing over her bed, watching her sleep like a couple of psychos."

I laugh and squeeze her tighter. "I'll be standing by her window with a baseball bat, making sure none of the local boys get any ideas."

"I'm sure she'll love that," Lydia says, and her tone makes it clear that Natalya will most definitely have something to say about her over-protective daddy. I've already decided I'm going to give her self-defense training and teach her how to use some weapons. My little girl is going to know how to protect herself. She may not appreciate it at first, but it's happening.

Lydia grabs my hand and leads me from the room, keeping the door open enough so we can hear when she wakes up. We go down the hall, and when she crashes onto the couch with a tired sigh, I sit down next to her. Putting an extra pillow behind her, I position her so she's stretched out with her legs resting in my lap. When I start to rub her feet, she lets out a sigh of pure pleasure.

"Don't look at me like that," she says, giving me a lazy smile. "You know damn good and well I think your cock feels better than a foot rub." Her smile widens. "But this does feel damn good."

I laugh and press my thumbs into the arch of her foot, pulling another moan from her. Turns out I love bringing her pleasure in more ways than one. I've become an expert on foot and back massages, and I'm more than happy to give them to her anytime she wants. Anything that gets my hands on her body is a win.

After I've rubbed away the tension from her feet and calves, I get up, and when I return, her whole face lights up when she sees the bag of Twizzlers I'm holding.

"Do you have any idea how much I love you?"

I laugh and hand her the bag while I sit down and pull her up against me. We share an ottoman while she finds us a movie to watch. I went from having the exciting life of a notorious hitman to being the kind of guy who thinks the perfect evening is staying at home with my wife and baby, and I couldn't be happier.

Everything I need is under this roof, and I'd be a damn fool to not realize how unbelievably lucky I am. I take the licorice Lydia offers me, because as much as I hate to admit it, the damn things are tasty, and kiss the top of her head. Our life together is amazing, and I'm convinced it's only going to get better. All we need is a houseful of kids to make this absolutely perfect. Our little girl needs some brothers to play with. With that thought in mind, I relax into the couch with a smile on my face, already imagining the future that's headed our way.

* * *

Lydia
One Year Later

Natalya grips my hand as she stomps her cute chubby feet into the sand, laughing when a new wave comes in, soaking her legs. She's a beach baby to her core. Ever since the first time Kirill held her against his chest and walked her out into the blue water of the Ionian Sea, she's been mesmerized by it.

Looking down, I watch her grey eyes widen before she raises an arm, pointing at the birds flying above us. She gives a squeal when Boris comes up and licks her hand.

"Dog!"

I laugh at the sound of her cute voice. She doesn't know too many words yet, but she's got dog down. They all adore her. Peanut runs around at her feet, darting away anytime a wave comes too close to him, but everything gets put on hold when she turns her head and spots her daddy.

"Da-da!" she screams, immediately trying to run for him.

His gorgeous face lights up when he hears her screaming for him. I laugh as she squeezes the hell out of my finger and walks as fast as her unsteady toddler legs will allow. He closes the distance with a laugh and scoops her up into his arms, talking to her in Russian while he covers her face in kisses. She giggles and rests her hands against his face. Her curious fingers find the scar that trails down the side of his face, but when Kirill pretends to try and bite her arm, she laughs again and drops her hand to rest on his shoulder. He's in nothing but black swim trunks, and the sight of him is hard to look away from, especially when it's our daughter he's holding up against that sculpted, tattooed chest.

I realize he's caught me staring when he leans close and whispers in my ear, "Later you can tell me what you were thinking while eye-fucking me, *zaika*."

Before he pulls back, he gives my ear a soft suck that nearly has my eyes rolling back in my head. How can one man be so damn good with his mouth? He pulls back and gives me a wink. Grabbing my hand, he pulls me to the water. I follow him in, the three of us enjoying the clear, blue sea while the sun shines down and the dogs play on the beach.

Natalya laughs as Kirill holds her out so she can kick her legs and arms. He doesn't let her go, but I'm guessing she's going to be swimming before too long. With a lifejacket and floaties, and maybe a leash tied to her ankle, of course. I hold my arms out and when she tries to get to me, Kirill hands her off. I pull her close while he grabs me and pulls the two of us against him.

"Life doesn't get any better than this," he says, pressing his lips to mine.

"No, it doesn't," I agree.

"I mean, we need several more babies, of course, but what we have here is pretty damn perfect."

I laugh and kiss him again. I know he's more than ready to get me pregnant again, but I need more time between them. I haven't even lost all the baby weight yet, and I'm just now feeling like I'm not walking around like an exhausted zombie.

"Whenever you're ready, little bunny," he says, reading my thoughts. "Just let me know, baby, and I'll make it happen."

I have no doubt about that. Since I stopped breastfeeding, I got on the pill so we don't have to worry about condoms, but he's made it clear that whenever I want to throw them out, he's A-okay with it. I rest my head against his shoulder while he holds us and the waves gently lap against our bodies.

When Natalya starts getting hungry we head inside. Kirill and I cook supper together while Natalya plays next to Peanut. After we've eaten, it's bath time, and then Kirill rocks her while he reads her a story in Russian. She points to the pictures of animals after he says the word in Russian, and I swear this little genius is going to be fluent in English, Greek, and Russian by the time she's five.

I smile at the way she looks at her daddy. She has no idea she's cuddling up with a lethal hitman. She just sees her daddy when she looks at him—the man who loves her unconditionally, reads her bedtime stories, and always has time to play and laugh with her. She's lucky to have him. She's lucky to have a dad who looks at her like the whole world is centered around her. Some people say you shouldn't spoil babies, but I think everyone deserves to be the sun in someone's universe at least once in their life. When Kirill looks up and smiles at me, I realize how lucky I am that he makes me feel that way every damn day.

We tuck Natalya in and smother her with kisses so she'll fall asleep feeling safe and completely loved. With the nightlight on and Peanut in the dog bed that he now prefers to sleep in by her crib, we leave the nursery while she drifts off to sleep.

I don't get very far before a pair of strong arms come up on either side of me, blocking me in against the wall. His mouth finds my neck, giving me a hard enough bite to make me gasp. He licks the sting away and nibbles a line along my shoulder. I reach a hand behind me, running it over the front of his jeans. A moan escapes when I feel the hard length of him.

"Find something you like, sweetheart?"

"Yes." I squeeze him through his jeans, smiling at the deep groan he gives.

"Let me hear it, little bunny. Tell me how much you want my big cock."

He presses harder against me when I move my hand. The hard length of him against my ass makes it hard to think, but when I rest my hands on his and he runs his tongue up my neck, I find my voice.

"Please," I beg. "Please fuck me."

"You want my dick, baby?"

"Yes," I say in a breathy rush.

"You wet for me?" His teeth nip at my earlobe, sending a shiver of pleasure down my spine. When I nod my head, he whispers, "Prove it."

He doesn't have to ask me twice. I slide one hand down my pants, running a finger along my soaking wet slit before bringing it up to his waiting mouth. He takes one look at my glistening finger before letting out a deep groan and wrapping his lips around it and sucking it in. The feel of his tongue running along my skin has me more than ready to feel it between my legs. I'm squirming by the time he lets me go.

"Good girl," he growls before picking me up and carrying me into our room. Setting me down, I immediately fall to my knees before him, earning me a pleased smile as he runs his hands through my hair. "Take off my belt, baby."

My hands shake as I reach up and undo the black leather belt that always makes me blush a little bit when I see it. When the leather strap slides loose of the last belt loop, I hold it up for him, but he just slowly shakes his head. He waits to see what I'll do with it. I think about binding my wrists like we've done before, but tonight I'm feeling a little feisty. Tonight, I want to try something new. His eyes narrow when he sees me put the belt around my neck, slowly tightening it. It's tight, but not tight enough to cut off my air. By the time I hook it closed, his jaw is so tense I can see the veins in his throat standing out against his skin. I meet the eyes that are definitely hurricane-level stormy grey and hold the belt strap up for him to take.

He grabs it, wrapping it around his hand until I'm forced closer. "In ten seconds you better have my cock out and down your throat, or you're going to feel the sting of this belt on your ass."

"Goddamn," I whisper, nearly orgasming on the spot.

"One," he says, reminding me that I'd better get my ass in gear. I reach up and work on his pants, but my hands are shaking in my excitement and it takes longer than normal. He's already to seven by the time I'm pulling his thick shaft free. I waste one precious second admiring how beautiful he looks with the veins trailing up his length and the arousal that's already coating him. By the time I wrap my lips around him, he's at nine. I suck in a quick breath and lower down, taking him in fully, not even giving my gag reflex a chance to realize what's going on.

"Jesus fucking Christ," he growls, fisting my hair with one hand and the belt with the other. "That's my good fucking girl."

He keeps me impaled on his cock, unable to breathe and completely at his mercy, just the way I like it. With a groan he tugs on the belt, slowly pulling me off him.

"That's right, baby, keep sucking."

I run my tongue over him, loving the way it makes him growl, and right when I get to his head, he pulls on the belt, sinking himself back into me. He raises and lowers me until he's seconds away from losing control. I can feel how tense he is, how hard he's trying to not come. When I run my tongue along the ridge of skin that always drives him crazy, he forgets his English and fills our room with the sexy sound of Russian.

Pulling me off him, he lifts me up and strips me. This isn't a sweet, gentle undressing. This is a rough stripping from a man who's desperate to get inside me. He sheds his own clothes in record time, and when he hovers his body over mine, he pins both my hands to the bed with one of his and uses his other hand to hike one of my legs up. I suck in a quick breath because I know this angle, we both do, it's the one that allows him to go so deep I feel like I'm going to lose consciousness.

"Take me like a good girl, *zaika*," he murmurs against my lips. "Take all of this big cock. I want you to feel it in your fucking throat, sweetheart."

"Mm-hmm," I moan, more than ready for him to fill me.

He presses his lips to mine in a hungry, bruising kiss while he slams into me. The shock of it has me bucking up against him and screaming into his mouth. He kisses me through it, fucking me in a brutal rhythm that has me seeing stars right before my whole body explodes with the force of the orgasm. He doesn't let up, slamming into me over and over again, forcing me right into another one. I clench around him, my whole body tensing and bucking beneath him, and when he growls against my lips, thrusting hard and deep as I feel him pulse inside me, I smile against his lips, greedy for everything he can give me.

"My god, I love you, baby." His voice is ragged and breathy, and when I start to laugh, he joins in, holding me as we ride this high together.

"I love you too," I tell him, wrapping my arms around him when he lets go of my wrists.

He runs his finger over the belt at my throat. "I like this a lot."

"I thought maybe you would."

"My baby does know me well."

He cups my face and kisses me gently. It always amazes me how damn sweet he can be. He can fuck me so hard, making me feel like I can't breathe and like I won't be able to walk for a week, but he can also be so sweet it almost makes me cry.

"You're the best thing that's ever happened to me," he whispers against my lips. "And every morning I wake up so damn grateful that you're by my side."

I brush aside a strand of sweaty hair from his forehead while I wrap my legs around his waist, keeping him inside me.

"Good," I say, making him laugh.

"There's that smartass girl I love so much."

I laugh and kiss his lips. "I feel the same way about you, and I've never been happier. You and Natalya are everything to me, and our family is just going to grow. This is just the beginning."

"I like the sound of that," he says, rolling us over so I can rest against him.

I kiss the old bullet wound on his chest and feel my eyes grow heavy because he truly wore me out. His fingers caress my back and ass while I drift off to sleep, feeling completely safe and loved and happier than I ever thought possible.

About the Author

Just like her last name, Sonja loves morally grey characters and alphas with a hidden heart of gold. She loves strong men with mile-wide soft spots for the women they love and who will stop at nothing to keep them safe.

She writes mainly dark mafia steamy romances where the lines between good and bad blur into a beautiful, sexy shade of grey.

Zero cheating and HEAs are always guaranteed!

Printed in Great Britain
by Amazon